THE JESUS INJECTION

Visit us at www.boldstrokesbooks.com

THE JESUS INJECTION

by

Eric Andrews-Katz

A Division of Bold Strokes Books

2012

ISBN 13: 978-1-60282-762-2

THIS TRADE PAPERBACK ORIGINAL IS PUBLISHED BY
BOLD STROKES BOOKS, INC.
P.O. BOX 249
VALLEY FALLS, NY 12185

FIRST EDITION: NOVEMBER 2012

CREDITS
EDITORS: GREG HERREN AND STACIA SEAMAN
PRODUCTION DESIGN: STACIA SEAMAN
COVER DESIGN BY SHERI (GRAPHICARTIST2020@HOTMAIL.COM)

Acknowledgments

The journey from story idea to publication is never traveled alone, and there have been many people who have helped Buck see life on the printed page. I can't say "Thank You" enough to Len Barot and Greg Herren (and eventually the team) at Bold Strokes Books for sitting down at the Saints and Sinners Festival and listening to my pitch. Thank you to the Palm/Card Reader at the House of Voodoo on Bourbon Street who predicted the event and the outcome of said meeting two days prior.

An endless amount of gratitude goes out to my friends and clientele. They have kept me going so I could afford to simultaneously pursue my writing career. There are many who read through my work and gave feedback, some listened and discussed it with me, and others just listened (or they might have blocked me out and gone to sleep). These people definitely deserve mentioning: Amy, "Big Red," Brad, Dea, Dorothy, Garth, Harold, Irene, James, Jay, "Leely O'Hara," Lloyd, Mazzi, Patrick, Runette, Sandra, Scott, Stephen, Vincent, and so many others for their support.

Much appreciation goes to Susan who took time out of her mothering schedule to speed read and give great feedback.

For Jaima: My extreme gratitude for years of past, present, and future friendship.

A note of thanks must go to the entire team at the *Seattle Gay News*. They have allowed me to hone my craft over the years as I continue to find my voice and style.

Another note must go to my parents, Ervene and Gary Katz. I consider myself very lucky to count them among my close friends.

Although they often don't understand my life, their support and love remains consistent and I'm grateful for it.

While visiting Roger and Brad in Brussels, they warned me not to notice the belligerent drag queen in the doorway. I noticed and knew one day she would appear in print.

A very special and personal "thank you" goes to "O" and "H" (you know who you are). All I am allowed to say is "thank you" (and you both know why).

Never least, my unending gratitude goes to my husband, Alan. Whether out of love or duty, he helps me brainstorm ideas, reads through most everything I've ever written, offers suggestions, critique, and corrections as I go along not only with my work, but also in life. Most of all, he shows an indomitable amount of patience with everything I do—even if it is only humoring me by letting me be my silly self. His encouragement has been there from the beginning and his support continues daily. For so many more reasons, he is my Hero.

There are many more people I have accidentally omitted although their support is always present. They are more than my intimate circle of friends; they are my family. I am truly blessed.

For Alan

You are more than my Muse
And far beyond my Best Friend

CHAPTER ONE

The sour notes drilled through the air and into Buck's ear with equal ease. The voice made the tune harder to recognize. This musical equivalent to fingernails dragging on a blackboard put his guard up—along with the hairs on his neck. Scanning the pedestrian walkways for the source, Buck reached into his jacket and took off the safety on the gun in his shoulder holster. His light blazer covered the piece easily, but intuition had nudged him. A good agent was a man who listened to his intuition, and Agent 98 was such a man.

Buck restarted his journey to dinner when the voice began a distracting second chorus. Approaching a doorway, he noticed a form slumped within its darkened frame. A yellowing light reflected from above bathed the creature in amber shadows, without giving away details.

"La vie en rose!" finished the gravelly voice. The shadows moved and grew larger, taking an ogre's form. *"Bonsoir, monsieur. Un peu de confort une nuit humide?"*

From the shop door's shadow stepped an extremely tall drag queen. Her red wig was askew and hung unkempt past her broad shoulders. The makeup was thickly overdone in a failed attempt to cover the hints of a stubbly beard.

Approaching hesitantly, Buck tried not to look too much at the figure looming in the doorway. She seemed to be staring at him. He smiled briefly, hoping it would convey his polite disinterest.

"Ah!" The drag queen called out to him, slurring her overly pronounced accent. "You look like an American!"

Buck reached into his pocket and pulled out a few euro coins. Walking past the doorway, he threw them into a bowl holding several other coins and a chocolate candy.

"Good monsieur," she begged, taking a firm hold on Buck's arm. He glared at her, and the drag queen pulled back her hand slowly. "Why in such a rush? The night is young, and so are you. Tonight is meant for lovers! Why be alone?"

Buck gave her a quick study. If she weren't stooped over with alcohol, she would probably stand six feet five—not including the cascading red wig. The dress was obviously second or even thirdhand, as the style hadn't been seen in decades. Despite the eyebrows being shaped and the face painted well, the makeup base was not properly blended at the neck, an amateur's mistake.

Drag was clearly something new to her. She had yet to find good taste.

"I'm not alone," Buck said, taking a step back. He retrieved his cell phone from his pocket. "I'm actually running a few minutes late and need to let my friends know."

She teetered forward, stepping out of the door frame. "Take my picture to show her. So she won't be jealous when you say you were detained by a beautiful woman."

Buck laughed. He stepped backward and set his phone to camera. She framed herself in the doorway with a dramatic flair. She tugged at her dress, ripping the collar until she exposed a broad shoulder with retreating wispy strands of hair. He snapped several pictures.

"It's very kitten with a whip, no?" the redhead said.

"No," Buck said with a shiver. *"Bonsoir."* He pocketed his phone and returned to his quest for dinner.

"You are very handsome, monsieur." She took an unsteady step forward, squinting her eyes. Her voice became as direct as her focus, and she spoke very slowly. "You look familiar."

Buck smiled. "I get mistaken for Orlando Bloom a lot," he

replied. The drag queen studied Buck's dark brown hair, staring into his hazel eyes with a blank expression. Throwing another euro into the bowl, he turned to make a quick exit.

"I get mistaken for Ann-Margret," the drag queen called out, causing him to stop in mid-step. She threw her head back and let out a cackled cry of delight, cut off by a coughing jag. "Monsieur, don't rush off! I'll take a picture of you now. For your friend? Look around you! You are standing in front of one of the oldest buildings in Belgium. Look how each statue stares down as if they see you, as if to say 'I know who you are!'" She gestured at the building across the street. Her eyes grew large, and she pulled herself to her fullest height with menacing speed. Buck jumped backward with surprise. The wet ground caused his shoe to slip and he tripped off to the side before he was able to catch himself.

Something flew past and struck the drag queen with a thud. Buck looked at her stunned expression, and downward at the dagger's handle jutting out from between her fake breasts. She wavered, swaying before collapsing onto his chest. She was heavy, and Buck struggled to lay her down carefully.

The wig spread out in a puddle like a red halo under her head. She coughed and raised her head, her eyes focused on Buck.

"Three. One. Four," she croaked out before a gunshot made her body jump.

Buck looked around quickly for any form of cover. He dove behind a set of stone stairs and pulled out his gun. He listened, but heard nothing aside from other pedestrians yelling and running for cover. Slowly, he peered around the stairs and looked through the iron rails.

The statue from in front of the Barber's Guild moved toward the dead body with great stealth and agility. The figure was covered in grayish white makeup, and he must have been waiting there for some time without moving a muscle. He was naked except for a hat pulled low to hide his face and a pair of marble-colored shorts that did little to hide the well-defined body that wore them.

Buck pulled out his camera and took photos of the statue

retrieving his knife from the drag queen's body. The statue looked up and their eyes met. The statue raised his gun and fired three shots. Buck ducked behind the stairs. He crouched down, counted quickly, and sprang out from behind the cover, gun raised and ready to shoot. After a hard landing on the pavement and a quick roll, Buck was in kneeling position, aiming and taking his shot.

The figure immediately fell to the ground, unharmed, aimed in his direction, and fired two more shots before distant sirens were heard. Buck was about to return fire when he realized that being caught by the Belgian police while on vacation would not be the best of choices. In the moment's hesitation the marbled figure leapt to his feet and darted off.

He was quickly lost in the night.

"Now, that statue has an ass you could chip a tooth on," Agent 98 mumbled. He stood, holstering his gun. The sound of approaching police sirens snapped him out of his reverie. "I'm going to get in trouble for this," he muttered, and walked back to the body of the drag queen.

The eyes stared, glazed over and lifeless. The knife was gone, and a crimson blossom spread from her chest where the knife had entered. He checked for a pulse and found none.

"Bye-bye, Birdie," Buck said, shaking his head. He could see the police cars screeching to a halt at the end of the pedestrian mall. "No time to mourn. Or eat," he said, and took off running down the street.

Buck darted between two buildings and zigzagged through several alleyways. His attention was divided between his sense of where to go and making sure no one was following him. The shouts of the public and the police were muffled, but it wouldn't take long to get a police investigation going.

He slowed his pace when he approached the parking garage. The attendant was long gone, but Buck didn't want the video cameras catching anything that might look suspicious. He regulated his breath, his heartbeat pounding against his chest—but at least the cameras couldn't see that. At the back of the first floor, Buck reached into his pocket and clicked the button on the side of his keychain. His M3 convertible BMW answered with a chirping sound and a brief flash of headlights, and the car's door unlocked.

Buck slid behind the steering wheel and started the engine with a gentle twist of the ignition key. The motor softly growled before he put the car in gear and backed out from the parking space. He scanned the garage for any sign of life. Finding nothing, he drove out into the night.

Once safely out of the city and cruising along the highway, Buck relaxed with a long breath. Reaching into his jacket, he reset the safety on his gun and was just reaching for his phone when music signaled an incoming call.

"Yeah, I knew that was coming." Buck sighed as the name *Muffin* flashed across the phone's screen. He put the phone into the empty cup holder and pushed down until it clicked into the hidden docking device. Immediately, the GPS screen pulsed into life. A flat line spread across the middle before opening a picture.

"Agent 98." The tone of the pear-shaped man appearing on the dashboard's screen was harsh. The stern expression clearly showed his displeasure was parental. His resemblance to Alfred Hitchcock was unmistakable—the round face, two hair clusters on either side of his head, and a healthy weight. "You have been on vacation for two days. Must you draw attention to yourself so quickly?"

"What can I say?" Buck said. "The paparazzi seem to love me."

"You are the queen social bee, aren't you?"

"Don't drone on, Muffin."

The tone became sharper after the unappreciated nickname. "I've asked you not to call me that."

"Yeah, yeah." Buck ignored him and reached down to press a button on the phone. "I'm sending you several photos. Do be a good boy and find out who that stone guy was, and why he was trying to kill me."

"Kill you?" the man on the screen said. He clasped his hands behind his back and rocked on his heels. "You weren't the one who got killed."

"Oh please," Buck argued as the photos were uploaded and sent through the system. "The only reason the assassin missed me is because that drunken drag queen saw him first. In a way, I guess I owe that queen my life. I should at least find out who she was. Look into that, too, would you?"

"The pictures are coming in now," Muffin replied, looking at pictures off-screen. "She does look familiar, wouldn't you say?"

"No." Buck hissed between clenched teeth. "I wouldn't say."

"Maybe not."

Irritated, Agent 98 shifted in the car seat. "Just skip the commentary and find out who she was, and more importantly, who her friend is, okay?"

"I struck a nerve, didn't I?" Muffin said with a gloating smirk. "Anything else I can help with?"

"Actually there is. Before she died, the transvestite said something odd: 'Three. One. Four.' Any idea what it could mean?"

"Now, how would I know that?" Muffin released a deep breath. "Maybe it's a date, or a country's phone code? It could be an address."

"It could be a lottery number," Buck said, exasperated. "It could be anything."

"Indeed," Muffin said. "Don't worry about that for now. We'll look into it. You just get to a different country. Check in with the embassy so we know where you are, and then finish out your vacation in peace and quiet."

The car's silence was profound and momentary. "I don't think that's going to happen."

"Really," Muffin said, holding up his palms to the screen for reassurance. "There's no need to be rash. Just go enjoy…Italy. Rome should be beautiful this time of year."

"No, Muffin, I think we're beyond that." He ignored the protests. "There's no way I'm going to relax now. I'm heading to

Antwerp and will be catching the first flight out. I'll meet you in the office tomorrow morning, about ten? Have coffee ready, will you? Only a little cream, thanks. See you then!"

"No. You don't need to, really!"

Buck silenced Muffin's arguments with the press of a dashboard button, and the screen went black.

Agent Buck 98 drove on, listening to the gentle purr of the tires on the road. His mind raced along with the car's speed, which was over the posted limit. Without taking his eyes off the road, he moved his hand to the dashboard again and pressed two more buttons. Audra McDonald's dulcet, light-operatic vocals boomed out of the car's speakers, surrounding Buck with angelic sounds. He settled into the pre-set warmed car seat, relaxing in comfort behind the wheel. His foot gave the gas pedal a nudge and the BMW sped toward the airport at Antwerp.

CHAPTER TWO

The elevator stopped and Buck let his stomach settle from the bullet ride up to the fifty-second floor. The doors opened to reveal someone standing on the other side, blocking the exit.

"Agent 98!" Muffin's voice startled Buck into taking two steps backward. Agent 69's figure in a solid black suit was imposing enough, but the complete whiteness of the room beyond temporarily blinded Buck. While it was common to be greeted at the elevator, rarely did Muffin wear such a sour scowl.

"Going down?" Buck asked with false hope.

"Precisely." Muffin stepped aside, waiting.

"You're not usually so uptight, Muffin, what gives?"

"I've rarely been this upset by you," he replied.

"This is you upset?" Buck stopped at the end of the short corridor. Only a drawer marked *Refuse*, with a handle, could be seen. "Wow. Muffin's upset. You may want to show some emotion sometime, otherwise how would I know?"

"How's this for emotion?" Muffin asked, his face completely void of expression. "The next time you fuck up on your vacation, bringing in the international police and causing diplomatic problems we now have to clean up, we will denounce you, leave you to fend for yourself, and deny we knew of your existence. You can rot in a foreign jail for all we care. And we won't lift a finger to help."

Agent 69 turned away from Buck and leaned in, pressing the

top of his head against the wall just above the refuse drawer. His fingers crawled on the surface until he found a small button barely etched into the panel, then pressed it twice. The drawer opened and a red retina scanning light shone upward. Once the scan was completed, he stepped aside, letting Buck have his turn.

"I guess that's pretty succinct," Buck mumbled, trying to avoid Muffin's eyes.

"I do hope so," Agent 69 replied. He took hold of the handle and, putting his weight into it, pushed against the door that materialized in the wall.

"It's not like I planned it that way," Buck explained. "How am I to have control over demented drag queens or killer statues that try to murder me?"

Agent 69 carefully closed the door behind them. From this side, it looked like a normal office door. "If it happens again, murderous statues will not be the worst of your concerns." He emphasized his point with a tight-lipped smile.

"Nice try," Buck said, falling back to his usual ill-timed humor. "But it doesn't compare to this one, eh, Muffin?" He flashed a full-toothed grin.

"When will you stop calling me that?" asked the non-amused agent.

"I refuse to call you Agent 69."

"Why? Does it leave a bad taste in your mouth?"

"Wow." Buck's reply was nonchalant. "That was almost funny. Almost."

He waited for Muffin to take the lead down the aisle between several rows of computers. All stations were empty, except for the very last seat in the far corner. The worker was dressed completely in white—the only color on his person was his thick black hair and glasses. He never looked up at the approaching agents, keeping his eyes focused on his computer screen as he diligently entered data.

The two men made their way to the back wall and paused in front of a heavy door.

"Besides," Buck said as Muffin punched in his code number on the keypad, "I use my name all the time and there's not a problem."

"You use your first name only. For some reason, the Agency looks the other way." He pulled the metal safety door open and ushered Buck through.

"That's because I do my job," Buck replied. "And I do it damned well."

"And above all, with modesty and humility." Muffin pulled the door shut and clicked on the light. Despite its heaviness, the door moved with little effort and in silence.

The room seemed deceptively large due to the contrast of color from the starkness of the previous areas. A window with a one-way viewing advantage looked out into the workspace with the lone typist. In the center an elongated table stretched the length of the room, with three comfortable chairs pushed in on each side. At the far end, a large retractable screen hung down from the ceiling.

Buck helped himself to a cup of coffee with milk and sat down at the table. He jutted his chin toward the viewing glass before taking a sip from the mug.

"You're getting a little slow, Muffin. Don't you usually have a trap set to test me? Something coming at me or someone attacking? I thought for sure the Stepford Stenographer out there was going to start shooting at any minute or attempt to wrestle me to the ground."

Agent 69 walked slowly to the edge of the table. He never took his eyes off Buck until he reached the front window's edge. Without a word, he picked up the small remote from the tabletop and pressed the button on the side.

The stenographer continued typing for several more sentences. Without a warning the keyboard exploded in his face. The force pushed him backward. The collision happened so fast that Buck jumped and spilled his coffee on his jeans.

Muffin remained completely calm. "The keyboards are equipped with tiny but powerful explosives."

"Evidently," Buck said. He put the coffee cup down and brushed his jeans off as best he could. "You could give a guy some warning, you know."

"I guess I'm just too slow to think of such things."

"So what the hell are the killer keyboards for, anyway?" Buck settled back down at the table and hesitantly attempted another sip.

"Assassination without being anywhere in the area," Muffin replied. The remote in his hand buzzed. "Yes, we're done with the demonstration," he said into the device. Turning his attention back to Buck, he continued, "We have them set to detonate when a preprogrammed word or number sequence is typed out on the keyboard. I can even program them to activate other explosives to set off a chain reaction, within a limited radius, of course."

A team of workers in hazmat suits came in and began cleaning up the outer chamber. Muffin clicked the remote, and a set of blinds made its way across the window, blocking out the view. Lighting automatically came on and dimmed to a comforting level.

"So what's the code word to set them off?"

Muffin's stoic expression revealed nothing. "Unless you're planning on becoming an office worker, you don't need to know." He added, "And if you don't watch yourself, I'll personally see that it happens."

"You're a harsh man, Muffin. A harsh man."

Agent 69 clicked the remote and the lights dimmed further. The screen at the table's end bubbled into a mass of swirling life before focusing and becoming a picture of the man dressed as a statue standing over the drag queen's body. The picture was one Buck had taken.

"Do we know who he is yet?" Buck asked, sinking down in the cushions of the wing-backed chair.

"Not yet," Muffin said. Several of Buck's pictures flashed onto the screen. "As you can see, there's not much facial exposure."

"Hey! *You* try to avoid bullets and take pictures at the same time. All I wanted was dinner."

"Don't get defensive, Agent 98. I only meant that his camouflage was good, and we can't get any positive identification."

"What about the tranny train wreck?" Buck asked.

"Ever sensitive toward others, I see. As a matter of fact, though, we did identify her."

The screen blinked into a split, holding two pictures. On the left was Buck's photo of the drag queen framed in the storefront doorway. The picture on the right looked completely different. An elongated-faced man with thinning, stringy brown hair in a comb-over peered out of deeply set almond eyes from under a heavy unibrow. The jagged edge of his nose bragged of surviving several breaks, and the stained, angled teeth added to his ominous appearance.

"Don't tell me that's the same person?" Buck said incredulously.

"Which is why I'm not surprised you didn't recognize him." The drag picture disappeared and another version of the mug shot photo took over the screen. "Karl Langlier, forty-five years of age, born in what is now the Czech Republic to parents of average financial income. Despite the Communist regime, he privately studied the Bible, and at age twelve, announced he wanted to enter the clergy. His parents were furious and disowned him at once. Langlier escaped to Austria and entered a religious school in Vienna. He left the school and the church five years later, and shortly thereafter went to prison for setting a church on fire—the church adjacent to the school he'd just left."

"Any survivors?"

"None." Muffin blinked through several photos dealing with Karl Langlier's life. "He was returned home and did jail time, but during the change of the Czech government somehow slipped through the cracks and was released. Eventually, he made his way to the United States and has been seen in the company of several major underworld crime bosses. We've never been able to connect him to anything, so there are no warrants out, but he's definitely suspect. In the last four years, he was seen several times in new company."

The slideshow continued. The new picture that morphed onto the screen showed a woman, caught by surprise and looking over her shoulder in the camera's general direction. Her brown bushy hair was unkempt, rolling just past her stiffly held shoulders. The oval shape to her head and her hair color contrasted sharply with the paleness of her skin tone, similar to Meissen china. Her hips held the spread of Italian peasantry, but her breasts were average in size and appeared small for her body type. Her attractiveness was not from looks or the use of minimalistic cosmetics, but from an inner strength evident even in the photograph.

"Now, her I recognize," Buck commented.

"I would hope so. Dr. Raven Evangelista," Muffin summarized. "Born here in the United States, in Greensboro, Alabama. The daughter of a Southern Baptist preacher, she was raised in strict religious schools, eventually graduating cum laude from Rutledge College. Her degrees are in chemistry and bioscience research, with a strong background in political science."

"So why do I recognize her?"

Several pictures crossed the screen. "She was married to the brilliant scientist Dr. Timothy Shoulwater."

"That's it!" Buck sat up in his chair, implanting the pictures on his memory. "Dr. Shoulwater was the guy that made the breakthrough in HIV studies, right?"

"That would be him."

"Didn't he come up with a vaccination or something to cure HIV?"

"Not quite," Muffin said. "He came up with a vaccination that would allegedly reverse the process of the virus. It would eventually eliminate all traces of HIV in the system and start to produce T-cells once again. Even in the most extreme cases in studies, the virus seemed to be controlled."

"So why the 'allegedly' comment?"

"Because he died before it could be advanced any further. A fire broke out in his private lab, and his notes were destroyed.

Unfortunately, Dr. Shoulwater didn't survive and his body was too badly burned for an autopsy."

"Any evidence left over?" Buck asked.

"Nope," Muffin answered. "It was ruled as an accident due to some faulty wiring and gas gauges."

"And do I detect doubt in your tone?"

"You certainly do," Muffin said. "It just seems a little too neat and convenient. All of his notes gone with no traces of any backed-up material."

"That was two years ago," Buck argued. "If someone else was going to publish them, they'd have done it by now, wouldn't they?"

"One would think," Muffin agreed. "But we have had recent evidence that there may have been alternative reasons for wanting Dr. Shoulwater dead." A picture of Shoulwater talking with another colleague flashed on the screen. The second man was handsome, and the smiles on both faces revealed more than just the shared laughter.

Buck sat forward, quickly assessing the picture of the two men. "Did the good doctor have a secret?"

"That is what we've come to believe."

After a long silence, Buck jumped to the next question. "Do you think that his wife, what was her name... Evangelista! Do you think she knew and...killed him?"

"You're getting a little ahead of yourself," Muffin said. More photos of Dr. Shoulwater and his companion flashed on the screen. "Divorce proceedings had already been initiated before his HIV discovery. But he had allegedly agreed to come out of the closet only after his divorce was final."

Buck finished the thought. "And Evangelista didn't want to be left out of a profitable discovery. Okay," he summarized. "Shoulwater makes this breakthrough discovery for an HIV cure, right before he comes out of the closet but after he's filed for divorce."

"Technically, his wife filed."

"But how does all this tie into the drag queen or the statue guy that tried to kill me?"

Muffin studied him carefully before speaking. "Your interest only really picks up once the subject turns back to you, doesn't it?" he continued with a heavy sigh. "We believe that Dr. Raven Evangelista contracted Karl Langlier to kill her husband and to steal all his records and notes."

Buck looked flabbergasted. "How did you come to that conclusion?"

"Langlier burned down the school and the church in Vienna on March fourteenth. Want to guess what date Dr. Shoulwater died? March fourteenth. Most contract killers have some sort of signature card, maybe this was his." Muffin rolled his eyes. "Really, Agent 98, sometimes you can be so dense." He shook his head and continued, "After doing some research we found a history of major criminal activity on that date. The assassination of Cardinal Santiago seven years ago, the shootings in New York five years ago, and the bombings in Croatia three years ago all occured on the same date: March fourteenth...three-one-four. Langlier was seen in those areas, but there is nothing to connect him to the events themselves. Except the date. I'm sure there's more, we're still researching." Muffin took a deep breath. "Skip ahead until two years ago and Dr. Shoulwater is dead. Raven couldn't steal his research and take credit for the breakthrough on her own—the world knows she doesn't have that kind of background."

"I'm sure they checked out her alibi first, being the spouse," Buck said.

"They did," Muffin concurred. "She was in a meeting and seen by over forty-five people."

"Do you think she's keeping it quiet for alternative reasons?"

"We do, but we aren't sure what they are yet," Muffin said. "She's rediscovered her conservative religious upbringing and has become quite vocal in her organization against the 'new liberal media,' as she humbly puts it."

"What organization is that?" Buck asked hesitantly.

"She is one of the founders and anchoring supporters of the Sisters of the Southern Cross."

The name registered quickly. "That loud-mouthed religious nut group? Didn't they predict the date of the Rapture…three times?"

"Say what you want, but she is personally responsible for taking that 'loud-mouthed religious nut group,' as you call them, and making them a major force behind the scenes of national politics. There has been a slight backlash against the media in this country, and her organization donates—generously—to some very prominent political campaigns."

"I can only guess her causes." Buck's sarcasm was clear. "More prayer in school, less Planned Parenthood, *no* sexual education, doing away with the evils of evolution and…"

"Doing away with the legalization of same-sex marriage," Muffin concluded. "She has several members of Congress deep into her pocket. We can't know how many for certain, but we can speculate that there are more than the few we know of."

"Does Evangelista have any personal political aspirations?"

"She hasn't shown any to date," Muffin said. "But she has written several papers on the glories of the Reagan and both Bush administrations."

"Just what we need—another closed mind. So back to me again," Buck, said taking a sip of coffee and ignoring Muffin's rolling of his eyes. "Why would Evangelista want to have *me* killed? How did I get onto her radar screen?"

"We aren't sure," Muffin said. "Maybe she knows your reputation. Maybe she knows your sense of humor."

"You know, Muffin," Buck said. He leaned across the table and pointed his finger in Muffin's direction. "You keep circling Funny Airport without ever coming in for a landing."

Muffin replied with his usual stoicism. "Get yo' finger out of my grill. If Langlier was working for Evangelista, why distract you for such a long time before attacking—and why was he working with a partner, which he had never done before? And why not use a name instead of three-one-four?"

Buck shrugged it off. "I think the drag queen was distracting me so her statuary accomplice could get a clean shot."

"But why kill the drag queen?"

"He wasn't trying to," Buck said. "I tripped and fell. The statue was trying to kill me and when I slipped, the knife went into the drag queen. The shot missed me and finished her off. It was just good old-fashioned luck."

"Not so much for the drag queen."

"What would Evangelista have to gain from her ex-husband's notes, now that she's turned into a right-winger? Surely she wouldn't want to save the lives of gay men," Buck said. "So what good are the notes to her?"

"We think she has another use for them," Muffin explained. "We believe that she is working on a very top-secret project that somehow involves Shoulwater's notes, but we're not sure what it is or for what purpose she's going to use it."

The pictures continued to flash across the plasma screen. Buck studied her image as much as possible, trying to get a feel for her. A stern oval face held-dime shaped eyes set symmetrically to a sharply sloped nose. Evangelista didn't seem a fan of cosmetics and appeared to apply them so randomly that it looked like the work of a novice. No matter how she appeared in any of the pictures, her skin looked as if she had never been out in the sun. Outside of an aura of strong confidence, which she seemed to exude in every picture, the only thing she had going for her was a pair of lengthy legs.

"I don't get it," Buck said to the photos as if they would give him the answers. "It goes against everything she stands for now. Why would a woman like Evangelista want to help cure AIDS?"

"Now, that's the million-dollar question, isn't it, Buck?" answered a female voice from behind them.

Buck immediately sat up rigid in his chair, pressing both palms against the tabletop. His eyes shut as his jaw clenched tight. A chill raced along his spine. He recognized that voice immediately. It was unmistakable.

It just wasn't one he wanted to hear.

CHAPTER THREE

I don't get it. It goes against everything she stands for now."
   She opened and closed the door without being noticed, and slipped into the room while Buck was speaking and studying the photos on screen, half of which she had taken. Assuming she was meeting Agent 69 alone, she was taken back when she heard another voice, and not too happy when she recognized it.

   "Why would a woman like Evangelista want to help cure AIDS?"

   "Now, that's the million-dollar question, isn't it, Buck?" Watching him go completely rigid so quickly was almost worth the aggravation he was going to cause her. She approached the table with confidence and a smile.

   "Agent 69," she began, genuine respect in her tone, "thank you for inviting me into this mission. You neglected to tell me I'd be carrying the weight of a team."

   "Don't underestimate yourself, Agent 46." Buck spoke with padded sincerity and a charlatan's smirk. "You carry the weight of two teams."

   "You're both pretty girls," Muffin said, standing and leaning over the table. "Now, play nice."

   Buck smiled and gave his fellow agent a polite nod of the head. "Good to see you, 46."

   She acknowledged the concession and nodded back, slowly sliding into the chair on the opposite side. "You as well, 98."

"Now," Muffin said, adjusting the buttons on his remote. The screen returned to its swirling and retracted slowly to the ceiling. The sconce lighting brightened enough without being garish. "I've asked you both here without the other's knowledge for a reason. You both excel in your fields, and when you've worked together previously...I don't want to hear it! You were both incomparable." He turned his attention to Buck. "Agent 46 here has been doing field research and investigating Dr. Raven Evangelista ever since Shoulwater died two years ago. She knows what she's talking about and has a gift for complete subtlety when obtaining invaluable information. There is no secret she can't find out. She's also one of the best, well-connected agents we have with connections in high places throughout the world. Her sources range from Hollywood celebrities and well-placed political figures, to the average person in small podunk towns. She's very smart, as you know, and you could stand to learn a thing or two from her."

"Got that, Bucky?"

"And as for you..." Muffin turned his attention to her. "Agent 98 has more field time than any other special agent. Period. Because our enemies haven't figured out he's gay, he has served us well in ways that female agents have failed. He can be subtle when he wants to, which admittedly is rare, but it can be done."

"Are you sure?" she asked with incredulous amusement. "Because I'm thinking that Helen Keller would walk by him, point and screech, 'Gaaaaaaaayyyyyyyy!'"

"Muffin!" Buck said indignantly. "How the hell am I supposed to work with that?"

"I'm sorry, Buck," Agent 46 said between breaths of laughter. "He set me up, and how was I supposed to resist?"

"Next time, you could at least make an effort."

"Agent 46," Muffin reprimanded. "You're not helping, and I'd expect better behavior from you."

"What's that supposed to mean?" Buck demanded.

"Enough already!" Muffin shouted. The room came to a quick silence. "Agent 46, say what you will, but you could learn a lot from him. And as for you, Buck—when Agent 46 isn't acting as childish as you usually are, she knows what she's talking about. Don't you remember France?"

As soon as he said it, he knew he'd crossed the line.

"Can we please *not* discuss France!" came from both agents.

Muffin put his hands up to silence the shouting. "At least there's one thing you agree on. You can start there. Anyone?"

Agent 46 watched Buck seethe in his chair. His arms were crossed so tightly she imagined he would crush his own ribs. The thought brought a malicious smile to her lips. Leaning back, she mentally counted the moments before he cracked.

She was quite surprised when he didn't.

"Come on, now," Muffin said.

Agent 46 released a heavy sigh and leaned forward on her elbows. "Look, Buck, someone's going to have to say something, right? You're not exactly my first choice of partner either, but here we are: together again." She waited for a response, and got nothing. "I know that you know your shit. I admit that in many ways, you are a superior agent. But! I know my shit. And in my fields, there are none better. We're working together. We have no choice. Do you want some douche at your back, or do you want the best in the field?"

Buck took her outstretched hand reluctantly. At least her handshake felt sincere.

"Good show, old man!" Muffin said. He got up and walked to the door.

"Besides," Agent 46 said with a sly grin, "you used to be somewhat amusing. If memory serves correctly."

"And it does," the two answered in unison.

"Very good," Muffin said, one hand on the door handle. "I'll go get the instructions for both of you, and then you can go home to pack. The rest of the briefing you can do on your own."

"Muffin!"

"You leave for Arlington, Virginia, tonight," Muffin called as he opened the door and started through. "The Sisters of the Southern

Cross are throwing a big gala at the Robert E. Lee Hotel. I'll be back in a few moments. Play nice!"

"Great," Buck muttered.

"You're going to wear a hole in the tabletop if you keep tapping like that," Agent 46 said. His fingers immediately stopped and he put his hands in his lap. She decided to throw out some bait. "Dating anyone?"

Buck spoke quickly, trying not to seem interested. "I was dating this one guy…but you know…"

They simultaneously declared: "Saving the world gets in the way of all relationships." The awkward laughter allowed them to share a brief smile. She allowed the silence to settle. It was clearly his turn.

Buck looked her over. "What about you—boys or girls? Or was Gerta a fluke event?"

She studied him with a subtle mixture of loathing and honest admiration. "Why start with that?"

"What'd I say?" Buck said, with faux shock.

"You go right for the gut without warning? Have you no decency, man?" She shook her head with pity. "All the years you've known me, how many women have I dated? One: Gerta. If you remember, that didn't work out so well."

Buck mumbled to the empty chair next to him, "How was I to know she wasn't out to her embassy?"

Agent 46 was about to reply when the door opened and Agent 69 reappeared. He resumed his seat and placed two identical briefcases on the table.

"The first thing you need to know is about the key." He held out a small silver key to each agent. "It's set for the elevator. After today, you'll need it to reach this floor. It's a safety precaution, but you will not be able to get above the fiftieth floor without this. The fifty-first floor below is empty and a buffer."

"No biggie," Buck said reaching for the key. It was quickly pulled out of his reach.

"There are things you both need to know first," Muffin continued. "The key looks like any round bicycle key, and it's pretty sturdy. If you look inside you'll see two tiny delicate prongs. Don't let anything happen to them. If they are altered in even the slightest way, they will automatically trigger the elevator's alternative mechanism. These keys are specially made and cannot be duplicated by any means."

"Okay," Agent 46 said, after a moment's silence, "I'll ask. What is the elevator's alternative mechanism?"

"Let's just say it's the faster way down."

Buck said to the lady, "I think I'll let you open your briefcase first."

"Nope," Muffin concluded. "You can do that on your own. There are things to be taken care of before you leave this evening."

"I need to get my nails done," Agent 46 whispered. "Do be a good little boy and get our IDs and airline tickets."

"Don't you think there are more important things than getting your nails done?"

She smiled a salacious grin. "Never underestimate a woman with French tips."

"Ah, Buck," Muffin interrupted. "I need to discuss something with Agent 46, so you might as well get the paperwork going anyway."

"Yes, Bucky." She waved her fingers at him as he walked out of the room. "Run along now."

❖

Agent 46 glared down at the personal identification card in her hand. Clenching her teeth, she swallowed her anger and snapped the plastic card against her leg.

"I don't know why I'm surprised," she said over Buck's howling laughter. "I knew you had something planned."

Buck thanked the driver with a moderate tip and gathered the bags. "At least it's a good picture. Better than most have on their ID cards."

"It's not the picture I object to; couldn't you have picked a better name than…" She looked at the card and read it disdainfully. "Miss Noxia von Tüssëll? And I'm guessing that you booked all the reservations under this name, didn't you."

"As a matter of fact, I did."

"Great. Now I'm going to have to deal with this ridiculous name for the rest of the mission. Noxia von Tüssëll."

"Actually," he confided, "I think the accent is on the first part, TOO-sell. It's not ridiculous. I'm not sure, but I think it's German."

"You're a real son of a bitch," Noxia seethed.

"Hey, at least I didn't give you some ancient age."

"No," she sneered back, picking up her few bags. "At *most* you didn't give me some ancient age. And do tell, what is your name for the mission?"

"Mr. Buck Miller."

"Of course it is. Don't even try to get out of this with that over-capped, toothy grin. It doesn't work on me."

"They are not capped!" Buck said indignantly. "And it works on everyone."

"We'll see." She started into the airport ahead of him, leaving him to wrestle with his two bags.

He called after her, "I did book us first class!"

Noxia walked up to the counter.

"May I help you?" asked the attendant politely.

"Yes, my name is…" There really was no choice now. "Noxia von Tüssëll."

"I beg your pardon?"

"Here." She slid the ID card across the counter. "It's just easier."

"No problem, ma'am. You'll be boarding first class at gate 20C."

"Are we checked in yet?" Buck asked as he bounded up to the

counter. Noxia rolled her eyes at him and glared. "I'll just meet you at the gate. I need to use the bathroom first."

Noxia said nothing, but walked off as fast as she could. Waiting in line for security with her shoes in hand, she went over the name again: Noxia von Tüssëll. It wasn't the best, but at least it had some flair. Buck could be so annoying sometimes, but she had no other choice but to put up with him, if the mission was to succeed.

"Agent 46," came a deep, whispered voice.

Noxia looked up to see a friend of hers in a security uniform. "Timothy." She gave him a sincere smile. "I didn't know you were assigned security. Whom did you piss off?"

Timothy smiled back. "Too long a story to go into right now. What are you waiting in line for? Come with me." He let her gather her things and led her around the security gate. "She's a good friend of mine," Timothy whispered to the checking guard.

"Timothy," Noxia playfully said. She leaned on his shoulder as she put her shoes back on. "Do you want to have a little fun, *and* do me a favor at the same time?"

His smile impishly grew. "What did you have in mind?"

Noxia leaned forward and whispered into Timothy's ear. He looked at her with newfound admiration. "You are an evil woman."

"Yes," she agreed.

"Oh, Noxia!" Buck frantically waved at her from the other side of the security. "Noxia, wait up!"

"I'm assuming that's him?"

"Yes, Timothy, that's him."

"Attractive," Timothy replied. "This'll be fun." He moved over to stand behind the x-ray machine.

Holding his Italian loafers in his hand, Buck emptied his pockets into the plastic bin. Waiting until his bag was going through the machine, Buck walked through the metal detector. The red light flashed immediately.

"Wait," the guard said, stopping Buck in his tracks. "Please go through again, sir." The second time was no different. "Please step over here." Buck moved to where he was told. The guard held the wand and waved it over his body. When it passed over the front of his pants, the wand buzzed.

"What's up?" Buck asked. "I'm not wearing a belt."

"Any coins in your pocket?"

"There should be nothing there," Buck insisted as the wand waved over his pants and the alarm sounded again.

"I'm not touching that comment," Noxia said with a smile. "I'm going to the gate. Hopefully you'll make the plane."

"Noxia! Wait!" The call was in vain as she walked away, waving her fingers over her shoulder.

Buck did a mental check. "No rings, watches, or bracelets. My belt is off and my phone is in the bin. There should be nothing triggering this."

Timothy waved the wand over Buck's body again, and once more it buzzed as it passed over the front of his slacks.

"Sir, I'm going to pat you down to make sure there's nothing here." Timothy did as he promised. Looking at the guard across the machine, Timothy announced in a voice louder than needed, "There's nothing in his pants. I felt absolutely nothing in his pants."

"Could you phrase that differently, please?" Buck insisted. "You could have a little tact."

Timothy turned around. "Sir, I'm afraid that we're going to have to give you a more thorough search. Hopefully it won't make you miss your plane." He took the protesting Buck by the arm and had another security officer drag along his bags.

Fifteen minutes later Buck ran down the Jetway and entered the plane as they were about to close the door.

Noxia watched him take his seat next to her and get buckled in and settled. The plane immediately started down the runway. She could hear his angered breathing over the jet's engines.

"Do you want the window seat?" Noxia offered. "I'll be nice and switch if you'd like."

"No!" Buck replied. "I prefer the aisle."

"Calm down," Noxia said. "I've ordered you a Cape Cod. You still drink them, right?" Buck didn't say anything, but gave the briefest of nods in her direction. "Oh, get over it, Buck. Nothing happened, besides a little inconvenience. Between the two of you, I'm willing to bet Timothy got the worse end of it."

"Timothy?" It dawned on Buck she'd arranged the entire thing. "So that's payback, is it? Just wait, you'll get yours, you crazy bitch!"

Noxia turned in her seat and smiled at Buck. Without warning, she plunged her hand into the seat between his legs. She twisted her fist until the nail of her index finger dug deeply into Buck's crotch.

"Do you feel that?" She pushed her manicured nail deeper against his perineum. "That's the tiny razor that Agent 69 put under my French manicure. I'm sure you feel it now?" She felt the nail cut through the slacks and press into his flesh. "I'm not putting up with much of your shit this time around. So you're going to take it down a notch. And never call me a bitch—I really don't like it."

Noxia sat back in her seat and began leafing through the SkyMall magazine. The attendant brought Buck's drink and a chilled glass with a mini bottle of champagne for Noxia. "Look, you got a little manhandled by a very handsome gay friend of mine. It lasted a few minutes and I thought you'd like it." She got no response. "I have to live with this ridiculous name for the rest of the mission, and there's no telling how long that'll be."

"I told you," Buck said sullenly. "It's not ridiculous, it's German. And these *were* Prada!"

"Get over it," Noxia said. "You got alotta Prada."

"Now I'll have to take them to my tailor."

"Small price to pay," Noxia said. She put away the magazine and took out her laptop. "I'm going to watch a movie, you want to share it with me?" She pointed to the complimentary headphones in the seat pocket in front of them.

"What are you watching?" Buck said, starting to let his guard down.

"One of my favorites—a good friend of mine is in it, actually. *Any Given Sunday.*"

"Wait," Buck said taking a deep drink of his cocktail. "That stars Al Pacino, Charlton Heston…"

Noxia finished the list. "Cameron Diaz, Dennis Quaid, and Ann-Margret."

"Great. Just great." Buck let the headphones drop into his lap. "Can this flight get any worse?"

CHAPTER FOUR

Noxia entered Dixie, the hotel bar, looking and feeling fantastic. Her hair was carefully crafted atop her head, reminiscent of Audrey Hepburn. Knowing her olive skin highlighted the little suntan she had, Noxia used her makeup expertly to draw attention to her high cheekbones and piercing brown, almond-shaped eyes. She only wore an inch heel due to her height. She was a strikingly handsome woman, shapely and sensual looking. She spotted Buck first, sitting at a banquette in the back and looking handsome in a black pinstriped suit. He was texting something on his phone and didn't notice her entrance at first, but as if on cue he looked up and waved her over.

"It's always a bad sign when the man looks prettier than the woman," she said, approaching the table.

"Not if you're the man," Buck replied. He began sliding out of the seat.

"Don't bother," Noxia said with a sigh, sitting down next to him.

"I ordered you a drink, a French 007 if memory serves correctly."

"And it does."

Buck gave her a quick once-over. "That dress is very nice."

"Thank you," Noxia replied quickly. "But this dress isn't nice. 'Nice' is what you say when you've heard a friend's nine-year-old

do the entire score from *Wicked*: 'That's nice, dear, now run along.'"
She listed the differences. "This dress does everything a Vera Wang
original is supposed to do. This dress isn't nice; it's fabulous."

"Okay. It's fabulous, then." He shrugged. "I just texted Muffin,
and he's supposed to send me a blueprint of the hotel."

"Why do you call him that?" Noxia asked. "It can't be just
because of the '69' thing."

"No. It really isn't. It started off that way but it's turned into
something more, like a term of endearment."

"For you, maybe."

"Don't let him fool you," Buck said with a knowing nod.
"He knows how I mean it, and if it really bugged him, he'd let me
know."

"Yours is on the house, sir," said the handsome blond waiter as
he put the drinks before them.

"Thank you, Evan," Buck replied graciously.

"If you need anything else," Evan said, pausing provocatively,
"just let me know."

Buck flashed the full-toothed smile. "I may well do that." Noxia
turned away, sipping deeply from her champagne. Evan lingered for
a moment before meandering back behind the bar.

"Friend of yours?" Noxia asked dryly.

"An acquaintance for now," Buck said. "Possibly a friend later.
This is my second drink, and I've yet to pay for either."

"You're amazing," Noxia said, unimpressed.

"Hey, membership has so few advantages. Is it my fault I know
how to work the ones I have?"

"Aren't you concerned about expectations?"

"Definitely. And I'm looking forward to them."

"One drink can be a simple flirtation; two drinks…" She took a
sip of her cocktail. "That's an implication of things to come."

"Possibly. Being gay is a different game with a different set of
rules," Buck said. "For now, as long as I don't ask for the drinks, I
have no reason to pay off. Plus," he gazed over to the bar to find Evan

chatting to another server; both were staring directly at him, "you don't have to feel sorry for me, it's not that much of a hardship."

Noxia leaned back against the banquette's cushion. "It wasn't you I was feeling sorry for."

"Your dinner companions just arrived, *Noxia*; Bitter and Jealousy. Oh hey, girls!"

Noxia forced a smile and took a full sip of her cocktail. He puffed himself up proudly, a smug look on his face.

"Look," Noxia said quietly. "Why don't we bury the hatchet here and now, what do you say? Otherwise, it's going to be a *very* long mission."

"Terms?"

"Simple," Noxia said. She downed the rest of her cocktail. "Do you need another? No? I'd like one." She turned and signaled to Evan, who quickly brought her another drink. "I have a little anger about something," she continued when the drink arrived. "If you just apologize about the French incident, I can get over it and move on. Sound good?" She held up her drink for a toast.

"Ah, no." Buck took a deliberate sip of his vodka cranberry. "I don't like those terms."

"Come on, Buck. One of the top Agency rules: Never leave a fellow agent in danger."

"You weren't in any *real* danger."

She stared at him incredulously. "I was hanging by my wrists under the Viaduc de Millau, and you don't think that's 'real danger'?"

"Help was on its way," Buck said with an indignant squirm in the seat. "Gendarmes were notified."

"I was swinging like a pendulum under the highest bridge in the world!" Noxia said. Her voice hissed with controlled quiet. "It was three hours before they got me down, and you were less than five kilometers away at the time!"

"I was in pursuit of someone."

"You were in pursuit of a date!" Her voice grew louder. "I

was left strung up over eleven hundred feet with a diamond tennis bracelet cutting into my wrists!"

"Keep your voice down, people are staring," Buck said, glancing around. "And if that was the case, you should have just used it to cut your restraints."

Noxia sat back. "You could have come got me, and you didn't."

"Pierre was leaving town that evening. I didn't know when I was going to see him again."

She shook her head. Narrowing her eyes, she asked, "*Have* you seen him again?"

"That's not the point."

"You're right, that's not the point," she said calmly. "The point is that aside from any set of Agency rules, I thought we were better friends than that. It hurt that you tossed our friendship aside for your *tryst de amore*. Don't you think you owe me the smallest of apologies?"

Buck stared at the tabletop lost in thought. He reached into his inside pocket and took out a pen. Hovering over a napkin as if it were his college exam, he scribbled something down and slid it over to Noxia.

"How can you write that small? I can't even read this. What does it say?"

"It's the smallest of apologies." Buck let the slow grin grow into a full smile.

Noxia gave in and laughed with a shake of her head. "Thank you," she said quietly.

"I'm ready for that drink now." He raised his hand to catch Evan's attention; it wasn't difficult. "Another for you, so you can catch up?"

"Sure," Noxia said, feeling the tension dissipate.

"Thank you, Evan."

"My pleasure. For the lady." He placed the drink in front of Noxia. "And for the gentleman. It's on me," he added with a wink, and returned to the bar.

"I have to say," Noxia said after a few moments of silence, "I do admire that you have such a strong sense of conviction, this inner self-confidence and determination to continue, whether you are wrong or right."

"You say that like it's a bad thing," Buck answered. "Just when did it get to be socially unacceptable to have a strong sense of self-confidence? I find it funny in some places you can be self-confident, then in other places it's called 'arrogance.'"

"Yeah, but," Noxia continued, "in all the years we've known each other, you just charge forward with such a lack of fear. Aren't you afraid of anything?"

Buck's answer was immediate. "Nope. Nothing."

"Nothing at all." She threw out the bait and watched him avoid eye contact with her. She could feel the grin tugging at the sides of her mouth. "I bet I could find something that you're afraid of," she purred.

"Do your best then, Miss Noxia von Tüssëll."

She pounced. "Let's make it interesting. I need to figure out what is the one thing that scares you the most. Loser pays all expenses including four airline tickets, for us both and our guest of choice, winners in first class, losers in coach."

"Wait. Why do the losers get to go?"

"They get to be a servant for twenty-four hours while we are there. This applies to us only. Our guests aren't required to do anything but watch the fun. Then there are gloating privileges, of course." Noxia smiled.

"Where to?" He leaned in closely, eyes wide.

"Belize, for a week's vacation."

"How long do you have to figure it out?"

"The end of the mission." Her smile appeared. "It could be two weeks, it could be a year."

Buck sat back, mentally reviewing his potential vacation guest list. He reached for his cocktail and held it up for her. "My dear Noxia, you have a bet." Their glasses clinked, sealing the deal. "What time do we need to be upstairs?"

Noxia glanced at her watch. "We should probably start to find our way to the gala."

He signaled to Evan they were leaving. A moment later, Evan brought over the black check holder and left it on the table. "Have a good evening," Evan cooed at Buck. "Come back and see me again, soon." Evan winked and walked away, Buck watching his every step.

"Before we head out," he said, "tell me a little about this hotel."

"The Robert E. Lee," Noxia began, "was taken over and renovated last year by Dr. Raven Evangelista herself. Probably used as a tax break. She holds meetings here, and major fund-raising parties. She doesn't live in Virginia, and it can be assumed the hotel's proximity to Washington DC is the reason behind her investment."

"And who is the beneficiary of tonight's gala?"

"Undetermined," Noxia answered. "It's just a political fund-raiser for the Sisters of the Southern Cross."

"So, basically I schmooze and eat, and you go tap into the computer system?"

"Not quite," Noxia corrected. "I'm better at observing than you are, and you're definitely more tech savvy than I. You tap into the computer and I'll schmooze."

"Fine by me." Opening the check holder, Buck chuckled aloud.

"What's so funny?" Noxia said. "Membership doesn't have as many advantages as you thought?"

"Not that at all," Buck said, closing the black book and sliding it over to her. "Membership privileges are great, but you need to be a member. This is for your drinks. I'll wait for you outside."

Buck walked outside of the bar into the lobby of the Robert E. Lee hotel. The room looked more like an outside courtyard than a hotel lobby. The center area was filled with wicker furniture with plush cushions. A dark oaken desk ran along the wall to his right, serving as the concierge check-in area. Two elevators were hidden along the back wall, disguised in the trunk of a huge weeping willow tree. The branches were painted along the walls above the elevator cars, and actual tree branches crept along the ceiling and hung downward with tiny sparkling lights.

"Great," Buck mumbled.

"What is it?" Noxia asked as she joined Buck in the lobby.

"Look at the elevators." He pointed. After the third floor, the elevator shaft was made of clear glass. The entire lobby could be viewed from the elevators as they traveled from the third floor to the penthouse. "I don't care for glass elevators—they remind me of Willy Wonka."

"You have to admit," Noxia said. "It's creative and beautifully done."

"I feel like I should be on a veranda, with a fan in my hand and someone making mint juleps."

"Well, Big Daddy," Noxia said, wrapping her arm within Buck's, "let's go see what kindness we can find in these strangers."

They walked casually to the center of the lobby and looked around, observing the crowd. Well-dressed figures cut the formal occasion's edge, and the scent of *nouveau riche* hung in the air like old-world magnolia blossoms. Couples and small groups milled around, conversing before making their way to the elevator tree trunks.

A handsome gentleman with skin the color of rich chocolate stood at attention between the elevator cars. The uniform he wore clung to the shape of his body, framing him in the waiter tuxedo of an old-fashioned Southern server. His hands were clasped behind his back and his broad shoulders winged back at attention. "Good evening," he said.

"Good evening," Noxia said. She reached into her black clutch and took out the finely printed invitation, reading off the title of the evening's event. "The Nights of Southern Comfort?"

"Very good, ma'am," the attendant said after looking over the invitation. He turned and pressed the call button with one white-gloved finger. The yellow lights above immediately came to life. The far car arrived and opened. Noxia took a step toward it. "Excuse me, ma'am. For this evening, that car is for hotel guests. This car has been designated for tonight's event."

"Oh," Noxia said taking a step backward.

"I swear," Buck whispered to the attendant. "I can't take her anywhere."

"I can hear you," Noxia said through a faux smile. The car arrived and another identically dressed attendant stepped out.

"I'll take them up, Sebastian," the attendant said after throwing Buck a coy glance. Sebastian looked from his coworker to the couple and nodded. He stepped aside.

The three got into the elevator and stood in opposite corners. The attendant withdrew his keycard and swiped it through the slot next to the floor buttons on the panel. The doors immediately closed and he pressed the button for the penthouse ballroom on the twelfth floor.

The elevator began its ascent.

As soon as the car's view opened to the lobby, Buck put his back to the glass, grasping the handrail, and turned to face Noxia and the attendant. "Is there always a separate car for the penthouse?" Buck asked immediately.

"No," the attendant answered. "Usually both cars are open for guests below the eleventh floor. Anyone going any higher would need a specially programmed key to get to the Presidential Suite, the Penthouse Suite, and the private ballroom on the penthouse floor. But for tonight's event this one car has been reprogrammed as an express to the private ballroom on the top floor."

"Won't we need a key to get down?" Buck asked.

"No, sir. The key is to get up only."

"I always thought the key was—knowing how to go down."

Noxia jumped into the momentary awkwardness. "You've been very kind, personally taking us and all. What's your name?"

"Randall. I am Randall Hardin."

"Miller," he said with keener interest. "I'm Buck Miller."

"Nauseous," Noxia mumbled. "I'm getting nauseous."

The car came to a halt. Noxia politely stepped aside and

motioned for Buck to exit first. He walked out but spun around to hold the elevator door open for her. It was unnecessary, as Randall had already done it. Their hands touched, and the elevator door closed, separating the two men. When Buck turned around he was startled by the incredulous expression Noxia was giving him.

"Don't hate me 'cause I'm beautiful," he said with a Southern accent and a toss of his head.

"I don't," she answered, turning the corner. "I hate you because you're a dog!"

Tiny tea lights guided the path down the hall strewn with colorful flower petals. At the far end a set of draped double doors stood closed and waiting.

"Is this a benefit or a sacrifice?" Buck whispered.

"From what I know of Raven Evangelista," Noxia answered, "some from column A, some from column B."

CHAPTER FIVE

They were greeted by the sounds of "The Blue Danube" upon entering the ballroom. The music came from an orchestra on a dais directly under the hanging flag on the back wall. The flag was a variation of the Confederate battle flag. The background was still red, but the blue bars that ran down the center formed a cross instead of an X. In the upper right corner were sewn the initials "SOSC."

"I'm guessing," Buck said after taking a moment to find his breath, "that Raven has never been accused of putting the 'b' in subtle."

"That's an understatement," Noxia said.

They moved into the room with the next wave of arriving people. The food servers weaving in and out of the crowd were all wearing matching tuxedos reminiscent of an era long past. They were all African American, in contrast to the majority of guests.

"I'm not seeing the bar," Buck reported.

"It's around," Noxia said, scanning the crowd about her. "What I am seeing is three senators, one Supreme Court Justice, and four congressmen, including Mr. Julian from South Carolina—he's the one that interrupted the president's speech on repealing Don't Ask Don't Tell, remember?"

"Oh, yeah, the typical conservative Republican who preaches about the sanctity of marriage until caught with a fifty-dollar hooker in the Cloud Hotel?"

"That's him. It didn't hurt his career all that much, though."

"Is he still married?" Buck asked, watching Noxia carefully follow the congressman's movements.

"Separated and she's filed for divorce," Noxia answered. "But that hasn't been made public yet. Besides, marital discord never hurt a politician's status. He definitely is handsome," Noxia replied. "Look, Buck, there's going to be a lot of people in this room you are bound to disagree with. I'm not sure if you are aware of this, but your internal editor quit a long time ago, and when you get nervous or uncomfortable with people, you can be…a prick."

"Good line—internal editor quitting; I'll have to remember that," Buck replied. "And thank you for at least not calling me a little prick."

"When you get that way, you are definitely a big prick. I'm asking nicely. We're on a information seek and find here, let's try to keep things on the down low until you can figure out how to get into the computer system, all right?"

He crossed his heart with an exaggerated motion. "I promise to be Mommy's Little Helper and not get into trouble. Too much."

"Go get a drink," Noxia said with an exasperated breath. "I have a congressman to flirt with." She ran her hands over her shapely hips and almost immediately became lost in the crowd.

"Easier said than done," Buck muttered just as a waiter whisked by with one lone filled champagne flute. He managed to grab it before it escaped and took a sip, testing the quality. "Good champagne," he assessed. "Evangelista must be hoping for a large return."

Something delicious-smelling breezed past him and Buck turned to find out what it was. He followed a server carrying a tray that seduced his senses of smell and appetite. Pushing his way through the flash mob around the server, Buck managed to get one of the last remaining hors d'oeuvres before they were snapped up. Popping what looked like a seasoned saltine with a dab of chili on it into his mouth, he wasn't expecting the burst of flavor, or the slight burn of spices on his taste buds. The heat burned through his nasal cavity as he took a deep breath.

"Now, that's good," Buck moaned to no one in particular. Glancing around, he saw no sign of other servers. "Who do you have to fuck to get another one of these?"

"So glad you liked them," said a soft-spoken voice from behind him. Buck spun around to find himself looking into the amber eyes of a very handsome man. "I'm the chef."

The smooth skin and jet-black hair made discerning the man's age a challenge because of the elfish way his hair hung straight down on either side of his ears. The men stood at equal height.

"I beg your pardon," Buck said, taken off guard.

"No problem," the man said with a polite smile. "Thank you for the compliment."

Buck blinked several times. "I'm sorry," he said. "My name is Miller. Buck Miller. Yours?"

"Richard Pye, chef and owner of Rebel Catering."

The two men shook hands. Something electric passed from one to the other, connecting their breaths with deeper heaviness. Their shared smile grew as their handshake stopped but their palms remained locked. Buck cleared his throat. The heat passing between them spread a little too far through his body.

"What's in those little bites, the spicy crackers?" Buck asked. "Or is that a trade secret, so you'd have to kill me once you've told me?"

"You're no good to me dead, Mr. Miller," Richard said with a playful smirk before hastily pushing forward. "They're called Southern Firecrackers, and it was one of my first recipes. Homemade flatbread with simple spices, but they're always a favorite."

"I've always said," Buck replied with a lingering meaning, "they may sing for their supper, but if you're a good cook it's your choice if you want them to stay for breakfast."

"I can appreciate that sentiment," Richard said. "I take it you serve a grand breakfast?"

"A spread you'll never forget," Buck said, keeping their eyes locked. "But alas, much like Professor Higgins, I'm a 'confirmed old bachelor and likely to remain so,' and being married to my work, my dating life is nil."

"What is your line?"

"To bet a handsome chef that I can make better hors d'oeuvres and hope for the best."

"When you're not making people feel slightly awkward or speechless," Richard said, his cheeks flushing. "What is it you do for work?"

"I have an antique store in Palm Springs," Buck replied, remembering the cover story. "It's called History Repeats, and it allows me to mix my hobby with work."

"What brings you to Virginia?"

"A love of classics—there are a lot of antique dealers out here. And of course, our hostess this evening." Buck let his smile grow, showing his white teeth. "Tell me more about yourself. How long have you been in catering?"

"I've had a passion for cooking for as far back as I can remember." Richard's voice was low and even. As he spoke his face softened and his eyes sparkled with memory. "A woman down the street used to take care of me when I was younger; I was raised by a single mother who worked all the time. Anyway, this woman used to cook Southern comfort foods and soul food from her days in Alabama." He smiled, his pearly teeth showing through his soft lips. "She used to say 'comfort foods feed the soul,' and that's what Southern cooking is all about."

"I thought Southern cooking was all about 'fat equals flavor'?" Buck joked. "Sorry." He bit his lip, knowing it made him look boyishly cute. "My internal editor quit, and sometimes my mouth gets ahead of my brain."

Richard laughed. "Your internal editor? That's funny. In the South both of those expressions are tried and true. Besides, when did you ever see a thin Southern chef?"

Buck raised his eyebrows. "I don't know, you look pretty svelte."

"Thank you," Richard replied, looking away. "Being image conscious is something I learned from my main patroness."

"And who is that?"

Richard looked at Buck and smiled. "Dr. Evangelista, of course." He said it nonchalantly. "You may not know it to look at her, but Raven Evangelista is just a good ole girl at heart. She's been very appreciative of my work and has become a generous patron. I'm pretty much top chef here at the Lee, and when she hosts an important event, she'll take me to wherever she hosts it."

"Don't you find working for her to be," Buck tried his best to put it discreetly, "a slight conflict?"

"Why?" Richard asked surprised. "She's an employer like anyone else. She pays better than most and I have benefits, including dental." He smiled his sensual, pearly grin. "She has her political views and I don't comment on them. If anything, I try to avoid discussions on the subject. Raven also introduces me to many important potential clients."

"So you're a capitalist who cooks like Mammy Yokum."

Richard looked confused. "I'm not sure how to take that."

"I'm sorry," Buck said sincerely. His hand crept out and took hold of Richard's wrist. The momentary connection rekindled the electricity they shared, and Richard began to soften. "I told you my mouth gets ahead of my brain. When I get nervous, I say stupid things."

"Are you nervous, Mr. Miller?" Richard flashed a smile. "Don't worry about it. You're a clever man and I can appreciate your candor. But," Richard nodded and took a step back, "I do need to get back to work. I hope you'll excuse me."

"Sure." Buck nodded.

"Enjoy the night, and I'm sure we'll see each other again." Richard stuck out his arm.

"I hope so," Buck replied. They shook hands. It was brisk and the previously felt connection was gone.

"I do have to run, sorry." Richard clasped both of Buck's hands in his own. "It was a pleasure to meet you."

"The pleasure was mine." Buck started to smile, but Richard flashed a brief grin and ran off into the crowd.

Buck's heart beat quickly, but his skin felt a distinctive chill. From the infinite playlist in his mind, Broadway divas belted out songs about the fears and delights of potential romance. The lyrics filled him equally with hesitation and delight.

"Excuse me," came a chilled voice, cutting through his mental fantasy and dousing him with cold reality.

Buck replied without turning around. "That depends on what you did." The light laugh he offered fell on deaf ears.

"I try my best to personally meet everyone at my fund-raisers," the woman said. "I am Dr. Raven Evangelista."

Buck gave her his complete attention. Russet bangs hung down her forehead, and her dark brown eyes studiously bored into him. Wisps of hair hung loosely down the sides of her rounded face, and her nose hovered over tightly clasped thin lips. Most of her hair was pulled back and concealed by a white snood hanging against her nape. It gave a soft feel to an otherwise tightly pulled figure. The black trim along the pale gown's edges accentuated her curvy hips.

"Buck Miller," he said, extending a hand. "It's my pleasure to meet you." Shaking her hand was like holding wet spaghetti.

"Have we met before?" She peered at him. "You look awfully familiar."

"I get that a lot." He laughed. "I doubt it. When I come to Virginia, it's usually to hunt for antiques or for an estate sale." He slowly unleashed his charm. "I think I would remember you."

"You're very kind, Mr. Miller."

"Well, you seem to be a woman of very distinct taste. Your hair is beautiful, very Eva Perón. Before the chignon."

Her face remained stoic. "Was that supposed to be a compliment?"

"Sure it was."

"Than I'll forgive you, and take it as you intended." She smiled. It was an eerie effect through the wrong-colored lipstick.

"I beg your pardon, I meant no offense." Buck showed more

tooth, hoping to smooth over the choppy water. "As hostess, maybe you can answer a question." He pushed through the obvious transition. "What is the fund-raiser for this evening? I have to admit, I'm not sure."

She studied him for a moment, her eyes blinking as if taking memory photos. "It's for the Sisters of the Southern Cross."

"I'm sorry," Buck replied, when no other explanation followed. "I'm not familiar with them. Are they a local charity?"

"No," she said with an exaggerated, polite chuckle. "They're a national organization."

"What do they do? Are they like Civil War enactors, or the Daughters of the American Revolution? Or do they do civic work, cleaning up streets?"

Raven's jaw clenched tight, and her chin jutted out defiantly.

"We definitely help clean up, Mr. Miller, but our goals are higher. Our aim is to clean up the morals of America. Our country has fallen into debauchery, like ancient Rome, and as with Rome, it will be our undoing." She spoke like a well-seasoned orator.

"Some would interpret that by saying we are growing as a country," Buck reflected. "That we are having a moral renaissance after a petty dictator's regime."

Raven barked out an exaggerated laugh. "If we are having a renaissance in this country, it is because people are realizing the power of prayer is strong, and that strength is found in the Lord. There is a steady stream of religious viewpoints becoming a stronger voice in our nation. What our country is seeing is not so much a renaissance as it is reclaiming its greatness from the liberal media. The United States needs to be back onto a true conservative and proper path to righteousness."

"What kind of righteousness are we talking about?" Buck asked. "Are we talking restrictions on what theories can be taught to children, or what words can be said in public schools? Or are we talking the basic rights of marriage for all people?"

"Two excellent points," Raven said. "Schools need to be stricter with what they are teaching our children. They are our nation's future. They need to be protected."

"Protected from what, or should I ask from whom?"

Raven clasped her hands together. "Protected from those who can bring them harm. Degenerates, or those who break the law."

"Which laws?" Buck pressed.

"Man's law," Raven barked. She drew a quick breath and recomposed herself. "And of course, God's law."

"The two are very different."

"They can be." She smiled. "They can also be one and the same. Enjoy the evening, Mr. Miller." Keeping her smile frozen in place, she nodded politely and walked past him. Several people followed in her wake.

Buck remained still and pensive. As a waiter flashed by, he reached out and grabbed another snack from the tray.

"I've been watching for the last few minutes, but didn't want to interrupt." Noxia sauntered over with two champagne glasses in her hands. She offered one to Buck. "What did Evangelista have to say?"

"Well," Buck sorted out the last bit in his mind, "it wasn't so much what she said, more of how she said it. I felt like she was issuing a warning."

"To you personally?"

"Maybe, but I don't think so," Buck said, sipping from the champagne flute. He allowed her to ease her arm through his as they milled around the room. "I think she was trying to be ominous, but it comes across like the German warning scene in *The Sound of Music:* 'The Anschluss *is* coming, Captain'; a little melodramatic."

"You really can turn anything into a musical reference, can't you?"

"Hey," Buck said. "You can learn everything from musical theater, so don't knock it."

"Well, how are we going to solve that problem, Maria?"

"I'm not sure, but I'm about to solve another. Give me a

moment, will you, Noxia?" He slid his arm free and walked over to where Richard stood talking to a server. He tapped Richard on the shoulder and waited politely.

"I just wanted to say I hope I didn't offend you," Buck said, not giving Richard a chance to say anything.

"No. Not at all." The pearly smile expanded. "Actually, I was coming to find you, Mr. Miller."

"Buck, please. Really?" He hoped his excitement didn't betray him.

"Buck." Richard said the name as if trying it out on his tongue. "I wanted to give you this earlier, but…" He held out his card.

"Buck, dear, who's your friend?" Noxia said, joining them.

"Noxia, this is Richard Pye, he owns Rebel Catering and provided the food for the evening," he said coldly, resenting the interruption.

"My sincerest compliments," Noxia said. "Everything I've had has been delicious."

"Thank you," Richard replied. His confused look flickered from Buck to Noxia and back again.

"Noxia's a dear old, *old* friend. She was afraid she wouldn't have any fun, so she twisted my arm into coming tonight."

"As an escort?" Richard said, only half-jokingly.

Buck answered before Noxia could. "More like a chaperone. She's never been able to hold her liquor."

"Hey," Noxia said. "I'm not really a pathetic lush, but I can take a hint. Buck, I'll be over there when you're done talking. Take your time. Richard, the food is fantastic. A pleasure to meet you."

"The pleasure was mine. You don't have to go." He smiled. "I actually need to get ready for the next wave of appetizers." Stopping a passing waiter, he took a small, rounded sandwich and handed it to Buck. "In regard to your challenge earlier, I'll let this Muffaletta Pinwheel be my entry. I doubt you'll be able to beat it."

He held it out. With the first bite, Buck's eyes closed and an ethereal look of pleasure crossed his face. "That is delicious."

Richard leaned in close and whispered softly. "Trust me,

breakfast won't be that easy." He locked eyes with Buck. "Have a good night. I hope to hear from you." He looked over Buck's shoulder, giving Noxia a polite nod before turning and disappearing into the crowd.

"Another club member, I take it?" she asked, rejoining Buck.

"Oh yeah," he moaned. "As far as I'm concerned, he can be president."

Noxia moved her hand in front of his eyes several times in succession to no avail. "Good Lord, Buck's been hit by lightning. This was unexpected." The smile on her face turned inwardly malicious. "This'll be fun to watch. In the meantime, hello! What about Raven Evangelista?"

The sound of the name pulled Buck out of his trance. He blinked a few times.

"What kind of feel did you get from her?" Noxia prompted. "What's she like?"

"If the iceberg that hit the *Titanic* could smile and take human form…" Buck began.

The band broke out into the classic tune of Dixieland. The crowd stopped talking amongst themselves and turned to face the dais. Raven climbed the side stairs as the band finished their melody.

"Warn the captain," Noxia whispered. "I'm seeing white peaks in the water."

"I've already heard enough of her," Buck said. "I think I'm going to go find a way into the computer system. I'll meet you back at the hotel suite." He patted her shoulder and discreetly took his leave.

CHAPTER SIX

B uck retraced his steps to the elevator and pressed the button. His foot tapped the floor impatiently; his eyes scanned the lit numbers, watching them race to the top.

"All I have to do now," he mumbled, "is to find the computer room, break in, and connect my little spy device into their port system. No problems. I should have let Noxia do this while I stayed and listened to a bad speech with great food."

The elevator opened and four guests got out. They followed the flowered carpet toward the ballroom and entered without a look back.

"Going down?" asked the attendant.

"Mr. Hardin." Buck immediately put on his charming smile. "You read my mind." He stepped into the elevator's opposite corner from the attendant. "You're like a rescuing angel."

"Not enjoying the benefit, Mr. Miller?"

"It's not that, but not really, no." Buck faced the attendant, an idea forming in his mind. He glanced over the descending numbers. Eleventh Floor, tenth, ninth... "The hotel is beautiful. What else can you tell me about it?"

Eighth floor, seventh, sixth...

"What else did you want to know?"

Fifth floor. The ride was slowing down.

"Maybe I could get a hotel tour? Providing you have the time."

The offer hung in the air. A splash of crimson colored Randall's cheeks. The elevator came to a stop, and the doors opened. The small cluster of people stepped aside, waiting for the occupant to exit.

After an awkward moment of silence, Buck clasped his hands behind his back, giving Randall a polite nod of his head. "I guess you don't have the time," he said softly. "Have a good night, Mr. Hardin." He took a step before feeling the tapping at his arm.

"Give me ten minutes."

A nod of the head confirmed it.

❖

"Now, that's impressive," Buck said with absolute astonishment.

"Glad you liked it." Randall said, reaching for his underwear.

"It's just so big." He stared at it in disbelief. "And you said the President of the United States has been on it?"

"Several times."

"It's a shame we both couldn't be on that together. Is it extra king size?" Buck stood before the Presidential Bed, impressed by its massive frame. His fingers reached out for the soft comforter lining as if reaching for the Holy Grail. Pressing down on the mattress, he marveled at the softness and let out a small groan. "Not that the floor wasn't delightful, but this would have been wonderful."

"That bed is a pain in the ass to make up," Randall warned. He looked around for his pants, finding them half-pushed under the bed. He bent down to retrieve them, talking over his shoulder. "It has special sheets, blankets, and everything, and requires laundering if you even sit on it, so don't!"

Buck looked down at one of Randall's finer attributes. "It's just a shame I couldn't experience the bed."

"I wonder how long I've been gone," Randall said, clutching his wrist. "It couldn't have been too long."

"Thanks a lot," Buck said.

"You know what I mean," Randall replied. He pulled his pants up, hastily buttoning them.

"You missed one," Buck said. He reached out and buttoned the hotel uniform pants properly. "There. Now you look smooth and sharp." He ran his hands over Randall's hips and buttocks in an attempt to remove all the telltale wrinkled signs from the material. "Thank you for the tour of the hotel, especially the Presidential Suite. It was all quite impressive."

"We really need to get going," Randall said urgently.

"I understand." Buck wrestled his feet into his shoes. "How about you give the place a quick once-over, and I'll wait by the front door."

"Appreciate it, thanks. I'll be there in a minute."

Buck walked to the front doorway and leaned against the wall to adjust his shoes. The hotel keycard he'd slid out of Randall's pocket was slipping toward his toes, and he wanted it securely under the arch of his foot. When Randall hurried around the corner, he took hold of his shoulders and gave him one last kiss, buying him the extra moment he needed.

Randall opened the door and they walked out. Buck stepped forward and pressed the call button. The elevator arrived and they both got in. While Randall fiddled with his uniform and nervously tapped his fingers against his leg, Buck leaned against the car's handrail at the far back of the car. Neither man said a word as the elevator slowed, came to a stop, and the doors opened.

"Thanks for the tour." Buck flashed his smile. "You're definitely one of the finer assets I've come across at this hotel."

Buck walked across the lobby and sat down on one of the wicker chairs. Glancing at his watch, he counted to twenty in Italian. It bought him thirty seconds, and that was enough to let the elevator doors close and a fresh sweep of people to brush through the lobby. He stood and set off to find the lobby's bathroom.

A man was washing his hands when Buck entered the restroom. Past the sinks were five stalls opposite six urinals on the right. Buck chose the farthest stall. Pulling the door outward, he entered the stall, closed the door, and set the hook-and-latch lock in place. Sitting on the closed toilet lid, Buck slid his right shoe off and retrieved the stolen keycard. Inspecting the heel, he put pressure at the base of the sole until a small hinge gave and swung away.

Daddy's little toolkit, Buck thought, not sure if anyone else was in the bathroom. Inside the hollowed heel was a small keyboard the size of a cell phone, and a holder with a coding strip.

He slid the key's magnetic edge into a slot on the side of keyboard, where it was firmly held in place. Pecking the keys, he entered the words "Robert E. Lee—Arlington, VA." The keyboard's lights flashed as it began the process of setting the card to be a master key. Buck placed his hand over the heel so the lights wouldn't show.

"Great!" A voice exploded in the outer bathroom. "This is just what I need!"

"Dude," a second voice replied. "Calm down. We'll find him."

Buck pulled his legs up.

"My instructions were clear," the first one said. "Find that faggot!"

"Ray, we'll find him."

"He was under our noses all night long. And now this!"

"Dude, he can't be that far ahead of us."

"Ahead of us or not," Ray said, "Raven was quite clear: We need to find him and take care of him."

The heel of Buck's shoe announced with a chirp that it had reset the key.

"What was that?" Ray asked.

Shit! Buck thought. *This is not what I need right now.* The sounds of each stall being roughly pulled open began. He took the keycard out of the holder and slid it into his pocket. His thumbs closed the hidden heel compartment when the stall's door next to him was thrown open.

"Come out, little birdy," Ray taunted.

Through the crack between the stall walls and the door hinge, Buck saw a form move in front of his door. It moved back a step and stood perfectly still. An eye peered through the narrow opening.

"I see you, little bird," Ray called. "There's nowhere to fly."

Buck kicked both legs against the door, sending it flying outward. The man on the other side jumped back. The shoe that came flying afterward struck him squarely between the eyes. Buck leapt out of the stall, grabbing the stunned man by his collar and hurling him toward his accomplice. Two bullets met the flying body halfway, jolting him with dulled thuds. He crumpled to the floor.

Charging the gunman, Buck collided headfirst with his stomach and the two men fell backward, hitting the locked bathroom door. Buck firmly grabbed the blond man's hand and brought the wrist down hard on his knee. The force made the hand release, and he dropped the gun. Buck kicked it away. The man slammed his forehead into Buck's, and he dropped the stranger's right arm. The other fist connected with Buck's jaw.

Buck rubbed his jaw and ran his tongue over his teeth. "You're damn lucky there are no broken teeth. Big mistake hitting the moneymaker."

The man beckoned with his good hand. "Let's dance, asshole."

Buck threw a swing. The man ducked and slammed a fist into Buck's stomach. He reeled back into the sink counter, trying to catch his breath. He avoided another swing by leaning backward over the sink countertop. Using his hands for leverage, Buck threw his weight onto the counter, raising his feet and slamming them into the chest of his assailant, sending him flailing backward.

In an instant Buck crossed the room and grabbed the man by the collar. Swinging him around, Buck held him tightly in his left hand, pounding his face with his right fist. His fist broke the blond man's nose, taking most of the fight out of him. When the guy stopped resisting, Buck let him slump to the floor.

Buck pulled himself upright, staring down at the assailant and trying to catch his breath. He studied the face, trying without success to recognize the guy. "Now, what am I going to do with two men in a locked bathroom?"

He walked across the room and retrieved the kicked gun. Then he looked down at the dead Ray. "What the hell was that about?" Taking hold of the body under the arms, Buck dragged him into the stall and positioned him sitting on the toilet.

"I'm guessing he drives a four-by-four with an extended cab, huge tires, and a horn that plays three, maybe five different tunes," Buck said after placing the second assailant in his own stall. He pulled the doors closed.

Splashing water on his face, Buck took out his phone and pulled up the copy of the hotel's blueprints Muffin had sent. Between the earlier tour given by Mr. Hardin, and the blueprints, Buck planned his route up the stairs to the fourth-floor computer room. Unlocking the bathroom door, he pulled it open and walked back into the hotel lobby—which was in complete chaos.

"What fresh hell is this?"

The lobby was full of people moving in every direction. Formal gowns and tuxedos from the benefit mingled with cut-off shorts and T-shirts worn by hotel guests, all moving faster than a disturbed colony of ants. Buck ran to the elevators but a sign was posted in front of them: "Do not use elevators—use stairs." He made a dash for the doorway.

I feel like a salmon, he thought, pushing his way against the heavy flow coming down the stairs. At each level a hotel attendant was directing people and spouting instructions.

"Please don't run or push!" an attendant said as Buck made his way over. "Move down the stairs, sir, please."

"What is going on here?" Buck asked.

"Nothing to panic about, sir." Everything was said in a monotonous voice. "Go ahead and move down the stairs in an orderly fashion. There's nothing to worry about."

"Are you kidding me with that?" Buck grabbed the boy by the shoulders. "I'll kick your ass down the stairs if you don't tell me what the hell is going on."

The twentysomething kid looked panicked. "A bomb exploded in the area," he stuttered. "A few doors down. They think it might have been a terrorist attack. The police think we might have been the intended target."

"Great," Buck lamented to himself. "Now Raven can be a martyr." Pushing the boy aside, he continued up the next several flights of stairs until he came to the fourth floor.

Exiting out onto the floor was considerably easier than climbing up the stairwell. The remaining people were moving rapidly toward the stairs, and Buck moved about the hallway with ease. Finding the computer room, he removed the keycard and slid it into the lock. It clicked open.

After a little searching, Buck found the main computer base. His fingers explored the different wire connections with a surgeon's skill until he found the USB port he wanted. Reaching into his pocket, he retrieved a matchbox and slid it open carefully.

A small rectangular metallic object fell into the palm of his hand. The conductor was the size of a fingernail, with a connection port on either end. Leaning behind the main computer, Buck unplugged the brain system from the port. Lights blinked and the motor ran down. He snapped his device into the computer's outlet and reconnected the main cord into the other end. A single green light blinked as the computer rebooted.

Buck took out his phone and pressed the coded buttons. The tin sounds chimed, signaling the connection was made. On the screen, an icon of a muffin top appeared. It flashed several colors before disappearing.

"Now," he said aloud. "Let's get the hell outta here!"

Retracing his steps, he joined the steady stream of people in the stairwell, glad to blend in and happy to allow them to steadily move him along. The lobby was just as chaotic as it had been earlier, and he stayed with the crowd until he was out in the street.

The block was roped off, allowing the fire trucks, police cars, and ambulances to drive through. Police barricades lined the streets and the crowds packed against them. Not far away thick plumes of smoke rose and a raging fire was being extinguished. The air was thick with the smoke from the charred building and the scent of burning flesh from the poor souls that were trapped inside. Voices shouting orders cut through the air.

Buck viewed the destruction. It was overwhelming. He spun around, grabbing the first officer he could find.

"Is the Robert E. Lee safe?"

"What?" the confused officer asked.

"Is this hotel safe!" Buck yelled.

The officer screamed back. "I only have a little information, but yes, the Lee is safe as far as we know. The bomb exploded about a quarter mile down the street. We're evacuating as a precaution."

"What got hit?"

"Some bar, I think. I'm not sure."

Buck let the officer go. Official trucks flew past on the street, and people were either rushing to leave the scene or crowding the barricade trying to get a look. He pulled out his phone, but there was no service.

"Noxia," Buck whispered, genuinely concerned. Without hesitation, he took off down the street, pushing his way through the crowd.

CHAPTER SEVEN

After Buck left her, Noxia watched Raven receive her applause from an enthusiastic crowd. A cart was wheeled onto the stage and a gift presented to her, a cake decorated exactly like the flag of the Sisters of the Southern Cross. The applause continued for several moments.

"Is that applause for me or the cake?" Raven asked the audience. Jovial laughter answered her. "We'll have this cut up and ready for everyone in just a few moments, but first I want to talk to you about this evening's cause."

"I'll take that, thank you," Noxia said, grabbing a full glass of champagne from a passing waiter.

Raven took her place at a podium, bringing the reception noise to a minimum.

"Ladies and gentlemen, distinguished guests, welcome. Tonight is a special night and I want to personally thank you, not only for your generosity, but for your attendance as well."

Polite applause spattered the hall.

"Tonight, I want to start out by telling you a story. I have a close friend who has a seven-year-old child, a sweet innocent girl with blond hair and green eyes. One night over dinner, my friend asked her daughter, 'What did you do today in school?' The daughter answered: 'We saw a movie, *Dr. Doolittle*.' Remembering the film fondly from her own youth, my friend asked: 'What did you think of the giant pink sea snail?'"

Raven spoke softly, her voice low and steady, letting her words seep out into the audience. She paused, allowing each person to conjure their own fond memories for the classic film for children.

"What my friend was shocked to find out was that it was not the beloved film with the charming English title character. The child never heard any of the lighthearted classic songs. And the legendary pink sea snail never appeared on screen.

"What was shown to this class of six-, seven-, and eight-year-olds was the remade version instead. What they were subjected to was virtually an hour and a half of pure profanity. There were no talking parrots or dancing llamas. Instead, the class was subjected to watching rats making jokes about passing gas and dogs commenting on the sexual behavior of humans. On top of that," she paused melodramatically, "the movie itself is rated PG-13! My friend was not informed of the teacher's movie choice. She was not asked if it was okay to subject her innocent child to such perversity. Not even as much as the courtesy of permission slip was ever sent home. And *this* is what passes as acceptable for our children in today's America? I say no!"

The crowd applauded.

"She's something else, isn't she," asked a voice behind Noxia's ear.

"Something else, indeed." Noxia turned to be face-to-face with the handsome congressman from South Carolina. The salt-and-pepper at his temples caught the dim light, softening the ruddy farm-raised complexion to a country-boy charm.

"I noticed you earlier, but we didn't get a chance to be introduced. I'm Dexter Julian." He paused to let the name sink in. "Congressman Dexter Julian from South Carolina."

"It's a pleasure. Miss Noxia von Tüssëll."

"That's a unusual name. Was it Mrs. or Miss von Tüssëll?"

"It's a German name." She smiled at his adept ability and extended her hand. "And it's Miss. No introductions are needed for you, Congressman. Your reputation precedes you."

"Oh?" His eyebrow arched.

"I know you graduated top of your class at the University of South Carolina School of Law," Noxia said.

"I'm impressed. Do you work for the media?"

"No," Noxia replied. "As Roosevelt said, 'It is the duty of every American to question their government and to not do so would be unpatriotic.' I like to keep informed of who is holding what seat in Washington DC, no matter which state they are from. It all adds up to one government, does it not?"

"I like the way you think," he said. "With that line of logic, I hope then at least that you are one of my constituents?"

"Wrong again." Her smile encouraged. "I'm not from South Carolina."

He smiled and crossed his arms, leaving access to his champagne flute in his right hand while hiding his left. "And what else are you informed about?"

Noxia tried to ignore his condescending tone. "I know that while you spearheaded the campaign for the child predator Internet laws, you were also one of the main voices behind keeping the rebel flag flying on all municipal buildings, not just in your district but for the entire South. How am I doing?"

"There's nothing more attractive than a smart woman who knows her politics."

"Congressman, you're very kind."

Raven's speech continued: "It is important, today in our country, to remember that Christ died on the cross for the sins of the innocent. Now our country is asking us, the innocent, to die for the sins of the lawmakers; they are trying to rewrite not only our laws, but our language as well! 'Pornography' is passed off as 'Erotic Art'; 'Back Alley Abortion' is rewritten as 'A Choice'; 'Country Dictatorship,' we are told, has become 'People's Democratic Republic'; and 'The Sanctity of Marriage' is trying to be changed into 'Equal Rights.' I ask you: When does it stop?"

She emphasized the last words by banging on the podium. Her words gained speed and her tone strength. Noxia could see

Raven's eyes rapidly blinking to the enthusiastic applause of almost everyone in the audience. Raven studied the crowd briefly before pushing onward.

"Why is it that the liberal gays protest about not being accepted, or treated as equals, but they purposely root out gays on the conservative side, their own kind, exposing *them* and destroying *their* lives..."

"If a woman who know politics is your type, Congressman," Noxia said, with a slight flirtation, "then the good doctor here should be your fantasy girl."

"A little too knowledgeable. A little too political, and a lot too opinionated for my personal liking." He failed to hide his distaste. "But no matter what your opinion is of her, Dr. Raven Evangelista knows how to capture an audience and deliver one hell of a sermon."

"So did Hitler, Congressman." Noxia turned her head, exposing her long, swanlike neck.

"Unlike Hitler, Ms. von Tüssëll, Raven is a good lady who might just be able to accomplish some good for our country."

"For the sake of playing devil's advocate, Congressman," Noxia turned to directly face him, "Hitler built the autobahn and, like Mussolini, actually did good for his country before the madness of power brought their homelands nothing but a shameful legacy. Don't confuse being a good orator with being a good leader. Evil, very often and very quickly, travels down the road that goodness paved."

"Then I would *hate* to see the evil that follows you."

Noxia took a sip of champagne. "Maybe it's the good that I'm chasing. Ever think of that?"

"Yes, I did." The congressman's salacious smile was unmistakable.

"And we, as a country, need to reeducate our own," continued Raven's speech. "Give up on the fundamentalists, they that cling to fame. Reeducate..."

"Reeducation seems to be very big with her," Noxia said.

"I'll say." The congressman stepped closer to her side. Noxia could feel his breath on her shoulder. He ran a finger playfully over her wrist. His breath smelled of champagne and cigarette smoke. He lowered his voice. "That's her interest in riding the wave."

"Excuse me?" Noxia asked. "What's 'riding the wave'?"

"Riding the wave of politics." He pulled himself upright to a formal position, showing his most professional grin. "Dr. Evangelista knows how to stir up a crowd by knowing the latest political buttons and when to push them."

"Of course." Noxia nodded.

A security guard waited until Raven paused. As the audience applauded their approval, the guard whispered in Raven's ear and handed her a written note.

"Ladies and gentlemen," Raven said in a completely different tone. "I have just been handed a note that a bomb has gone off in a building not far from here. Please don't panic." As if on cue the hotel's security alarm system began ringing loudly. The crowd moved as one toward the doors. Raven was yelling into the microphone to be heard above the mayhem. "Hotel security has asked us to evacuate as a precautionary action only! Don't use the elevators! Take the stairs! There will be police and hotel workers in the halls to guide you…"

Noxia saw the mob coming toward her and turned to make her way out. "Congressman, I do hope to—"

But he was already halfway to the door.

The crowd pushed past her and Noxia was swept up in the turbulent wave of people. The mob shoved the double doors open, and smaller groups, despite the warnings, made their way to the elevators. Only a handful of people were beginning to get to the stairs by the time she reached the doors, and Noxia realized the gala must have been notified first. Taking advantage of the situation, Noxia made it down six floors before the crowd forced her to a much slower pace.

"Please don't push!" Attendants called out instructions from the corners of every turn. "This is just a precaution. Hotel guests will be instructed outside the main entrance! Visitors will find their cars waiting at the valet lot!"

Red lights blinked over exit doorways to show the way out. Recorded announcements rang out from speakers in the stairwells. "Use the stairs, do not use the elevators. Please proceed in an orderly fashion."

The repeated calls were difficult to hear over the sharp chattering and the footsteps on the descending steps. A new wave pushed forward as they drew closer to the lobby. Climbing down the stairs, Noxia glanced around for Buck, but there was no way to stop and get a good look. The crowd dispersed in every direction the moment they hit the hotel lobby. More instructions were called out. Noxia made her way out the main entrance keeping watch for Buck or the congressman; she saw neither of them.

Once outside, she could smell the fire and hear the sirens. Police barricades were just being set up, and an officer stood in the middle of the road clearing all traffic except official vehicles. Flames could be seen over rooftops, leaping into the air and transforming into an outline of blackened smoke against the night sky.

"Miss," an officer took Noxia by the elbow. "If you have a car, you need to go over to the valet entrance on the other side of the hotel. If you are a guest of the hotel, please follow the attendant over there."

Noxia blinked coming out of her stupor. "The valet, thank you."

Before she could ask another question, the officer was giving the same instructions to another set of guests coming out of the hotel. Noxia's mind raced. She moved quickly to the valet area and found her driver and limousine.

"Ma'am," the driver said, holding open the car door. "Is Mr. Miller not with you?"

"No," she said, pulling the dress into the car after her. "He'll find his own way."

"Should we wait for him?" the driver asked as he climbed behind the steering wheel.

"No," Noxia said after a moment's hesitation. "The instructions were to meet back at the hotel. So that's what we have to do."

CHAPTER EIGHT

W here have you been?" Noxia flew at him the moment he opened the suite door. Except for the shoes, she was still dressed in the evening's formal wear. Behind her the muted television flickered a news report.

"Mom, is that you?" Buck entered the room and closed the door. "Glad to see you're all right also."

"Don't know if you've heard," Noxia continued in a calmly patronizing voice, "but there was an explosion, and I've been waiting here for over an hour to find out if you were even alive. Excuse me if I was concerned."

"Not concerned enough to wait for me with the car, I noticed."

"Your instructions were quite clear," she said incredulously. "When it comes to following rules, I do what I'm told. You should give it a try sometime."

"And I'm doing fine, thank you!"

Noxia closed her eyes and took a deep breath. "Are you okay?" she asked sincerely.

"Yeah, sure," came Buck's flippant reply. He looked at his watch. "Quarter to midnight; it's still early. Want a drink?"

"I started without you," Noxia said, shaking her head and retrieving her cocktail. "I already called Muffin, and he's given me a full rundown."

"Great," he said. "Can you fill me in now?" He walked over to the overstuffed couch and helped himself to the open bottle on the coffee table. After pouring a pale pink vodka and cranberry juice for himself, Buck kicked off his shoes and put his feet up. "Excuse my feet, but they hurt from hoofing it back here, since *someone* didn't bother to wait."

Noxia sucked in her lips, flaring her nostrils and exhaling loudly. She tried again with controlled precision. "You told me to meet you back here…"

"Don't you think an explosion overrules that?"

"Agency rules are agency rules, but I'm sorry if your feelings were hurt. Can we move past this now?"

"So," Buck said calmly, "what was the bombing all about anyway? I've heard crazy rumors from terrorist attacks to assassination attempts to hate crimes. Was it related to the gala at all?"

"Not from what Muffin said," Noxia answered, taking a seat in a comfortable easy chair next to him. She unpinned her hair and shook it loose, letting it fall to her shoulders. "He says the bombing wasn't related to the gala at all, just coincidental that it happened to be the same night."

"And in the same area? I don't put much faith in coincidences," Buck said. "What happened at the party after I left?"

"Well," Noxia said, "definitely be glad you left before Raven started to speak. Ooosh." She rolled her eyes. "That is one conservative woman."

"How conservative?" Buck asked. "'Fire and Brimstone!' kind of conservative, or 'I don't mind gay folk; who else would cut my hair?' kind of conservative?"

"The worst from column A; the dregs from column B."

"She couldn't have advanced if she was that vocally prejudiced."

"Oh really," Noxia said with a raised eyebrow. "Ever hear of Maggie Gallagher, Sarah Palin, Michele Bachmann…I can go on."

"Please don't."

"My point," Noxia continued, "is that you can say all sorts of crazy shit to the media, it's all a matter of how you present it."

"You can wrap it up with all the pretty paper you want," Buck said. "But bigotry is still bigotry."

Noxia thought for a long moment. "I wouldn't say that," she answered carefully. "I get the feeling that although Raven might agree with Klan philosophy at its barest core, she still looks down on them as being low level differently than the rest of us. To her, the Klan is a group of bullies and thugs, and she considers herself to be more elite."

"A caste system for prejudice?"

She laughed. "Maybe, but she's more dangerous than any of the others could ever hope to be. She has intelligence and she's gaining power. She's a smart woman and knows how to apply her knowledge to get what she wants. Anyway, I did get to make nice with Congressman Julian. He said a few interesting things, and not all of them were about himself. For a man of wavering morals, he's actually quite charming. I was talking to him when the bombing news came through." Noxia looked at Buck and shrugged. "After that, we were ushered into the stairs and out of the building. You know the rest. What about your night?"

Buck filled her in on his activities.

"Busy boy," Noxia said, finishing off her drink. "Any idea who the guys in the bathroom were, or who they were working for?"

"Not a clue except for one guy being named Ray," he said, raising the bottom of his own drink. "They just said 'the faggot' and out I popped from the stall."

"If they didn't recognize you," Noxia pointed out, "it might not have been you they were searching for. Hate to break this to you, love, but evidently you're not the only faggot out there causing trouble."

"I'm not sure how to take that."

"You know what I mean," she said. "Were you able to make the connection to the hotel's computer system?"

"Despite all the craziness," Buck said, with a proud look on his face, "it was actually easy. Everyone was concerned with getting out of the building. With Muffin's blueprints as a guide, the only resistance I got was from the people evacuating in the other direction."

The bottom of the television screen flashed a news banner over the reporter's muted speech. The banner read: BREAKTHROUGH IN BOMBING.

"Turn it up," Buck insisted.

"…the Main Oar Bar and Tavern, a known Arlington hangout in the gay community. Authorities are treating the bombing as a suspected hate crime," the reporter was saying in a monotonous tone. "Rumors of a terrorist attack have been reported as false. Repeat, rumors of a terrorist attack…" Noxia clicked the mute button again.

"A terrorist attack." She chuckled. "People will believe anything."

"What do you mean?" Buck asked. "This close to DC, it's highly possible."

"Buck, you naïve little man, have you learned nothing?" she said condescendingly. "Muffin always feeds false news to one particular news team, to keep the general populace away from the investigation." Her expression changed. "Haven't you noticed that one particular major network news team is almost always absurdly wrong? Their logo should be ASS, not FOX."

"Why would Muffin go to that much effort?"

"It keeps people away so we can proceed unnoticed." Noxia spoke with a cocky edge to her voice. "The bombing isn't connected to Raven, it's a different situation. It's a serial bomber."

"How do you know that?"

She stood and stretched. Talking over her shoulder, she walked to the door of her bedroom. "Because of two messages that were found at the bar. The first is a Bible quote, something to do with Revelation. The second message is something we've kept out of the papers. Messages were found at all four locations—all have been gay/lesbian establishments: two bars in Fairfax, and a restaurant and a bookstore in Alexandria. Now this."

"What's the message?"

"Each box contained a note made of cut-out letters saying, 'Jesus Will Save.'"

"Jesus will save what?" Buck asked. "Pennies, stamps, coupons..."

"Ha. Ha."

"That still doesn't mean that Raven is ruled out," Buck argued. "She does tend to lean toward the zealot viewpoint."

"That's just it," Noxia said. "In viewpoint, yes. She's not one to blow up a bar, though, that's not her style. In a strange way she needs minority communities in order to feel better about herself. If there's no one she believes she's superior to, then how can she justify her superiority complex? It's an odd juxtaposition."

"Then what was it all about?" Buck asked, standing.

"I don't know, Alfie. Just a good old-fashioned hate crime, I guess. Either way, that's not our concern for the moment. It was fortuitous enough to let you plant the computer bug without being noticed. Speaking of," she opened her bedroom door, "I'm going to change clothes. You get your computer and we'll start downloading whatever that chip of yours can transmit."

"Agreed."

Buck was finishing setting up his computer connection to his cell phone when Noxia returned to the common area of their suite. She was wearing a pair of gray fleece sweatpants and a ripped sweatshirt to match. Buck was wearing the same, only in black. The soft vocals were courtesy of Buck's iPod.

"To answer your question," Buck called over his shoulder when he heard her enter the room, "Audra McDonald is the vocalist. Her voice makes me wet."

"Now, that's TMI." Noxia joined him as his computer booted up and the screen saver of a ragamuffin girl with a French flag behind her appeared. "You really are the reigning show queen, aren't you?"

"I reiterate," Buck said. "You can learn the basics of any subject from musical theater."

"And what musical have you learned from Raven's files?"

Buck plugged away on the keyboard. "It sure ain't *Dreamgirls*. There. Contact."

He pointed to a small muffin-top icon that appeared on the screen of his computer. It danced in place, spinning in circles. Clicking on the icon changed its colors, and the file opened with the beginning of a downloading time bar.

"Once this is done we'll be able to browse the hotel's files."

Waiting only a few more moments, Buck entered the files marked "REL" and began sifting through. "I'll need to set this to sort through e-mails sent only by the hotel and not the guests." His fingers played the keyboard. When the listings appeared, he scanned over the subject boxes, highlighting anything sounding remotely suspicious and all those without a subject printed.

"Nothing much out of the ordinary," Buck reported. "Wait, when playing chess, do you spell checkmate with a 'ch' or a 'cz'?"

"'Ch,'" Noxia said. "Are you that bad at spelling?"

"No," Buck answered hesitantly. "But Raven shouldn't be, either. There's an e-mail here from an account called Ravenflight, I think we can assume that's hers, and the subject is Czech Mate, spelled like the current Republic. I'm trying to get into it."

The muffin icon spun around changing colors again before exploding open in a starburst and delivering the e-mail. When the file opened, it was nothing but a gibberish assortment of letters and numbers.

"Is that some kind of code?" Noxia asked.

Buck answered, "Definitely some sort of encryption. Let me try a decoding program." He clicked away on the computer's keyboard. The picture on the screen wavered and morphed into another page with only parts of the e-mail translated:

Ravensflight@robertelee.com
Subject: Czech Mate
I don't cohj how you get it d8hn[d@ it. Find &k*ll i%
*f3# 314.
Don't diszp0*nt me!
R

"I'm not sure why," Buck said, "but I thought she'd sign her e-mails with a little smiley face, wouldn't you?"

"Right." Noxia raised her eyebrows. "Are there any more e-mails with the subject 'Czech Mate'?"

"Only one more." The e-mail was only four words: *It Will Be Done!* "That's it," Buck reported.

"What's the date on that last sent e-mail?" Noxia asked.

"It just says April."

"When were you attacked in Belgium?"

"April," Buck answered. An idea formed in his mind. "Langlier! The e-mail has to be to Langlier, with instructions to attack me."

Noxia studied the jumbled e-mail next to its response. "You may be right about that. I wish you could translate that sentence ending in f3#314. Is there any way to tell if the 314 part is part of the original or the jumbled translation?"

"Unfortunately not." Buck faced her. "It has to be Langlier, I'm telling you. It can't be a coincidence."

"You said you don't believe in coincidences," Noxia said, refreshing the drinks with the remains in the shaker.

"I don't, that's my point." Buck went back to his computer screen. "I'm going to save a copy of this and see if I can come up with any translations later."

"What else can you find in her files?" Noxia asked.

The computer keyboard clicked away under Buck's nimble fingers. Within a few moments another file titled "Scheduling" opened.

"The Sisters of the Southern Cross have a monthly meeting in Hall A, the Lilac Tree," Buck reported scrolling down the roster. "Blah, blah, blah...It seems that every congressman, senator, and everyone else politically conservative from the South has something booked here; weddings, conferences...nothing out of the normal, though. Yada yada yada, and wait."

"What?" Noxia asked, scanning the page.

"This doesn't make sense. Every month there's a meeting scheduled in the Grotto conference hall."

"Clichéd name," Noxia said. "But that's not a crime."

"No," Buck continued. "The group that reserves it is called the Rescued Right."

"And?"

"The Rescued Right is an ex-gay group," Buck explained. "One of those crazy zealot sects that think they can cure homosexuality through prayer."

"Like the ones touted by Michele Bachmann and her husband?"

"Same concept. Different group," Buck replied. "I knew I recognized the name, but it didn't dawn on me until I saw it listed here. Every month for the last..." He counted quickly. "Eleven months. Like clockwork, on the third Thursday of the month."

"That sounds like something she'd get behind," Noxia said, thinking out loud. "Just because it meets at her hotel doesn't mean she's affiliated with that group."

"Good point," he conceded. "But it's worth making a note of. Something isn't right there, I can just feel it."

"What's this?" Noxia pointed to one of the last reservations scheduled. It was for a medium-sized conference room called Dixieland.

Buck read where her finger pointed. "What's the Riding the Wave group?"

"I don't know," Noxia said. "But it was something the congressman said to me. He said something about Evangelista's interest in 'riding the wave.' When he saw I didn't know what he was talking about, he backtracked. I thought it odd at the time, but with the bombing and all, I totally forgot about it. Are there any other meetings scheduled before this one?"

Buck scrolled back. "Only one, two weeks prior. I'm not seeing any others. What is it?"

"I have no idea," Noxia said. "But I'd like to find out more. Open another window, do a search and see what you can find."

Buck typed "Riding the Wave" into the search engine. Over 600,000 hits came up. "This might take a while." Buck started to browse over the listings. "Mostly about a band with the same name. I'm scrolling…I'm scrolling…tons of surfing info…a radio station, and here's something."

He clicked on a link and an attractively appeasing website opened. The top of the page announced: "Riding the Wave: A journey into scientific discovery." Along the left sidebar was a listing of nationally prestigious awards and recognitions. Pictures of scientists studying through microscopes were alongside a lengthy explanation of what the group does.

"It's some sort of biogenetic study," Noxia said. "It sounds like they're bordering on some dangerous grounds."

"Like stem cells?" Buck asked.

"Beyond that," Noxia explained. "They're doing research following patterns of thought in the brain waves."

"That's nothing new."

"Let me finish or read it yourself," Noxia chided. "They're trying to get grants to continue research for the separation and isolation of thoughts. Their logic is that positive and negative impulses register differently on the brain, therefore they can be separated and controlled."

"Like a Jekyll and Hyde thing?"

"They're not using that analogy of course, but yeah, something similar." Noxia yawned and stretched. "I'm going to have to look into this more. But for now, I'm ready for bed."

"I'm not far behind you," Buck said. He clicked and searched through several more files. "What's this?"

Noxia turned back, intrigued by his tone. She slid close and looked over his shoulder at the screen. "What are you seeing?"

"A little file icon, right here." Buck pointed to the incidental note on the bottom page from the hotel files. "Your eye almost misses it, but if you look really close, it's a different font, and the color isn't black, it's very dark green. I'll try to enlarge it." He tried and failed several times.

Noxia practically put her face to the screen to read it. "The Jesus Injection?"

"I don't know what it is, but I'm downloading all of this." Buck put a flash drive into the laptop. Once the files were copied, he ejected the flash drive. Running his mouse over the words, he clicked on "The Jesus Injection."

All files closed in a reverse explosion until only the flashing muffin top was left. It continued to spin in several colors, but it slowed down until it teetered like a seasick drunkard. It finally fell over and then exploded, covering the screen in a blank white. The computer shut down and rebooted. As the hard drive remounted, the screen returned to normal, and everything appeared as it had been, except the muffin was completely stationary. Buck ran the mouse over the icon and tried to click on it. Nothing happened. He tried several times more but got nothing further.

"That can't be good."

"At least you have everything on the flash drive," Noxia said. "Although I wouldn't click on that Jesus Injection link again." She offered a sympathetic smile.

"So now what?" Buck asked.

"I'm going to bed."

"No," Buck answered. "You're going to see the congressman. Try to find out whatever information you can on Riding the Wave."

"I am?" Noxia said incredulously. "And what about you?"

"I'm going to see the Muffin Man." Buck whistled the children's tune.

CHAPTER NINE

A ctually," Noxia said to the cab driver, "right here is fine."
She paid the fare plus a generous tip and got out of the taxi.
Taking a deep breath, she slowly made her way down the street,
stopping before she arrived at La Fontana Ristorante. She was
already fifteen minutes late, but that didn't prevent an intimate smile
from curving her lips. Noxia never liked to arrive before her date;
it looked too anxious, and that wasn't her style. By this time, the
tardiness would still be counted as fashionable, and imagining an
expected heightening of anticipation from her company, she invoked
her inner coquette and proceeded.

Noxia entered the restaurant and realized she was the most
formally dressed of the dining guests. Her wine-colored business
suit did what it was supposed to; it subtly caused others to glance
her direction and become aware of her presence. Feeling confident,
she took a step into the waiting area and glanced around. A young
man dressed completely in black quickly approached her.

"Excuse me, ma'am. Are you Miss von Tüssëll?"

"Yes," she answered.

"My name is Kyle. If you would please follow me." He turned
and led her to the far back corner of the restaurant, without waiting
to see if she followed. They approached a table surrounded in
sheer black curtains, with the shadow of a darkened shape sitting
ominously inside. Kyle slid the curtain back and held it so Noxia
could pass underneath.

Sitting at the table's banquette was Congressman Dexter Julian of South Carolina, dressed in a black tailored suit with a pale blue shirt and a bold purple and black striped tie. The congressman stood as best as the rounded table would allow, waiting for Noxia to take her seat. Kyle opened a bottle of wine and left them to themselves, sliding the curtains closed for privacy.

"Very nice," Noxia said. "Private without being overtly intimate."

"I'd like to spend my time talking with you," the congressman explained. "Rather then explaining my time talking about you, if you understand."

"It might seem you were trying to hide back here," Noxia said. Her smile was playful and so was her tone.

"Not at all." Dexter was taken aback. "But a man of the public does deserve some private time."

"Hear, hear." She raised her glass and saluted.

"I thought we'd be a little less formal tonight," Dexter explained. "As you can see, the wine has already arrived, and a few appetizers should be arriving shortly. I hope that'll be all right."

"I'm sure it'll be fine."

"So, Miss von Tüssëll."

"Noxia, please. We've been through this."

The congressman smiled, letting it brighten his face. "And you must call me Dexter."

"All right, Dexter." Noxia smiled back.

"Well then, Noxia," Dexter began again, "I must say, I was a little surprised when you called. Pleased, mind you, but surprised nonetheless."

"I enjoyed meeting you at the fund-raiser the other night, Dexter." She shrugged. "And then everything got cut short."

"Yeah," the congressman huffed. "The Bomb-a-Bar-for-Jesus Guy strikes again. This is the fourth or fifth bombing, the media claims."

"What did you call him?" Noxia asked.

Kyle silently appeared between the curtains and placed a

plateful of lightly battered calamari on the table. They waited until he was gone before continuing.

Dexter smiled and spoke exaggeratedly slowly; his drawl made the words sound lyrical. "The Bomb-a-Bar-for-Jesus Guy. He's blown up a few different homosexual establishments here and in the surrounding areas. His signature seems to be leaving some Bible passage. So the media has named him the Bomb-a-Bar-for-Jesus Guy."

"You know," Noxia said, after repeating the nickname, "in a weird way, it *does* just roll off the tongue. I thought the other night was a terrorist attack. Where did you hear this piece of information?"

Dexter dramatically took a sip of wine before answering. "I have my sources."

Noxia spooned some of the calamari onto her plate and slid a little closer to the congressman. "Did the media mention any idea about who he is?"

"Not yet. But my sources say the FBI is getting closer. Anyway, it's probably the work of a deranged mind." He took a healthy sip of the wine. "Personally, I don't have any problem with *those* people. Our waiter's one, I'm sure."

It took Noxia a moment to realize he meant the waiter was gay, and not some lunatic. She blinked and shrugged. "I hadn't noticed."

"Really?" Dexter was legitimately surprised. "I figured you'd have better—what is it they call it—*gaydar* than that. Your friend, the night of the benefit, he was a little light in the loafers. Am I right?"

"Buck?" Noxia laughed. "I think he prefers to think of himself as under the gaydar. When did you meet him?"

"I figured it out just watching you talk to him, but maybe I have more of a trained eye." He put his hand over Noxia's and leaned in confidentially. "My sister's boy is a gay. Good kid, just likes his crust cut a different way." When he sat up, he used it as an excuse to move closer. Their bodies were practically touching. "Personally, I have no problems with them, I'm even a little flattered when some of the aides flirt with me. It may not be my kind of party, but it's always nice to be asked." He removed his hand from hers, reached for his wineglass, and saluted. "And they usually have the prettiest girlfriends."

"Buck does have his faults," Noxia said, choosing to let the compliment pass. "He is self-centered and can be very tiring. He's extremely childish, and often very challenging. But under that thick layer of self-protection, he's a caring guy. He has a good heart." She stopped. "He's really all you could want in a man: good companion, a sharp-witted conversationalist, and a great travel buddy."

"Is that all you need from a man, Noxia?"

She sat up, not knowing how to interpret the question. There were no overt traces of seduction in either his tone or expression, but the scent of his cologne mingled seductively with the light smell of the wine he drank.

Reading her confusion, he explained. "Are those all the requirements you have?"

"You'd be surprised how fast those requirements of mine become restrictions to others. Buck's great company; he helps me ward off unwanted advances, and I still have my freedom to pursue my interests." She paused, giving a glimpse of a girlish grin. "That is, should I find anything that interests me."

"You strike me as a woman of many interests. Doesn't that interfere with your friend's, ah, significant other?"

"No," Noxia said with a light laugh. "Buck's too submerged in his work to date anyone at any length, that's why he's such a good travel companion. He has no strings."

"And what happens when either of you start to date someone?" The congressman's interest went noticed.

"I'll cross that bridge when I come to it." Noxia was enjoying herself. "For now, Buck suits my purpose. He can usually travel when I ask him to, and since I have no time for long-term interests outside of work, he suits me fine."

"What is your work?"

Noxia replied, "Investments."

"And quite well, from what I've been told." The congressman flashed her an insider's smile. "I did mention I check my sources."

"I'd expect nothing less." Noxia saluted back, drinking from her glass. "It is interesting you should bring up my business, Congressman. There is an investment I'd like to talk to you about."

"Dexter, please." The lighting picked up the slight glow in his cheeks.

"Dexter, I'm sorry." Noxia slid closer. "I'm looking for a new investment, and when I was doing some research I came across a company that made me think of something you said at the benefit."

Dexter thought a moment and shook his head. "I can't recall us talking about investments."

"No," Noxia said, her face expressionless. "We didn't. I was looking into different research groups and came across one called Riding the Wave. Then I remembered you mentioning something about that the other night, right before we had to evacuate the hotel."

"I can't recall," Dexter said quickly. "Sorry."

"You said something about Evangelista's interest in Riding the Wave, and then you gave a haphazard explanation." Reaching out for his hand, she gently covered his with her own. "A really bad one, if you don't mind my saying. That's why I remembered it." She gave him a girlish wink. "I did some background checks, and I know it's some sort of research company, but I'm not sure what they do exactly."

The congressman looked at her hand on his, sniffing at the bait without taking it. "Why don't you make an appointment to talk to their CEO? If you're looking to invest, I'm sure they'd love to talk your ear off." His eyes shrewdly studied her. "Why ask me?"

"Because I know you're one of the seven main stockholders and I'd figure since we'd already met, I'd ask you." Her bluntness apparently stunned him into momentary silence, so she continued. "Don't look so surprised, Dexter. I told you when I met you, I know how to do my research." She pouted her lips before going into a perfect imitation of his drawl. "'I have my sources.'" The impression coaxed a smile and they both chuckled. "I'm not looking for inside information, nothing like that. I'd just like to know more about what the company does before putting any kind of money into it."

"That's private information. If you have sources that can tell you that, that's pretty impressive." Dexter took a healthy sip of wine, all the while never taking his eyes off her. She kept her stare locked with his, refusing to blink first. He placed the glass on the table. When he lowered his eyes and shoulders before giving in to a heavy sigh, Noxia knew she'd breached his defenses.

"Actually, it's been a good investment," Dexter said. "It was first brought to my attention by a friend a few years back. I looked into it and thought it might be a good way to stash some cash. I was surprised to find just how much potential the company possesses, and began to see the infinite possibilities it could become. Riding the Wave is just that, it's the wave of the future."

"How?"

"By studying brain waves and the patterns they make."

"Studying the brain waves?" Noxia asked, her eyebrows coming together. "It sounds a little science fiction, you have to admit."

"I thought the same thing until I actually read the reports and the details. They don't want to control anyone; it's nothing like that. What they are trying to do is learn how to read the brain waves, isolating the positive from the negative."

"By whose definition will the brain waves be judged—the positive and the negative? You've heard the expression, 'One man's meat is another's poison,'" Noxia replied. "So who gets to define? The government? The people? Or the individual?"

"All very good questions," Dexter said with a self-assured grin. His fingertips found the edges of hers. "And none of those things need to be thought through at this moment." He took a sip of wine and refilled both glasses.

Kyle parted the curtains with a platter of several cheeses, crackers, raspberries, and grapes. Plates were exchanged without a sound, and he retreated from sight.

Noxia said when they were alone again, "I do see possibilities, or else I wouldn't be wasting both of our time looking into its potential. Questions do remain."

"I understand," Dexter Julian admitted. "But again, what they're trying to do is find the basic core of the will to do 'evil.'" He used finger quotes. "Science is beginning to find early patterns in children who later on in life become serial killers. The theory is that if they can identify that kind of brain wave early enough, then they can isolate it." Dexter sipped his wine, proud of himself. "It's not control, it's a possibility of correction."

"What do you mean, correction?"

"If a child is showing signs of disturbed behavior, maybe through this kind of research we'll be able to isolate the disturbance and correct it."

"How would they correct it?" Noxia asked, her mind racing through many scenarios.

"I guess by changing the brain wave pattern or something like that. I'm not sure," Dexter humbly said. "That's probably what the research is for, huh?" He winked.

Noxia's smile was minimal. "What's to stop it from falling into the wrong hands?"

The congressman's face twisted into a concerned expression. "Wow," he mumbled, deep in thought. "I think you're getting way ahead of the company itself. That kind of detail is most likely in a galaxy far, far away, if you understand my meaning?"

"Thank you for making me feel foolish," Noxia said, with good humor.

"Not at all," Dexter assured her. "It's only natural to think that way with all the Hollywood media out there. No, I'm sure that when Riding the Wave ever, if it ever, gets to that point, I'm sure they'll take full precautions, and it'll be treated like anything else the government does."

"Now, I'll drink to that," Noxia raised her glass and kept her word. "How does Evangelista's interest in Riding the Wave come in?"

The congressman looked surprised at her. "You didn't do your research that well if you have to ask me. Evangelista's husband, what was his name? Showwater, Shoulwater, whatever, it was—he started plans for the company, and then left the fledgling works for his own personal research. Raven inherited the shares after his death and became one of the seven controlling stockholders."

"The unnamed majority." Noxia nodded. "That escaped my research." She saw Dexter's curious stare and disarmed him with a smile.

"How did you become interested in Raven?" Dexter said, jumping subjects. "I've not seen you at any other fund-raiser."

"Again," Noxia said. "Investments. Dr. Evangelista definitely has created a name for herself. I wanted to find out more about her before making any decisions about campaign donations." She looked at him with newfound inquisitiveness. "How did you become involved in her campaign?"

"You mean aside from being invested in the same company?" Dexter emptied his glass of wine, refilled it, and sat back against the banquette. "The good doctor has many views, many of which I agree with, some that I don't, although she can be a little more zealous than I in her opinions. She has a certain charisma that will carry her far. It's more of a decision of how far do I want to be associated with her before saying enough is enough. And does your friend Buck have the same interests in investments as you do?"

The abrupt subject change caught her off guard. "No," Noxia answered slowly. "Buck is in the antique business, he uses our trips together as buying expeditions. He has no interest in investments other than Louis XIV furniture. Why do you ask?"

Dexter's boyish charm relaxed her physical body but was slower on her mental state. "Just curious as to how much business you share together."

"That business is between me and him, Congressman."

"Dexter, please. Don't be insulting. I meant no offense." His charm was sincere. "Let's say, there may be an interest there." The congressman took a deep breath. When he exhaled, it was drawn out.

"Miss von Tüssëll," he said directly, sliding up to the table, folding his arms and leaning on his elbows. "I do hope you didn't come here just to talk politics and investments. There are many other subjects I'd like to discuss."

She could feel herself starting to blush. "And what would they be, Congressman Julian?"

"Anything but politics and investments."

Noxia found herself liking the farm-fresh congressman more than expected as the night went on. His conservative viewpoint irritated her, but his charm was evident and powerful.

Kyle stepped through the curtains and approached Dexter. "Excuse me, sir. You wanted me to let you know when it got to be nine o'clock."

"Thank you, Kyle."

The waiter nodded, subtly placing a black check holder on the table before disappearing.

"I do hope you'll excuse me," Dexter said. "I would much rather stay, but unfortunately, I have an obligation I must attend to."

"I understand," Noxia said. Surprisingly, she was disappointed to see the evening end. "You're a busy man."

"Thank you for being so understanding." He reached for the black holder and said, "Please, let this be on the good people of South Carolina."

Noxia took the holder from his hands and placed it by her side. "I'm self-employed and can write it off my taxes. How about we let it be on the government instead?"

The congressman smiled. "As generous as she is pretty," he said. "I do hope our paths will cross again soon."

"Me, too." She stared, holding him in her gaze. She slid out of the booth.

"Ms. von Tüssëll," the congressman said as he joined her. "Are you by chance going to Raven's benefit in New Orleans?"

"I'd not heard about it," Noxia said, intrigued. "Benefit for what?"

"It's for the Hurricane D'orthea victims. The benefit isn't for another two weeks, and normally I wouldn't travel so far, but I'll be down that way anyway and really can't get out of it." He took both her hands in his. "It would make Louisiana's sultry atmosphere a little more bearable if by chance you were there as well."

She let her left lip curl upward and her mouth slightly open. "It sounds very interesting, but…" she replied. Looking away for a moment, she let the coyness linger before saying, "I don't have an invitation."

"If you leave me your contact information," Dexter said, giving her hand a squeeze, "I'll arrange to have one sent."

Noxia blinked several times and took a step backward. "I thought you were inviting me as your guest."

"You'd be better company than the congressman from Mississippi, that's for sure," Dexter assured her. "Unfortunately, these things can't be undone."

"I'll check my schedule and see what I can do," Noxia said.

"There is a condition," Dexter said. "Although the invitation is for you and a guest, I'd be disappointed if you brought anyone else besides your friend Buck as your escort."

"And why is that?"

"I confess there's an alternative reason," the congressman said, looking into her eyes. "If he is there as your escort, I know I'll stand a better chance."

Chapter Ten

A wall with a painted sunset, instead of the usual vapid whiteness, greeted Buck and the elevator doors as they opened. The top floor button was still lit. Curious, Buck placed his hand over the doorway's opening and leaned out into the hallway hesitantly. It appeared like the painted hallway of any common apartment building. He shrugged and was about to step out when he noticed the wall placard: Floor 50.

"Shit!" Buck chided himself, stepping back into the elevator. The doors shut and the car remained still. Reaching into his pocket, he took out his keychain and, after fumbling for the bicycle key, inserted the tiny cylinder into the lock. He gave it a quick twist and again pressed the button for floor fifty-two. The elevator lurched upward.

"Forgot, didn't you?" Muffin said as soon as the doors opened. "You always learn the hard way." He led the way to the retina scan.

"Maybe," Buck said, his tone defensive. "But that's often the best way to learn." He got scanned. "And you know that when I do something, I do it well." He pressed open the doorway and entered, Muffin following.

"Well, there you have me," Agent 69 said in a monotone, his expression blank. "You're the best."

"Muffin," Buck spun around, smiling. "That's one of the nicest things you've ever said to me." Without warning, he swooped in and gave Muffin a bear hug.

"I. Hate. This," Agent 69 said through clenched teeth, his body completely rigid in Buck's arms. "Stop. Now."

"Admit it," Buck teased. "This just adds a little sugar to your day, doesn't it?" He gave Muffin a final squeeze before releasing him. He took in the emptiness of the stations in the room—except for the one computer in the corner. "Is this computer good enough to download my flash drive?"

Going between the empty rows, he called over his shoulder as he approached the computer. "I'm surprised at you, Muffin. No exploding stenographers. No tricked-out pendulums waiting to decapitate the unsuspecting, *ugh*!"

Buck fell to the floor with a heavy thud. He felt his hands stinging from sliding over the carpet, and a burning sensation at his ankles. Rolling over, he saw Agent 69 sauntering toward him with a self-satisfied smile on his face. "Proud of yourself, aren't you?" He extended his arm for help up.

"Laser trip wires," Muffin replied, stepping over Buck's prone body and ignoring the hand. He moved over to the computer, lightly touching the keyboard until the screen came to life. After a few more strokes, the screen waited for its next command. "You can set the laser wire at a moment's notice, for any grid, in any direction for up to twenty feet. It can trip a hummingbird or bring down an elephant, all depending on what you set it for."

"And what did you have it set for?" Buck said, joining Muffin at the computer station.

"Jackass."

"You could have at least warned me."

"Why?" Muffin smirked. "*This* is what adds the sugar to my day."

"Nice trick to play on your friends." Buck handed him the flash drive.

"I hadn't thought of that."

"Don't click on that." Buck grabbed Muffin's wrist. "When I clicked on that icon a second time, my computer went dead."

"We can get into the files from the download without going

through the icon," Muffin explained. "The files you and Agent 46 sent can be pulled up in the conference room. This is just backup, until we can decode whatever crashed your system."

"Noxia didn't send them," Buck answered defensively. "I'm the one who snuck into the computer room and sent you the files."

"That's what I like about you, Agent 98, total selflessness."

They proceeded through the hidden doorway in the back wall. When Buck was seated at the table, Muffin took hold of the remote, dimmed the lights, closed the shades, and lowered the plasma screen. After another few clicks, the familiar mug shot of Karl Langlier shimmered onto the screen.

"What we've come to learn so far," Muffin began, "is that Karl Langlier and Dr. Evangelista *did* have a parting of ways."

"Before or after he ended up in drag in Brussels trying to kill me?" Buck insisted. "Unless it was some sort of freaky freelance job."

"Very possibly. Langlier left Evangelista's payroll over a year ago," Muffin explained. "But there are still a couple of deposits made from her account to his. He then started to do a few jobs for a foreign service, and then nothing."

"So he was working on some private endeavor?" Buck asked.

"We're not sure. There's no evidence either way. What we do know is that there were two large financial payments from the Sisters of the Southern Cross, the larger going into a Swiss bank account which we have yet to gain access to. The other, enough to live on for several years, went to an account in Brussels, under the name Lan Glikërlar."

"Who the hell is that?"

"Mix up the letters and you tell me." Muffin clicked the remote.

The picture on the screen became smaller and the letters for L-A-N G-L-I-K-E-R-L-A-R appeared in order. With another click the letters swirled around and spun until they reformed, spelling out the name KARL LANGLIER.

"He may have been a clever assassin," Muffin said. "But he

lacked creativity otherwise. We managed to get this photo from footage in a Belgian bank. And you can see, Lan Glikërlar is definitely Karl Langlier."

A photo of a bank lobby appeared with three people standing in line. A camera focused on the first and then moved on. It stopped on the second person and focused in. A close-up of the face was pulled out and blown up into a focused image. The mug shot enlarged again and appeared next to the close-up. Ten red arrows appeared on the screen, all referring points of identification.

"We only need three points," Muffin said. "We have ten."

"So why the two payments after leaving Raven's employment?" Buck asked.

"Good question. We can only speculate."

Buck slapped his hand on the tabletop. "It was probably an advance payment for killing me."

"Possibly, but doubtful. Langlier was living on the Continent for at least four months by the time you showed up, Agent 98. The timing is off."

"Maybe Langlier came out of retirement for the last hurrah of killing me?"

"And waited for you in some country he had no idea you would ever visit?"

"Then there's something else," Buck confirmed. "A possible payoff for her husband's murder?"

"That's possible, too, although doubtful. That would be payment almost two years after the murder took place. Most hired guns wouldn't wait that long for payment, especially if they're starting to dislike their employer."

"Do you have any good news, Muffin?"

Muffin paused dramatically. He spoke very softly. "We know the identity of the Bomb-a-Bar-for-Jesus Guy."

Buck gave Muffin his full attention. "When did this happen?"

"Last night, while you were on the red-eye," Muffin said. "He blew up another bar, this time in DC. The police caught him three blocks away."

"And?"

"And what?" Muffin said. He clicked another few buttons and a face appeared on the screen.

The picture was that of a living skull. His face was gaunt and drawn out, with cheekbones practically ripping through the sallow skin. He was completely bald. Cloudy eyes in sunken sockets stared out from under heavy lids and resided over skin thinly stretched over bone. His neck was thin and long, but his head hung forward, his shoulders rounded and stunting his true height.

"It's like someone deflated Mr. Clean," Buck said.

"Yes," Muffin agreed. "His name is William Haggen, although the police don't know that yet. He apparently eradicated his fingerprints, possibly with hydrochloric acid. That's why they never picked up any at the crime scenes. His teeth are dentures, so identification that way was impossible. He didn't want to be identified."

"So how did you?"

"Sheer luck," Muffin said. "A missing persons report was filed with good descriptions of his two tattoos, the Greek letter lambda and a dove carrying an olive branch. The first is older and fading, the latter was done in the last year. One of our agents working missing persons was at the station when Haggen was apprehended. The police assumed Haggen's tattoos were fresh, but when our agent got a look, he noticed they weren't *fresh*, they were freshly *altered*."

"How?" Buck asked.

"The lambda tattoo had another line added to the center, and a circle around it, which turned it into a peace sign. The dove was colored in black. The inks didn't match and were only partially healed. He's being held for psychiatric evaluation."

"How long do you think it'll be before the police figure out who he is?"

"That shouldn't take them too much longer," Muffin answered. "It'll be just long enough for us to determine whose jurisdiction the case falls under."

"Has the bomber said anything?" Buck asked.

"Nothing," Muffin said. "Nothing except Bible quotes and nonsensical ramblings. If he says anything that is coherent, it's usually a Bible verse."

Buck sat pensively. "How old is this guy?"

"In his late thirties, maybe early forties, I believe. Why?"

"The lambda," Buck answered. "It's the Greek letter meaning 'sameness,' but it's also an old-school symbol of gay rights, before the rainbow was adopted. Most people younger than thirty don't know its meaning."

"I wouldn't say that," Muffin replied. "There's Lambda Legal, Lambda Literary, Lambda—"

"Yes," Buck interrupted. "They may use Lambda in the title, but you'd be hard-pressed to actually *find* a lambda represented anywhere on most of those logos or websites. You can know the word without knowing the meaning. Besides, it would fit in his age range. The question is why would it be on his arm if he's going around blowing up gay establishments?"

"A case of self-loathing, perhaps," Muffin replied.

The plasma screen went black and retracted into the ceiling. Muffin clapped his hands and the lights slowly brightened.

"What now?" Buck asked. "Do I wait until you've had a chance to go through the computer files? Do I head back to Virginia to investigate Evangelista more?"

"She's not there."

"Then where is she?"

"New Orleans," Muffin answered. "The Sisters of the Southern Cross are holding a benefit for the victims of that devastating hurricane three months ago. As president, she's assuming hosting responsibilities. Noxia has managed to get an invitation from the congressman."

"She gets to go to New Orleans," Buck complained. "And I get stuck with Virginia?"

"Oh, don't worry, Agent 98. You're going, too."

"Really?"

"You'll be going with Agent 46 to help keep an eye on Evangelista."

"Are you actually hoping we'll get into a confrontation?"

"We're counting on that," Muffin replied.

Buck tilted his head. "You're using me as bait?"

"You do catch on quick, don't you? In a word, yes."

"What is it you're hoping she'll do?"

"I'm not sure," Muffin replied. "She won't have the home field advantage, and she'll have to improvise."

"Thank goodness for small favors!"

"Agent 98, don't be such a baby. What's the worst thing that could happen?"

"I don't know," Buck answered. "There's the bayou with snakes and alligators. That's good enough reasons to avoid it."

"You'll be in the French Quarter at a very nice hotel," Muffin assured him. "You'll make do."

Buck folded his arms with a pout. "I'm sure that's what the hostess of the Donner party said when the food ran out."

CHAPTER ELEVEN

The lobby of the Fleur-de-lis Hotel in New Orleans was decorated lavishly in fine oaken splendor divided by five supporting columns. Overstuffed octagonal sectional pieces were scattered between the pillars in no particular pattern, inviting guests to sit, sink, and become lost in their easy comfort. Welcoming tables for the evening's event were being set up along the inside wall to the left. Attendants were anxiously arranging the table buntings with the Sisters of the Southern Cross logo and placing information cards on how to donate to the Hurricane Relief Fund, while miscellaneous hotel guests meandered throughout the extensive lobby.

"We don't have to be here for two more hours," Noxia complained through clenched teeth and a faux smile. "Some of us need time to get ready for the evening. There's nothing here now. Why are you dragging me through this?"

"So I can take care of some last-minute preparations." Buck led her to the row of tables. He kept his voice low and his head turned away from her. "I just need you to be overbearing, pushy, and a little emasculating. You know how to do that, surely. And when I give you the word, storm out."

Noxia took her cue. "Must you always drag me through hotel lobbies?" She raised her voice. "What the hell is the difference between this one and any other we've seen?"

"I like the architecture," Buck said passively.

"There's plenty of architecture out there," she replied snidely. "You *always* do this. By the time we get out there, it'll be time to get ready and come back."

Most people around took notice of their voices and ignored them. Buck whispered to Noxia, "Be more of a bitch."

"I hate that word," Noxia whispered back. "Look, I'm not wasting my time doing this." She stopped walking, planting her knuckles on her waist. "I'm tired from walking, I'm sticky from the humidity, and I'm going back to the hotel *now*. Are you coming with me or not?" Noxia glared at him. She watched Buck's expression grow meeker until he looked away to study the floor's mosaic. "Fine." She stormed out of the hotel.

Buck remained where he stood, studying his shoes and looking deflated. He raised his head with a heavy sigh and gazed around the room. Every person nearby avoided making eye contact with him. He sighed again, gazing over the information pamphlets, and slowly made his way to the end of the row of tables.

"Are you all right, *cher*?" asked a soft-spoken voice. "Can I get you some water, or coffee, or maybe a brandy punch?"

"No. Thank you." He mumbled so softly she had to lean in to hear him clearly. Buck lifted his head to see a plump, well-dressed woman in a pastel blue gown. The dress freely flowed over her full frame. A translucent covering over her amble endowment lightly tinted the flesh beneath pallid blue. Her makeup was heavy, and her touched-up blond hair curled to her shoulders. The top of her head was hidden underneath an exaggerated hat matching her gown.

"I couldn't help but notice," she said in a hushed, melodic whisper, "that you don't seem to be doing well. Are you sure I can't get you some water? Maybe some iced tea?"

Buck smiled and noticed the woman's warm reaction to the gesture. "That's very kind of you, Mrs...."

"Lulu-Belle Hapshed," she answered, holding out her hand. "*Miss* Lulu-Belle Hapshed."

Instead of shaking her hand, Buck gently kissed it. Her cheeks grew darker. "A pleasure to meet you, Miss Hapshed."

"Oh," she said with an overexaggerated giggle. "Lulu-Belle, please."

"My name is Miller," he said, patting the back of her hand as if sealing in the kiss. He could barely feel any bones through the thickened flesh of her hand. "Buck to all of my friends, which I hope I can now count you among." Miss Hapshed blushed again, fluttering her heavily painted eyes.

"You just didn't seem to be having a good time," Lulu-Belle said. She placed her hand over Buck's and leaned in. "Your friend didn't seem to be very nice, bless her heart."

"No, she didn't." Buck took a heavy sigh. "But alas, I'm kind of stuck with her. She's my date for this evening's benefit."

"Oh, dear," Lulu-Belle said, looking a little distraught.

Through the sheer blue cloth that tinted Lulu-Belle's bosom, something caught his attention. With his best discretion, Buck glanced down at the sheer cloth covering. Something was sparkling there underneath. Nestled between her breasts was a cross pendant, embedded with three red gemstones, one in each of the three lower extremities.

"That's a lovely pendant."

"Thank you." She giggled, her round face puffed with pride. "They match the earrings, except the earrings are crucifixes." She turned her head and pulled back her blondish curls to reveal tiny earrings. "There's actually a tiny ruby in each of our Lord's palms and one at his feet. To represent his suffering."

Forcing sincerity, Buck responded carefully, "They're beautiful."

"If you'd like," she said confidently, "I can tell you where to get a pair for your girlfriend."

"Oh, no, no, no," Buck replied quickly. "That's very kind, but she's not my girlfriend—she's my cousin. I came down to visit and she had the invitation for this evening's event, but..." he said leadingly. "I don't think I feel up to sitting next to her all night, so I might as well not go."

"Oh, no!" Lulu-Belle let out a soft wail. "You mustn't let her stop you from enjoying what promises to be a wonderful evening. Plus, it's a benefit, and think of all the people that you can help. Don't let a silly thing like her stop you."

"I'm not sure, I just don't know if I can deal with sitting by her all night," Buck said. He let his pouty smile spread across his lips. "But if you're going to be here this evening, Lulu-Belle, I'll try to summon the strength."

She giggled and pulled her chin down coyly. "Are you trying to flatter me?"

"That would be like painting the peacock, wouldn't it?" He winked.

"Oh, Mr. Miller," Lulu-Belle said, gently slapping his chest. "You're too, too kind." Her face lit up. "I'll tell you what I can do." She leaned in so close Buck could smell her rose-scented perfume. "I happen to be in charge of the seating arrangements. Maybe there's something I can do for you. Follow me." She turned and led him to the farthest table along the row. Spread out on top was a stack of place cards with names neatly printed on them. Only a few had table numbers assigned. "Let me just see what I can do for you." She picked up a stack of stapled papers and began leafing through them. "Mr. Buck Miller, here you are." Lulu-Belle smiled at him over the papers. "You're sitting at table eighteen, that's all the way in the back. Hmmm." She looked over the papers and a printed chart of the tables. "I can move you to table eight, if that works better; but then we'll have an odd number there."

"Where are you sitting, Miss Lulu-Belle?" Buck said, moving around the table and standing behind Lulu-Belle, looking over her shoulder.

"Oh, *cher,* I can tell you're going to be trouble." She babbled with excitement. "I'm sitting at table six, but I'll be helping with hosting duties and won't be able to sit down too much. You know," she looked over the arrangements, "I can actually move someone from the main table and put you at the same table as our hostess, the prominent Dr. Raven Evangelista. How does that sound?"

"Are you sure? That's really too kind."

"*Cher*, it's nothin' at all. We'll just put your name down for table one. Oh," she said sharply. "That'll leave us an opening here. Let's see who we can move around."

Buck stepped as close as he could without being rude. His arm slid out around her waist and pointed to two names. "If we move this couple over here, where I was sitting with Noxia, we can move her to sit next to…" He glanced over the names and decided to throw a little courtesy in Noxia's direction. "We can put her here, next to Congressman Julian. She's a liberal Democrat. So that'll serve her right for being so nasty, don't you think?"

"Not so nice for the congressman, though." Lulu-Belle giggled.

"Aside from you saving a dance for me," Buck said as he leaned around to face her, "it should be the highlight of the evening."

"We'll just take care of this right now." Lulu-Belle flopped down in a chair and began writing out the names and table numbers. "Easy as pie," she said with a flirtatious wink.

"Miss Hapshed," Buck said, taking her hand between his own. He brought it to his lips and kissed it softly. "You are my own personal savior."

Lulu-Belle's eyes widened and then softened immediately. A muffled sigh escaped her lips as Buck kissed her hand. It took her another moment to catch her breath. "I look forward to this evening, Mr. Miller."

"And now," Buck said, "so do I. Until tonight." He gave her a polite nod before turning and leaving the hotel lobby.

Walking out into the Southern sunshine, Buck put on his sunglasses, congratulating himself on a job well done. He decided to stroll about the French Quarter. Humming a Sondheim tune, Buck relaxed and meandered his way down a pedestrian walkway adjacent to Jackson Square. Feeling the spirit of the city, he wandered past an array of fortune-tellers and decided to have his fortune told. Buck sat down at one random stall completely on whim.

Sitting behind a square-folding table was a withered woman of color draped in a lavender dress with a matching scarf on her head, covering the thinly braided strands that hung down to her breasts. Gnarled fingers bore many silver rings that seemed embedded in the flesh. Around her neck hung several silver chains carrying numerous keys, a whistle, and a couple of different colored skull charms. There were gaps between her yellowed teeth, and her eyes were almond saucers with a darkened amber tone shining through. Without so much as a welcome, she leaned forward and handed Buck a thick pile of playing cards that included several decks.

"Shuffle de cards and cut de deck into three parts with your left hand," the ancient voice said. She watched him carefully. "What is your birthdate?"

"June eighth," Buck answered as he placed the cards into three piles. As soon as he released the cards, her hand bolted forward and grabbed onto his wrist. She twisted his hand, thrusting her fingers into his palm, and began tracing the lines there.

"You have a long life in front of you. Dat's good." She traced another route across the surface and down to his wrist. "You are a good lover." She winked. "That's good, too. Eh!" Releasing his hand, she took the cards and turned face up several on the table. With one hand hovering over the cards, the other resumed its vise grip on his wrist and held it to the table, knuckles down. She studied the cards and his palm, comparing them like they were sacred texts. "You have danger in your life; here, here and here, much danger. But you have many spirit guides dat protect you. You are not married."

"No," Buck answered with a cough. "I'm not married."

"No. But romance is around the corner. So is danger; the two come usually together." She let loose a hacking laugh before resuming. "Ah," she said. "You will be going on a trip soon, and a famous person will join you."

"Oh, really?" Buck leaned forward with renewed interest. "Who? Who will it be?"

Ignoring the question, she looked down at the cards before giving him a puzzled look. Her twisted index finger pointed to the upside-down queen of hearts lying across the queen of spades. "Two ladies together plot against you: one with dark hair, and one with red." She looked into his face. "Surprises await."

"I'm not sure I like surprises. Especially from a pair of queens."

"You may not," she said, pointing to the cards, "but that is what they say."

"Well, thank you," Buck said as she gathered up the cards. "That was ten dollars' worth of anxious anticipation." He left fifteen dollars on the table before getting up.

Deciding to head back to the hotel and meet Noxia, Buck continued walking back up the alley until he came to Royal Street and turned right.

"I'm sorry," said a voice as Buck walked into another person.

"My fault," Buck said politely. "I wasn't watching... Richard?"

The man had taken a step away. "Oh my God. Buck Miller?" The two men exchanged a brief hug. "What are you doing here?"

"I'm here for the hurricane benefit." Buck's eyes quickly scanned Richard's body. The white linen suit he wore made his smooth skin look even more golden than it had in Virginia, highlighting his amber eyes and black hair. "Of course," he said. "You must be catering it since it's Evangelista's event."

"I am." Richard beamed. "You look great."

"Thanks. So do you in your fine linens." More color crept into Richard's cheeks. "I have to admit," Buck continued, "I was hoping to run into you again, but didn't expect to do it here."

"Anything is possible in the Big Easy," Richard said. "Is your friend with you this time around? You know, the one with the ridiculous name?"

"Noxia?" Buck smiled. "It's not ridiculous, it's German, and yes, she is with me, just not at the moment."

"My luck," Richard sighed. "Destined never to get you alone."

Buck flashed his white teeth. "Well, I wouldn't say 'destined.'

There's always a chance we can arrange something. I'm sure I'll be back in Virginia soon enough."

"I was hoping for something sooner. Maybe we can arrange for something after dinner. A late cocktail or something?"

"That sounds good," Buck said, never taking his eyes off Richard's. "What time and where?"

"Are you familiar with New Orleans?"

"Not really."

"I lived here for two years," Richard said. "I'm staying at the Monteleone, why don't we just meet there?"

"Oh?" Buck replied, suggestively raising his eyebrow.

"It's that famous hotel with the revolving Carousel Bar. We can meet in there. They serve a good drink. It's not far from here and easy enough to walk to, and if you get spun around, just look up for their sign on the roof. You can see it practically from anywhere in the Quarter."

"I think I can handle that," Buck said.

"Great," Richard concluded. "I can sneak out from the benefit as soon as dinner is served. How about I meet you at the Carousel Bar at eleven thirty tonight?"

"Sounds great," Buck said, trying not to let too much enthusiasm show.

"All right then." Richard reached into his pocket and took out his card. "Any problems, call me at this number."

"I doubt there'll be any problems."

Richard raised an eyebrow. "You never know." He looked at his watch. "You'll have to excuse me. Dinner can't be late tonight, and I have lots of work ahead. Until later tonight?"

"You're always running away."

"I'll do my best not to tonight."

"I hope not." Buck smiled. They embraced, letting the connection linger a few extra moments. Before breaking apart, Richard leaned in and gave him a quick kiss on the cheek. "Bye," he whispered and continued on his way.

Buck watched Richard's form disappear into the crowded

streets. He put his hands into his pockets and started back to his hotel, humming as he strolled along Royal Street.

When Buck entered the doorway to the suite, he was still humming. He was about to enter his bedroom when Noxia's door opened and she appeared, wrapped in a body towel with another one creating a turban on her head.

"I don't like the sounds of that!" she said hesitantly. "What happened?"

"Noxia," Buck said, with an offsetting melodic tone. "What are you being paranoid about?"

"It's not paranoia, Buck. I've known you for a long time," she replied. "What you whistle, or hum, or sing to yourself is a direct link to what's going on in that scattered brain of yours."

Buck laughed. "What?"

"Everything you hum has a meaning, you little show queen. When you're in a good mood, you hum. When you hum a Sondheim tune, it's usually because you're being playful or are just in a good mood. When you are being pensive, it's something a little darker, like *Chicago* or *Cabaret*. But when you sing Rodgers and Hammerstein, then that's danger; that means you've met some guy and are being distracted. And I recognize *South Pacific*. So I'll ask you again, what happened?"

"Nothing," he sang to her. "So what does singing *A Chorus Line* mean?"

"I'm not sure, but I don't like it," Noxia said, beginning to retreat into her own room. "But as long as you don't let it interfere, I guess I won't complain too much. You can tell me what happened when we sit down to dinner."

"Oh, Noxia," Buck said, his voice dripping honey. "Funny thing; we're not sitting together anymore."

"Oh, God," Noxia bemoaned. "Now I *know* I'm not going to like this."

CHAPTER TWELVE

Noxia allowed Buck to take her arm and lead the way up the stairs to the ballrooms on the hotel's second floor. Her height advantage got her glances, but it was her appearance that held them. The gown's blushing rose color accentuated the traces of sun she'd caught that afternoon. Her wavy curls hung freely to her shoulders. A pale scarf wrapped loosely about her neck, flowing over her otherwise bare shoulders.

Buck's navy blue suit was made of the finest linen from Dolce & Gabbana, perfect for the humid New Orleans twilight. His hair was carefully parted on the side, with enough product to make sure the moisture in the air wouldn't affect its style. As they climbed the stairs, he smiled at her and gave her a brief wink. It didn't help her sense of unease.

"Well," Noxia whispered as they approached the ballroom. Music greeted them even before they reached the top of the stairs. "She seemed very friendly."

"Who, Lulu-Belle? She and I go way back," Buck said flippantly.

"You would think that a woman of her"—Noxia thought carefully—"*experience* would know a gay man when she saw one. She was all about getting Bucked."

"Don't be hatin'. You sound almost jealous."

"Of you and her? Right!" She dismissed it with a laugh. "If you're sitting at the main table, where am I?"

"Actually, I did you a favor. I put you at the same table as—"

"Miss Noxia von Tüssëll," came a delighted voice from just ahead. She looked up, recognizing the soft drawl, and the sight helped ease her stress.

"Congressman Julian. Now, this is a delightful surprise." She gave a sideways nod of acknowledgment to Buck.

"The pleasure is all mine," the salt-and-pepper-haired congressman replied, joining them and extending a tuxedoed arm. "You are Mr. Buck Miller, if memory serves correctly."

"And it does," Noxia and Buck replied simultaneously.

"Obviously," Dexter Julian said with a laugh, "you've been friends a long time."

"Too long, some would say," Buck replied.

"Are you two heading in?" Dexter asked, overlooking the comment. "Where are you sitting?"

"I'm sitting at table one," Buck volunteered.

"I'm at number eight."

"My dear, how does fate have us at the same table?" the congressman asked.

"I'm guessing dumb luck," Buck answered quickly.

"I guess we'll just have to talk about you in your absence," Dexter said.

"I'm sure we'll find something better to talk about than him," Noxia replied. "The odds are in our favor."

"Noxia," the congressman said. "It would be my pleasure to escort you to our table." She tucked her hand inside his elbow. As they approached the double doors, the attendants moved and opened it for them.

Black and gold decorations covered the ballroom in everything from streamers to balloons to the table settings and coverings. The only exception was the flag of the Sisters of the Southern Cross displayed over the central dais. The congressman and Noxia wandered about the tables until they came to a circular one with the number 8 prominently displayed. Congressman Julian held out her chair before taking the seat next to hers. From where she sat, she could still keep a peripheral line of vision on what Buck was doing. Also sitting at the table was Congressman Jonathan Jackson from Mississippi, busily talking to another young woman, who looked like an exaggerated real-life Barbie, and two other couples who were members of New Orleans society. Polite introductions were made before everyone returned to their own conversations.

"So, really," Congressman Julian began. "Who arranged it so that we happen to be sitting at the same table—was it you or your friend Buck?"

"Does it matter?" Noxia asked flirtatiously.

"No, I just wanted to know who I should thank."

"You already thanked me with the invitation."

"Then," Dexter asked, "who does the seating arrangement benefit more, you or him?"

Noxia smiled and chuckled softly. "Definitely me."

"Glad to hear it. Have you ever been to New Orleans before?"

"Several times," Noxia said. "But this is the first time since the series of major hurricanes. I don't see how it's going to recover."

"That's part of what tonight is for," Congressman Jackson said from the other side of Dexter Julian. Both Dexter and Noxia turned in his direction. "But it's not just the damage from the elements," he continued. "It's termites as well."

"Really?"

"They're slowly moving through the city," Congressman Jackson explained. "The weather damaged the older wooden houses, and the damned insects are infesting them."

"That's awful!" bemoaned the yellowed-hair woman on the congressman's far side.

"Yes, my dear, it is," assured Congressman Jackson. He turned back to Dexter and Noxia. "Dr. Evangelista has already earmarked twenty percent of tonight's funds to go to termite tenting alone. She's a remarkable woman, wouldn't you agree?"

"That depends on what the other eighty percent of the money

goes to," Noxia casually replied. Congressman Julian was amused, Congressman Jackson not as much. Quickly recovering, she added, "I'm sure it's all going to help rebuild the city."

"And to clean up the city as well," Congressman Jackson added. "Bourbon Street is getting more and more out of hand."

"I used to work on Bourbon Street," the blond woman said with an eager nod of her head.

"Is there anything organic about that woman at all?" Noxia whispered into Dexter's ear.

"After a certain point," Congressman Jackson continued, "it attracts the wrong kind of element."

"And what kind would that be?" Noxia asked, practically leaning over Dexter. "The drunks, the druggies, or the whores?" The last word lingered.

"Noxia," Congressman Julian interrupted. "Would you like to dance?" The question broke the growing tension and she turned her attention back to Dexter.

"Yes," she said, gathering a breath. "Thank you."

Dexter took her hand and led her to the small dance floor laid out in front of the dais. A three-piece band was playing waltz versions of classic songs ranging from Strauss to more modern tunes.

"Jonathon can be a bit pompous," Congressman Julian explained as they moved to the rhythm of the music. "He means well."

"Like a wolf means well to a lamb?" Noxia said.

"He's a good ole boy from Mississippi, what do you expect?"

"You're right," Noxia agreed. "Why would I expect modern thinking from them in the twenty-first century? Mississippi is one of the only two states left that still makes gay adoption illegal. Hell, they're still flying the rebel flag down there."

"I campaigned for keeping that flag, remember?" Dexter said with stern politeness. "There's a great history associated with that flag, and a lot of pride."

"You're right. There's slavery, treason, class distinction…did I miss anything?" She could feel the congressman's body tighten up as they continued dancing. When she could, Noxia glanced over to where Buck was sitting. Raven Evangelista was approaching the table.

"You're surely not going to let that old dog Jackson ruin the night, are you?"

"What?" Noxia asked, turning her attention back to Dexter. "Sorry." She smiled. "No, he's not worth it."

"Besides," he continued, "it's not like he's going to go over and horsewhip your friend or anything. Jackson is just a mouth."

"The mouth of the Mississippi." Noxia chuckled. "That's fitting. But it votes in Congress. And that's scary."

"Despite my opinions," Dexter added, after a moment, "I like your friend."

"What do you mean, 'despite your opinions'? What are your opinions?"

"I think those people are fine," he whispered as they glided along. "There's no need to get your feathers ruffled. I just don't think there's a need to yell who you have sex with from every mountaintop."

"It's not that simple," Noxia said.

"They can do what they want to in private, but why do they have to flaunt it publicly in everyone's face?"

"It's funny," Noxia continued. "When we are here doing just this, it's called dancing together. If we were two men doing exactly the same thing, we're flaunting our lifestyles."

"If we were two men, I wouldn't be doing this with you," Dexter defended. "Don't get me wrong, I told you, my sister's boy is one of them, but I still don't like what they do."

"Then I recommend you don't do it," Noxia replied with a smile.

"I think we're heading in the wrong direction," the congressman said.

"Gay people are people. Simple. Done." Noxia could see something happening between Raven and Buck.

"I never said they weren't," Dexter continued. "I just don't believe they should be getting married."

"Why not? What does it take away from anyone else?"

"It may not take anything away, but it's not the same either. Leave them to their unions, or whatever they call 'em. But marriage is sacred between man and woman."

"Sacred how?" Noxia snapped. "Because they can naturally procreate and gay couples can't? What if a married couple doesn't want to procreate, does that nullify their marriage?"

"Noxia," Dexter said, with an uncomfortable tone in his voice. "We don't need to discuss this. You know where I stand. I make my opinion very public. Marriage is between a man and a woman, and nothing comes between that."

"Not even a hooker in a cheap motel?" She regretted the words as soon as they slipped past her lips. The reaction was immediate. Dexter stopped dancing. The verbal slap wasn't heard by anyone else, but it stung hard. "I'm sorry, Dexter."

"I am, too." His words were curt and cold. "Sooner or later it was bound to come up. I should have expected it." Saying good-bye with a nod, he left her alone on the dance floor. Back at the table, he made his excuses to the other guests, shaking hands all around.

"Ladies and gentlemen," came an announcement from the center stage. "Our hostess for the evening, Dr. Raven Evangelista!" Applause gathered as Raven took to the stage.

"Just a few words as dinner is being served, if you'll allow me. I'll keep this short and sweet, for a change." She led the audience in their laughter.

Noxia excused herself to the bathroom, giving Dexter privacy to make his exit. She washed her hands and checked her makeup. After only a few moments, she returned to the ballroom to find Raven finishing her speech.

"Please remember the greatness that is New Orleans, and know we can help to build a better tomorrow. And now, enjoy your dinners!"

The crowd applauded for several minutes. Noxia looked around for Buck. She glanced over to the main table, but he wasn't there. Noxia scanned the crowd, but didn't see Buck anywhere.

Dr. Evangelista made her way through the dispersing crowd, to her table where dinner was waiting. Giving a final glance around for Buck, Noxia decided to follow suit and went to her table. She sat down, noticeably alone, and stared down at her salad plate.

"I think I've lost my appetite," she muttered. With a brief smile, she excused herself from the table and made her way out the ballroom door.

"Eleven fifteen," she mumbled to herself, slowly going down the staircase to the hotel lobby. "That went by faster than I expected, and I didn't even have to hear the speech."

Noxia walked out into the balmy New Orleans evening. The noise of Bourbon Street to her right held no allure for her, so she went the other direction in search of the comforts brought by Jackson Square and the illuminated St. Louis Cathedral. Despite being well trained in self-defense, she didn't like to bring unwanted trouble to herself; that's usually where she and Buck differed. She stopped outside the gates behind the cathedral grounds and gazed through without really looking. The buried lighting hit the statue of Jesus, casting its monstrous shadow on the backside of the cathedral.

"That comment was unnecessary," Noxia chided herself, looking through the iron bars. "True, but unnecessary." She glided farther down the street, easily mixing with the people pushing to go in either direction. As she walked, she noticed something up ahead causing the occasional passing stare.

Skulls appeared miscellaneously in the crowd coming toward her. Several ghostly figures were bobbing up to look through the throngs before them and then quickly disappearing from sight among the masses. At first, Noxia dismissed the four figures as being part of the odd assortment of French Quarter nightlife and stepped aside to let them pass. When the skeletons followed her example, Noxia slowed her pace.

People still meandered the streets but the crowds had thinned out, allowing Noxia to see the four figures slowing their pace as well. She flexed her fingers. The razor under her manicure gave her the confidence to stop walking and wait. The skeletons fanned out around her, leaving her face-to-face with one. Two others flanked her, and the fourth circled behind her. They began a synchronized clapping of their hands as they circled around Noxia. Crowds stopped and watched the scene as if it were a street performance, picking up the contagious clapping.

The skeletons gathered with perfect symmetry, not saying a word. She remained still, watching the ghostly carousel revolve about her. The larger circle grew tighter as the figures danced slowly closer, boxing her in.

Four of them, she thought. *In this dress that might be a challenge. I can still handle them if necessary.*

She wiggled her razored finger by her side, ready for anything. They were getting closer and she could see traces of painted skin behind the rubber masks. The two on the sides were easily within arm's reach, and a quick jerk of her knee would ensure the one in front of her would regret any sudden attack.

The four figures stopped simultaneously, throwing their arms up in the air. Noxia remained perfectly still, her blood flushing through her body. Silence wrestled tension as a large group of onlookers waited and collectively held their breath. The skeletons let out an amplified screech, causing several crowd members to jump back in surprise. They threw their bony arms outward.

Noxia stood perfectly still as glittering confetti fluttered down about her. The crowd broke out into applause and cheers, stirring back to life and morphing outward along their individual paths. The skeletons remained still, eyes locked on Noxia, ignoring the steady flow of people around them.

She stared back into the dark eyes of the figure in front of her. The skeleton blinked and slowly rocked in place.

"Noxia?" the voice sounded above the noise of the passing crowd. "Noxia!"

She ignored the call, keeping her eyes locked on the costumed figure before her. The skeleton broke her gaze and glanced over her shoulder to see who was coming toward them. The figure leaned in closer until it barely touched her glitter-covered face. It let out a low growl, angered by her lack of response as much as by the approaching interruption. Then it moved past her, taking the other two with it.

Noxia kept up her stare even when the skeleton began to move. She slowly turned, following his retreat. Her name was called again, and a new form thrust its way in front of her, blocking her view.

"What was that about?"

Noxia quickly looked around and saw the costumed figures further disappearing into the crowd. "I'm not sure." She looked up into Congressman Julian's face. "What are you doing here?"

"I wanted to apologize to you," he said after a moment's hesitation. "I can't get upset by something I did. It's not like it wasn't in the papers."

"Don't worry about it," Noxia half mumbled, trying to see past him for any other signs of the skeletons.

"Who were they?" Dexter asked, looking over his shoulder and trying to follow her gaze.

"I don't know," she answered hesitantly. "But I got the feeling they knew me."

"Did they do anything?"

"No," Noxia said, starting to let her guard down. "Just covered me in glitter."

"Then it was probably just a French Quarter thing. You know this *is* the land of voodoo."

"Great," she muttered. "Just what I need, a spell put on me. Anyway, what are you doing here? How did you know where I was?"

"I saw you walking ahead, and thought I should apologize. Then I saw those skeleton guys."

"Apology accepted." Noxia began to walk away. The congressman quickly kept pace.

"I'd like to make up for my behavior. You seem like someone honest and trustworthy."

"I *am* someone honest and trustworthy." Noxia sighed. "That's half my problem."

"Heh," he snorted. "When will you and your friend Buck be back in Virginia again?"

She stopped walking and looked at the congressman. His face was pinched and his lips were tightly closed.

"Most likely in a few weeks," Noxia said hesitantly.

"Maybe this conversation can be continued then?" His eyes were full and hopeful.

"I'll make it a point to call," Noxia said softly.

The entire body of Congressman Julian practically melted with relief before her. "Good," he said. "I hope you will." He presented his arm to her. "Can I escort you back to your hotel?"

"We seem to be standing in front of it." Noxia gestured to the bed-and-breakfast behind her.

Dexter read the sign. "The Andrew Jackson Bed & Breakfast."

"I always prefer them," she said. "It's more cozy than a big hotel chain."

"Then I'll say good night," the congressman said. "And again, I apologize for my rudeness."

"Again," Noxia replied politely, extending her hand, "no need."

The congressman smiled. He gave her hand a firm shake and walked away.

Noxia watched him go. He reached the end of the street before turning around and waving with a smile. She returned the gesture and waited until he disappeared around the corner. She walked up the steps to the B&B's doorway and opened the door. She looked about the lobby and at the polite man standing at the welcoming desk before smiling. "Sorry," she said with a dopey grin. "Wrong place."

When she exited the Andrew Jackson, Noxia was confident no one was watching her. She moved out onto the streets and disappeared into the crowd.

CHAPTER THIRTEEN

Buck watched Noxia and the congressmen enter the ballroom with their arms linked. For the briefest moment, he felt a twinge of envy at the sight of the two of them, and then the feeling passed. He took a step toward the door when he heard his name being called.

"Mr. Miller. Mr. Miller!" The melodic calling continued. "It's me! Lulu-Belle." He looked up to see the blue hues of Lulu-Belle's dress fluttering toward him. She waved her hand, clutching a small white handkerchief, high over her head. "Mr. Miller, there you are. I've been waiting for you."

"Miss Hapshed," Buck said with a smile and held out his hands to her. "My savior has arrived." She took both his hands and leaned in, presenting her cheek. The dulled scent of worn tuberoses filled his nostrils with its sickeningly sweet fragrance. His lips brushed the heavily painted skin before he was able to retreat to arm's length.

"Now," she said with a giggling lilt. "You really must call me Lulu-Belle, and I don't want to hear another word about it." She slid her arm around his and pulled him close. "You are sitting right next to me."

"I thought you were at a different table," Buck said. "Don't you have hosting duties and all?"

"I got a reprieve," she said with a pat of her hand on his arm. "I thought to myself, 'Lulu-Belle! How often do you get to visit with a nice gentleman caller?' So I did a little rearranging, and now I can spend most of the evening at your table, the hostess table." She held out her name card with the big number 1 written in black ink.

She led Buck into the ballroom. They took a serpentine path, weaving between the black-and-gold-colored settings and the milling guests until arriving at their table. Lulu-Belle came to a stop and stood, waiting. Buck took the cue and held out her chair. As Lulu-Belle sat, he realized the challenge was getting it back into position.

Buck sat on Lulu-Belle's right side with the Mayor of New Orleans, a dark-suited man in his early sixties, and his attractive wife, a well-dressed woman in an emerald dress. Next to them sat Dan Faulkner, the thirty-three-year-old quarterback of the New Orleans Saints. Three seats remained empty—Buck assumed one of them was for Raven. He checked his watch; it read 8:30.

"It's much too early for that, sugar!" Lulu-Belle gleefully slapped the watch on his wrist. "So, Buck. You said your cousin brought you tonight. Do you travel together often?"

"Sometimes," Buck answered. "Where is she, anyway?" He shifted in his seat until he found Noxia in the crowd. She was happily talking to the congressman.

"Oh, she's just fine," Lulu-Belle assured him. She repositioned herself to block out his view. "Is this your first time to New Orleans? I've lived here most of my adult life. Actually, I live in Metairie, but that's practically a suburb of New Orleans. Leaving this area is just not an option. Who Dat Saints! Whoa! I guess I'm like Tennessee Williams, I got it in my blood." She gushed and giggled simultaneously.

"Don't all the hurricanes bother you?"

"Do you have any idea how many hurricanes have come through here in the last five years? Devastating."

"That's kind of my point," Buck mumbled.

"It's still my home. No matter what, it's my home."

"Were you here for any of the hurricanes, or did you evacuate?"

"Sugar," Lulu-Belle puffed herself up and counted off her fingers proudly, "I've lived through Hurricanes Ruth, Suzanna, and Tanya. As well as tropical storms Meredith, Natalie, and Lena. Do you have any idea of how many of these we get a year?"

"Talk about stormy weather."

Lulu-Belle released a sound like a bird's caw. The tiny crucifix earrings rocked back and forth. The little rubies in their palms flashed through the platinum hair. "Oh, that's funny! Well, it's not, but it is." She laughed. "We actually lived in our attic for three days during the last one. They had to airlift me and my two cats out of our home, but thank the Lord, we survived." She crossed herself and kissed her knuckle.

"How long have you been involved with the Sisters of the Southern Cross?" Buck asked.

"Oh." Lulu-Belle counted mentally. "I helped form the local chapter here three years ago. But I was involved long before that."

"Really. From the beginning?"

"Why, yes," she said with pride. "I've known Raven's family for many years. Our families have always been close. I was even a bridesmaid at her wedding."

"You don't say."

"I do," Lulu-Belle insisted. "We've known each other since God was a child, as my granny used to say." She laughed. "Well, at least since we were girls in Alabama. When Raven first started the Sisters, it was a social group in high school. After graduation, she kept with it and made the organization what it is today. We had no idea that it would become such a national success." She leaned in. "I joined from the beginning because it was a good way to blackball girls we didn't want to be around; you know, girls who could be wrong for the reputation." She nodded and winked, leaning in with the confession, "I also thought it was going to be more Civil War reenactments and such. Was I foolish, or what?"

"Or what," Buck jested. "How long did it take to get out of Alabama?"

"For me, it was another year when I moved here to go to

school. Go Tulane Green Wave, whoa!" The quarterback across the table smiled and nodded in their direction. "The Sisters spread like wildfire, and now there are chapters all over the South. We raise money for charities, and do lots of community and civil work."

"What kind of civil work?" Buck was only half listening. He signaled to a passing waiter to bring him a glass of champagne. He took several from the waiter's tray and drank half a glass immediately. Keeping one ear alert to follow the flow of conversation, he let his gaze wander. Noxia was talking with her congressman at their table. And he was sitting stuck with Miss Lulu-Belle Hapshed, the only Southern debutante without a sense of social skills. Sometimes life just wasn't fair. He looked at his watch: 9:15. At least he could soon make an excuse and be off to meet up with Richard.

"Unfortunately," she began, "New Orleans has no end of problems that need fixing. If it's not crime or decay of the beautiful old buildings, it's the city's decaying morals."

"I'm sorry." Buck dropped back into the conversation. "But what did you say?"

"The city needs to have its morals cleaned up," Lulu-Belle protested. "Bourbon Street is just getting too out of hand."

"I know I'm only a visitor," Buck said with incredulous disbelief. "But isn't that a major part of the city's revenue, not to mention part of its charm? I mean, coming to New Orleans is not like visiting any other part of the South. It's a country unto itself, like going from Rome into Vatican City. The openly encouraged diversity is one of the things that separates New Orleans *from* the rest of Louisiana."

"Dude," Faulkner, the football player, said. He patted two fingers across his chest. "Dat's da word!"

Buck shot him an uncomfortable smile and a polite nod. "Thanks."

"I'm not saying that all of it needs to change," Lulu-Belle backtracked. "I'm just saying that maybe it could take a step back, or even two. There's just too much out there, it's practically a Bacchanalia. People get mugged on the street and the average person does nothing to stop it. Or even worse, they think it's part of a street performance."

"You're never going to stop it," Faulkner added. "Partying is the New Orleans way of life. People come from all over the world to get drunk in New Orleans." He raised his glass and emptied the remains. His girlfriend nodded and followed his example.

"But too much debauchery is still too much," Lulu-Belle defended herself. "People are forgetting that there are still God-fearing Christians here. I think that one of the better programs that Raven has started is the Rescued Right. It has helped many people find their path back to God. Raven has been a large part of that."

"How's that?" Buck asked.

"It's one of the first things she does in a new chapter. She reaches out to the homosexual community and invites them to change their ways. She doesn't force them, but invites them with politeness, and shows them they can change."

"You make it sound like sexual orientation is a choice," Buck said.

"The choice is to be on the path of God, or the path to H-E-double hockey sticks." She nodded confidently. "Through diligent prayer, and if the sinner wants to change badly enough, and if they truly in their hearts renounce Satan's ways, they can change. They can live a happy and healthy heterosexual life. I've seen it happen."

"Really?" Buck said sardonically. "How did that go?"

"It's hard work, Mr. Miller. But I have seen it take. The Lord's light can clear anything away, as long as you let the darkness go."

"And you've had how much of a success rate?"

Lulu-Belle was silent for a moment. "There have been a few that have changed their lives for the Lord, but just won't let go of that one sin. I've seen it cause horrible fights in families and tear them apart."

"So have I," Buck said with genuine sincerity. "It's awful when it happens!"

"I know." Lulu-Belle dramatically clutched at her chest. "To see the parents tested that far when they know in their hearts their own child is so sick. It just breaks my heart when I think about them doing the Lord's work and having to send the serpents away from the nest."

Buck looked at her through a pasted polite expression. "How many of those kicked-out kids commit suicide?"

"That's another sin against the Lord." Lulu-Belle nodded emphatically. The crucifixes shook their sadness from her ears. "The poor souls of those lost children."

"And the damnation of those hypocritical parents!" Buck added.

"Mr. Miller," Lulu-Belle said with an edge to her voice. "The Sisters of the Southern Cross is a proud organization. We do a lot of good in this decrepit world and help a lot of people find their way. We are not hypocrites. We love the sinner and despise the sin," she concluded with a definitive nod.

"I'm sure that's a comforting thought to those kids," Buck said. "Right before they kill themselves."

"Mr. Miller," Lulu-Belle said, her face getting flushed. "We have helped many people. The Christian way is that of example. Raven would never ask anyone to do something she would not do herself."

"It's easy to say being childless, isn't it?"

"Raven was able to turn her own son away," Lulu-Belle said sharply. "If she can do it because of her love in the Lord, so can anyone else."

The words struck Buck like lightning. He blinked several times to let them sink in and took a deep breath.

"Raven has a gay son?" he asked incredulously.

Lulu-Belle's eyes widened and sucked in her lips. With a delicate grace, she turned to the tabletop and sipped at the almost empty champagne flute. "I probably wasn't supposed to say that," she muttered into her glass.

Buck's demeanor softened. He reached out and patted her fleshy arm. "Lulu-Belle," he cooed. Looking around, Buck found and signaled to a passing waiter with a tray of filled champagne glasses. "I assure you, everything you've said is held sacred to me and will not be shared." He smiled, placing another drink in front of her. "I never knew she had any children."

Lulu-Belle turned back to him, her eyes wide. She leaned closer, hanging over the imaginary clothesline. "Raven was just starting school when she met Timothy."

"That's Dr. Shoulwater?"

"Yes, they met at college. It was the end of the first semester that Raven found herself," Lulu-Belle softened her voice to a whisper and lowered her head with a disapproving look, "in trouble. She was only eighteen years old, bless her heart. She came here, stayed with me and had the baby."

Buck shook his head not following. "What happened to the baby?"

"Billy," Lulu-Belle sighed. Her breath was heavy with melancholy. "He was a beautiful baby, but she did the right thing and gave him up for adoption."

"I never knew," Buck replied, finding some compassion for Evangelista.

"But that's not the end of it," Lulu-Belle said, finishing off her drink. Buck slid another filled flute in front of her. "Years later, Raven hired a private detective and she found Billy. He was still here in New Orleans. After all that time, all that separation, and all the pain she went through to reconcile with him, and she found out he was a gay.

"She tried to work with him, and he began to see the light. He just wouldn't give up his gay lifestyle. She even had him come out to Virginia, she was already on the political path out there, and got him an appointment to see a specialist." She downed half the glass. "He went out there, but Raven finally realized he was never going to give up being a gay. It killed Raven, but she had no other choice and washed her hands of him altogether."

"What happened?"

"I don't know," Lulu-Belle answered. "Raven sent him away

and she never mentioned his name again. Out of respect, I've never asked."

"Do you by chance know the name of the family that adopted him?"

"No," Lulu-Belle said, shaking her head. "Raven never shared that with me."

"That's really sad," Buck said.

"I know," Lulu-Belle agreed. "He chose such sickness over a loving mother and the Lord."

Buck was about to comment further when the football star and his date suddenly perked up. "There's Dr. Evangelista now," he said. The entire table turned as one to watch the doctor's approach.

Dr. Raven Evangelista made her way through the crowd like she was Moses parting the Red Sea. She wore a simple red cotton dress with a similar-colored belt. Her brown hair fell down to her shoulders, and a faux red flower was clipped on one side to keep the hair pulled behind her left ear.

But it wasn't Raven that caught Buck's attention. Walking closely behind her at her heels was a blond man in a tuxedo. The center part in his hair brought attention to the two now-fading blackened eyes. A piece of surgical tape held the bridge of his nose together from a recent breakage. As the two approached the table, the blond man glanced at Buck. Loathing flashed across his face.

As the table's conversation came to a complete halt, Lulu-Belle was the last to look up and see Raven standing at the table.

"Speak of the devil," Lulu-Belle said gaily.

"Indeed," Buck added.

Lulu-Belle stood, causing every gentleman at the table to race to his feet, and immediately went to embrace Raven. She threw her arms around the doctor, but Raven kept her hands at her side and her eyes locked on Buck.

"Raven," Lulu-Belle presented. "This is my friend Mr. Buck Miller. Buck, this is my good friend and our hostess, Dr. Raven Evangelista."

"I think we've met before, Mr. Miller," she said coldly.

"And once again," Buck said, offering his hand, "the pleasure is mine."

"Yes," came the icy answer as Raven ignored his hand. "This is my friend, Terje Löggenbaur."

Terje glowered at Buck. "We've met before," he growled.

"Have we?" Buck said innocently. "Where?"

Terje said nothing and stepped closer to hold Raven's chair out for her. She sat gracefully down and Terje sat on the opposite side.

"Since I know you're into antiques," Lulu-Belle was saying, "I can take you around the Quarter tomorrow and introduce you to some of the dealers around here."

Raven was leaning over and whispering into Terje's ear.

"That's very kind," Buck said, doing his best to be polite while trying to eavesdrop on Raven's conversation. "But I'm leaving town first thing in the morning." Terje was whispering back to her. She nodded with understanding and stared directly at him.

"That's too bad," Lulu-Belle said.

Terje stood and left the table quickly.

"Mr. Miller," Raven said. Her stubby fingers tapped on the tabletop. "Have you seen the hurricane exhibit at the Presbytere yet?"

"What? No, not yet," Buck said. He smiled at Raven, trying to look over her shoulder and locate Terje. She moved back into his line of vision. It was too late anyway; the blond man had disappeared. Buck glanced over to locate Noxia, but he couldn't find her, either.

"It's not to be missed." Raven drew out the last word, sounding like a snake. "Have you taken a voodoo tour, Mr. Miller? Seen any of the graveyards that have added to the city's notorious infamy?"

"No," Buck said. Raven's expression was void, stoic and cold. "I try to concern myself more with affairs of the living than the dead."

"Be careful the twain never meet," Raven said. She forced a breathy chuckle.

Buck flashed a grin and looked at his watch: 10:45. Good enough. Raven was already standing and talking to someone else, walking away from the table and becoming lost in the crowd.

"Lulu-Belle." He leaned forward, placing his hand on her arm. "I'm sorry, my flight really is early, and I should try to get some sleep."

"If you need an early ride to the airport," Lulu-Belle said suggestively.

Buck was scanning the crowd. "Before I go," he said. "I really should say good night to our hostess."

"Such a gentleman," Lulu-Belle cooed as Buck stood.

"Dr. Evangelista," Buck said. He weaved through the crowd until he caught up to her. He tapped her on the shoulder to get her attention.

"Yes," Raven said.

"Sorry," Buck said, retrieving his hand from the back of her hair. "My watch got caught in your hair." His overly exaggerated smile didn't help. "I just wanted to personally wish you the best of luck with tonight's benefit."

Raven stared at him slowly, taking in every detail. She studied his extended hand before readjusting her stance and folding her arms across her chest. "What is it you want with me, Mr. Miller?"

"Sorry?" Buck asked.

"I had the feeling it was no coincidence that we met in Virginia," she said frostily. "And after tonight, I can't help but feel the same. So I'll ask again. What is it you want with me?"

Buck studied her eyes. They remained impassive.

"I'm sorry if I've given you the wrong impression," Buck said quietly. "There's nothing at all I want from you."

Raven's stare was cold. "Glad I could help you, then." She disappeared farther into the crowd.

Buck shook his head and gazed at his watch. Perfect. The time read 11:05. He had a date to keep. Grabbing several napkins from a stack on the table, he left the ballroom and made his way through the hotel lobby and out onto the street.

Walking down two storefronts, Buck stepped into an empty doorway and withdrew the napkins from his pocket. Squatting down, he opened one of the napkins until it covered his knee. He studied his watch until he found the brown hair wrapped around the metallic face. Using the fingers on his right hand, Buck withdrew the hair and gently laid it out in the center of the white napkin. Taking great care, he folded the napkin until it was an inch square. He slid it into the inner folds of his wallet.

Buck took out his cell phone and hit the speed-dial code. "Muffin, it's me. Who else calls you Muffin? I have an important question for you, and then you are going to do me a big favor, and I'm going to be your new best friend. Listen to me carefully: How soon can you do a DNA test?"

CHAPTER FOURTEEN

Buck walked down Royal Street with his hands in his pockets and deep in thought. Despite the hour the streets were still well populated, and he meandered through the crowd. After a few moments he realized he was softly humming a song from *The Sound of Music* and couldn't help but smile.

"Maybe Noxia has a point with this humming thing," he muttered. He kept his eyes focused on the broken sidewalks in front of him, and his thoughts changed to Lulu-Belle. His mind replayed the conversations from earlier, and quickly Buck became lost in his own theories. Forgetting to pay attention to his surroundings, he followed the crowd until he realized that he had crossed Canal Street and turned down one of the side streets.

Laughing at his own folly, Buck turned around and began to retrace his steps. Something ahead of him caught his eye. In the crowd coming toward him were three skeletons. Slowing his pace, he slid his hand into his jacket, reaching for his holster more from instinct than need. It was then he realized they weren't walking toward him, they were coming at him and stopped directly in his path.

"Sorry, guys. You startled me," Buck said. His heart was pounding. He looked at the three of them, all dressed alike in skeleton costumes with rubber masks over their faces. People meandered by, some casting odd looks at the costumed figures while others didn't flinch at all. The first skeleton stepped closer. Buck took a step back, thinking it wanted to pass. It moved exactly the same way, mirroring his image. He stepped aside, and again, the skeleton mimicked him. The other two fanned out to either side of him. They stood still and waited without a word. Buck looked at the three of them. "So what's up, boys?"

The skeleton in front stepped closer. Buck remained still. He stared back, trying to get a glimpse at what was under the mask. There were traces of dark makeup to hide the pale color underneath. Just under the eye, Buck could see traces of broken skin. This was not a fraternity prank.

"Costume party," Buck said with a cocky smile. "Or jazz funeral?"

"The only funeral is yours, dude," the skeleton said in a familiar voice.

"I hate being called dude," Buck said. "You'd think you'd learn after the last time I kicked your ass."

Buck smashed his foot down on the skeleton's instep. As the man fell forward, Buck's fist connected with his chin, sending him reeling and knocking him out cold to the ground. The skeleton on his right leapt forward and charged, colliding with Buck's side. The two of them crashed backward into a locked-up storefront. The two men were crammed in the small quarters, leaving the third attacker to stand back and watch, looking for a chance to join. Buck reached into his jacket for his gun, but the figure smashed a fist into his stomach, bringing Buck to his knees. The skeleton kicked his hand and the gun went flying from his grip.

The stranger brought his leg back to kick him in the head. Buck rolled and the foot narrowly missed him. Reacting quickly, he reached up and grabbed the costumed man by the ankle, twisting with all his strength. The foot cranked to the side. The ligaments tore. The skeleton's other leg gave way under the pain, and he toppled backward.

The remaining upright figure charged as Buck rolled away and leapt to his feet. When the skeleton stopped and turned to face him, both were ready for the fight. Both men rocked back and forth on the pads of their feet, ready to leap in either direction. The skeleton threw a punch, more to gauge than to make contact, and Buck ducked to avoid it. He threw two return punches into the skeleton's shoulders, knocking him a step backward.

"You really want to do this?" Buck said. His body was vibrating. Blood raced through his veins. Every sense was on edge, heightened by the pumping flow of adrenaline.

The skeleton threw another punch, and Buck returned with the same two responses.

"Persistent. I'll give you that."

The skeleton threw his next punch but this time was prepared when Buck made his attempt with the same gesture. The assailant knocked his arms out of the way and was able to connect a fist directly to Buck's jaw. The shock of the blow sent Buck reeling backward until he hit a wall. His head snapped back and into the cement siding. Slowly he slid down the wall. Seizing the opportunity, the skeleton turned and ran.

Buck could do nothing besides watching his assailant escape. His breath came hard and he rolled over to his side with some effort. He pulled himself to his knees, catching his breath and gazing about to make sure no other attackers were coming. Scanning the shadows, he saw the handle of his gun and quickly retrieved it. Keeping it pointed and ready, he approached the skeleton that still lay sprawled out in the doorway.

He leaned down, keeping the gun carefully aimed, and reached out his hand. The form didn't move and Buck cautiously reached his free hand out to check for breath. The man was still alive, but definitely unconscious. Without even trying to be careful, Buck took hold of the rubber mask and roughly pulled it off. The face was unfamiliar.

Standing up, he sauntered over to the second of the attacking skeletons. The figure lay broken, moaning and clutching his ankle. He wasn't going to be moving anywhere without assistance from someone, and Buck was not the someone to do it. Buck leaned down and grabbed him by the back of the neck. Roughly, he ripped off the rubber mask to find a matted mass of blond hair with a recovering set of fading black eyes. Terje spat blood on Buck's jacket.

"Maybe this time you'll get it," Buck said. He slammed his forehead into Terje's, again breaking the bones in his nose. The blond man's head rocked back and Buck dropped the unconscious man onto the cobblestone. "I *really* hate being called dude."

Buck stood up and wiped at his nose. Dark crimson streaked across the back of his hand. "Damn it! And I'm late for my date!" His arms hung heavily at his side and his legs felt like weights. With a determined sigh he looked around at the street signs and realized he was only a block or two away from Royal Street.

Wiping the blood from his chin, Buck made his way back toward the hotel. He ignored the looks of curiosity from other pedestrians. His suit was dirty, and torn in some places. Blood was splotched all over the front. His skin was ripped with cuts and scrapes, and he held his nose pinched close to avoid any further blood running down his face. Buck limped up to the prestigious hotel and was immediately greeted by a suited doorman.

"Sir," he beseeched. "Are you all right?"

"Fine, thank you," Buck replied. "Just went down the wrong street and met the wrong people."

"Shall I call the police?"

"No," he answered. "Thank you." His voice was nasal from the pinched nose, and his words were muffled as he spoke into his hand. "I'm supposed to meet someone here, so I'll just have a drink and wait."

"You can't go in there like that, sir." Buck wasn't sure if the statement was concern for his sake, or the hotel's. "Let me get you seated in the lobby, and I'll be right back with a towel and some ice." The doorman took him by the arm and led him to a seat discreetly placed in the corner of a very busy reception area. By the time Buck sat down, the man hurried off to get what he needed.

Buck removed his fingers from his nose and breathed easier when blood failed to run out. He glanced at his watch: 11:53. Richard was probably gone by now. There was little to be done. He was about to get up and leave when a fleeting figure dressed in white caught his eye.

It was Richard.

"Richard!" he called out. The figure in white stopped and looked around for the source. Spotting Buck in the corner seat, he walked over hesitantly.

Richard's white linens made his golden skin shine in the lighting of the hotel lobby. His black hair was shiny and wet from a recent shower. He approached Buck with a hesitant expression.

"Are you all right?"

"Yeah," Buck said, trying to smile. The bruises added to his boyish charm. "You should see the other guys."

"Guys?" Richard smiled. "I didn't realize you were into group S and M."

The doorman returned with an attendant, an ice pack, and a hand towel. "Here you go, sir. Oh, hello, Mr. Pye."

"Thanks, Marvin," Richard said, taking the ice and towel. He wrapped it up and gently applied it to Buck's nose.

"Is there anything else I can help you with?" Marvin asked. It took Buck a moment to realize he was speaking to Richard.

"No, thank you," he replied. "Actually, yes. Can you send a bottle of champagne to my room? And," he looked at Buck with a boyish grin, "maybe some extra ice."

"Very good, sir." The attendant walked off.

"You're a mess," Richard said. "Instead of the bar, why don't we get you cleaned up?"

"I thought I was too late," Buck said, accepting the hand up from the chair.

"Perfect timing," Richard said. "The benefit ran late. I had just enough time to get back here, shower, and get ready to meet you. I was on my way to the bar when you caught me."

"Must be kismet." Buck flashed his smile through dirty, bruised, and bloodied lips.

Richard led the way to the hotel elevators, speaking over his shoulder. "I haven't heard the cast album to *Kismet* in years."

Buck felt his heart leap at the Broadway musical's title. A grin crawled across his face and he placed one hand over his heart.

"The concierge recognizes you?" Buck asked as the elevator made its way to the twenty-third floor.

"I worked here many years ago for a short time," Richard said. "Plus, Raven books me here every time we come to New Orleans. She throws a lot of business in their direction, and they return the favor in spades. It's very simpatico."

"Does she stay here also?"

"No," Richard said, with a laugh. "She'd never slum in a four-star hotel. She has friends she stays with."

"And you?" Buck asked, dabbing at the corner of his blossoming lip.

"I know which side my bread is buttered on," he confessed. "But I do sleep a little easier when Raven's not so close. I like being my own man."

The elevator came to a halt before anything else could be said. "My suite's over here," Richard smiled, leading the way.

"Why don't you go get cleaned up," Richard suggested as they entered the suite and moved into the main room. "Take a hot shower if you'd like. No offense, but you look like you could use it. You'll find clean towels in the bathroom."

"Hey," Buck said, reaching out and touching Richard's shoulder. "I appreciate it. Thanks."

Richard stepped forward until they were practically in each other's arms. His hand reached around Buck's neck, and he massaged the taut muscles there. "Go get cleaned up. There's time for chitchat later."

They leaned in and let their lips softly touch. Richard's skin was smooth and tasted sweet to his lips. The cologne he wore was subtly applied. Buck felt his chest tighten. He heard Richard's breath grow heavy. "You're still a bloody mess. Go," Richard ordered, swatting the back of his pants.

"Yes, sir!" Buck responded playfully.

Buck inspected his facial cuts in the bright light of the vanity.

He dabbed at the scrape by his eyebrows, which ran a jagged inch down to his cheekbones. It wasn't deep, and shouldn't leave a scar once it healed. His bottom lip was swollen, but not bleeding anymore. The blood from his nostrils was crusted and dried, flaking off at the slightest touch. Leaning close to the mirror, Buck bared his teeth and inspected his favorite feature. Nothing broken. Not even a chip. With a satisfied breath, he reached over and turned on the shower.

Beveled glass separated the shower from the rest of the bathroom, with an open space at the end for getting in and out. The liquid soap was called "Peach Bellini" and smelled delicious. The scent curled into his nostrils as he lathered it into the soft, scattered coating of chest hair. He felt his muscles release their clench and the tension in his shoulders relax. The hot water felt good, and he stayed in the main spray, enjoying the feel of the water jetting against his skin.

Buck opened the bathroom door, allowing the light from behind to illuminate his frame. Steam filtered out, creeping around his body and dissipating into the air. The plush towel was wrapped around his waist midway between his hips and his navel—and there was a single trail of hair visible before it disappeared beneath the towel's lip.

"Well," he said, folding his arms across his chest. Buck leaned his shoulder against the door frame, crossing his leg and resting his foot on the curled toes. "Now, that's a pretty picture."

"Yes," Richard replied, staring at Buck in the doorway. "And it's even framed." Richard had undressed and slid under the blankets in the middle of the bed. He leaned against the headboard with his arms raised, his head resting on his palms. The smooth chest was stretched taut and showed off his strong upper body. The definition of his chest muscles was extraordinary. His flat stomach disappeared under the lush comforter. Pillows surrounded his bare torso. An open bottle of champagne rested in an ice bucket on one of the nightstands. Two glasses, half-filled and bubbling, waited in front.

Richard leaned over to retrieve the champagne flutes. The comforter pulled back and the curve of his buttocks was briefly exposed. Holding one glass for himself, Richard offered Buck the other. "Join me?"

"I was hoping you'd ask." Buck slowly walked to the edge of the bed. The towel came loose and fell to the floor. He slid under the covers next to Richard, taking the flute from his hand. They touched their glasses, letting a single chime ring through the room.

Buck kissed Richard's lips without taking a sip of the champagne. Richard's hand removed the flute from Buck's, and put both on the nightstand. Their lips barely parted. As their passion grew hungrier, their mouths opened and their tongues began to explore. Their arms wrapped around each other's backs. Fingers hesitantly resisted moving farther down too quickly, and each sensation was captured with every touch. Slowly, fingertip edges found their way to the firm curving of the buttocks. Body pressed on body. Flesh slid against flesh with sweat coating their skin. Together they moved as a single beast, raw and primal.

❖

Buck let Richard sleep for about thirty minutes before removing his arm from around him and gently sliding out of bed. Trying not to make a sound, Buck gathered his clothes and crept into the bathroom to get dressed. He looked at his watch: 4:30.

He primped his hair in the bathroom, doing his best to rid himself of the telltale signs of bed-head. Turning off the light, he slowly opened the door and crept out. He was about to leave the bedroom when he heard something behind him.

"Sneaking out without as much as a kiss good-bye?" Richard said. "You boys are all alike."

Buck turned and saw Richard still curled in bed, facing him with his eyes open. "I didn't want to wake you."

"I'm awake now," Richard said playfully. He peeled off the covering blanket.

"But I need to go." Buck hesitantly took a step closer.

"Oh well," Richard said. "Sucks to be left out." His hands began to explore his body.

Buck leapt onto the bed, landing on Richard and pinning him down. "You," he said between kisses on his neck, "are a bad boy. When was the last time you were spanked?"

"About an hour and a half ago," Richard said. His breath was short and panting.

"I have to go," Buck pleaded. "But I'm going to be in Virginia really soon, most likely within the next week. Any chance of seeing you again?"

Richard grabbed him by the arms. He stared directly into Buck's eyes. "I can guarantee it."

Buck leaned down and deeply kissed Richard. He fought the growing desire to tear off the clothes he'd just put back on.

"You have my card," Richard called out as Buck again attempted to leave the room. "Prove to me you can read it." He rolled over, putting his back to Buck. Making a production of settling back into bed, he purposely exposed his butt before pulling the blankets around him. Raising a hand over his head, Richard waved his fingers at Buck and nestled back beneath the comforter.

Going through the hotel's front revolving door, Buck stepped onto the sidewalk. The flow of pedestrians had dwindled to a trickle, some stumbling over the cobblestones. He moved down the street heading back his own room at the Lafayette Suites, with his hands in his pockets and a light spring in his step. He noticed the light streaming between the crooked old buildings and reflecting off the tiled roofs. It was simply beautiful and it inspired him to start humming as he walked. It was a Sondheim song, and life was good.

Buck entered the Lafayette lobby and went directly to the elevators.

He slid the card key through the electronic lock, and the green light flashed. Entering the room's hallway, Buck noticed something wrong almost immediately. The apartment lights were on, but no one was moving. The room was too quiet. Buck reached into his jacket and pulled out his gun. Checking it carefully, he held it before him and slowly entered the main room.

"Noxia?" he called out hesitantly. A painful moan answered him.

Chapter Fifteen

Buck approached the back of the sofa hesitantly, his gun ready. As he got closer, he saw the figure on the coach was Noxia, and he bolted to her side.

"Are you all right?" Helping her to a sitting position was not easy, given her condition. She was still wearing her gown, but it was disheveled and wrinkled. Her hair was coming loose from its pins, with strands curling about her face. The side of her forehead was reddened and swollen.

"Where the hell have you been?" Noxia demanded. She pushed herself up to a sitting position. She took several deep breaths, trying to clear her head.

"I was out, obviously. I'm just getting in."

Noxia looked at the clock on the table. "I could have used your help," she said.

"Well, how was I supposed to know that?" he replied. "So what the hell happened to you?"

"I left the benefit early," she explained. "You were nowhere to be found, so I left. I started back here when these guys dressed like skeletons surrounded me."

"You, too?" Buck said astonished. "I think I met up with three of their friends later."

Noxia winced. "There were four of them when they found me. One stayed behind and followed me back here."

"But what happened?"

She winced again at the volume. "I came back here. There was a knock at the door. I opened it, and it was one of the skeletons. He clubbed me, and that's all I know."

"Why in the world would you open the door?"

"They said it was the front desk and they had a message for me. I really didn't stop to think about it, okay?"

"You're lucky, that's all," Buck said, standing and getting the ice bucket from the wet bar. "I'm getting ice for that lump on your head. Check yourself over, and we'll see if they took anything."

Buck filled the bucket from the machine at the end of the hall. He closed the door behind him. The door to Noxia's room was closed. Buck put the bucket by the wet bar before cautiously calling out, "Noxia?"

"Changing out of these clothes," she called from beyond the door. "I'm checking through my things—so far nothing's gone."

Buck went to his door and opened it. The bed was made. The closet doors were closed, but not all the way. Moving his gun back into position, he silently padded over to the sliding mirrored doors and reached out with his left foot. With his big toe, he gave the doors a strong push and they flew to one side.

No one was inside. He leaned in closer, looking up on the shelf and down on the floor, but nothing was there except his clothes and the courtesy ironing board. His shoes were still aligned on the upper rack. He spun around at the sound of a knock on the door.

"Nothing's missing from my room," Noxia said. "Except I can't find my phone. What about you?"

"Someone definitely went through my things," he answered. "All of my clothes are pushed to one side, and my shoes aren't in the same order."

"You have an order to your shoes?" Noxia asked.

"Mock all you want," he defended. "But that's how I know someone's gone through here."

"Did they take anything?"

Buck looked around the room. "My phone was with me. The only thing I'm not seeing that's possibly missing is...my laptop."

"I didn't bring mine. So, it's your computer and my cell phone."

Buck led her to the center room couch. She sat down as he loaded the small plastic liner with ice. Handing it to her, he sat down at the other end of the couch. "Tell me about your run-in with the undead," he asked, and she explained her encounter. "So they didn't attack you or anything like that?"

"No," she said. "They just surrounded me and tried to intimidate me. That's why I thought it was just a frat prank or something. They took off as soon as the congressman showed up."

"And how was your evening with the congressman?"

"He's highly conservative," she announced.

"Check."

"A philanderer."

"So the papers have announced."

"But damn, he's attractive and charming."

"Bingo," Buck said. "That's why he's in politics."

Noxia agreed with a smile. She readjusted the ice bag and placed it back on her head. "What about you? How did you shake the bones?"

Buck relayed his fight with the three skeletons.

"Why were you in that area anyway?" Noxia asked.

"Well," he said sheepishly, "I had a date."

"Another dependence on the kindness of strangers?" she asked, wincing as the ice touched her head.

"See," Buck said. "Why do you always make it sound so tawdry?"

"Because with you it usually is."

"Well, this time it wasn't," Buck replied. "This time it was an honest-to-goodness date, with Mr. Richard Pye, no less."

It took her only a minute to recognize the name. "Evangelista's caterer? What happened with the policy of not getting involved with anyone while on a case?"

"That's more of a suggestion than a rule, isn't it? Besides, I thought he might be able to help me do undercover work."

"I bet," Noxia said gruffly. Her stare was as icy as the bag in her hand. "Why I am not surprised?"

"Hey," Buck said. He bolted to a sitting position. "You can't blame me for this one. How was I supposed to know you were being attacked by a skeleton man?"

"So, while I was getting knocked out, you were having a piece of pie." Noxia stood up and dropped the ice bag in the sink of the wet bar. "Save it," she commanded when he tried to say something. "It's not your fault. Really. It never is."

Buck stood up to go to go to bed. As he moved around the back of the couch, he saw a manila envelope on the floor not far away from the suite's front door.

"What's this?"

"What's what?" Noxia asked.

Buck retrieved the envelope and sat back down on the couch. "This?" He waved it at her.

"It wasn't there when I let the skeleton guy in, so how the hell would I know?"

The envelope was sealed with a piece of tape and the small metal clasp on the envelope. Buck reached for a pen from the table and slid it along the edge, opening it carefully.

"It's the paperwork from Muffin I asked for," Buck muttered. "Oh, I got you. I got you now, you bitch! Not you!" He looked up at Noxia in brief panic and quickly reassured her. He smacked the papers against his palm and leapt up from his seat.

Noxia was left on the couch, confused and staring.

"Are you going to tell me, or what?" she called after him.

"Let's just say, it's about time we got a break in this case." His smile was both reassuring and unsettling.

"Where are you going now?" Her exhaustion showed.

"I have to go change our plane tickets," he said, walking out the door. "We're heading back to Virginia immediately!"

❖

The plane leveled out as it cut across the blue skies above the clouds. Noxia's drink remained on her tray untouched, engrossed as she was reading the contents of the envelope. Buck sat relaxed for the first time in several days, resting lightly in the aisle seat and reclining back as far as the first class accommodations would allow.

"I can't believe this," Noxia repeated. She gazed out the plane's window and then looked back over the paperwork.

"You've said that several times," Buck replied, basking in the knowledge that he'd impressed her.

"I can't believe she had a son and hid it for so long."

"She's a conservative Christian," Buck said nonchalantly. "It happens all the time."

"Yeah, but there's a difference here," Noxia continued. She leaned over and pulled out the mug shot picture from the envelope. "Most people didn't give birth to the Bomb-a-Bar-for-Jesus Guy." Noxia sat back in the plane seat. "I still can't believe you put this together."

"I'm not a complete moron, thank you. Besides, DNA doesn't lie," Buck said with a cocky air. "Once Lulu-Belle made her slip, it just all fell into place."

"What kind of mother turns her back on her own son?" Noxia said, bewildered. She glanced over the paperwork, rereading in disbelief.

"I'm guessing she felt shamed," Buck replied. "For Raven it must have been a huge sin to be unwed and pregnant. Today's views are a lot more liberal than when we were all younger."

"Maybe," Noxia sighed. "But to cut your own child off like that, just because they are gay?"

"Not everyone is made out to be a parent," Buck said. "It's usually those that shouldn't be that eventually are. Society requires a license for boats and cars, but not for parenting. Something's wrong there." He let out a breath and tried to settle into the seat.

"When did Lulu-Belle say they found each other?" Noxia asked, scanning the paperwork.

"About a year and a half ago."

"That would be after Dr. Shoulwater's death," Noxia said. "Any idea if the kid knew who his father was?"

"No clue on that one," Buck admitted.

"Wow." She replaced the papers in the envelope.

"Exactly," Buck said. "Raven told Lulu-Belle that they had a fight because of his homosexuality, and sent him back to New Orleans. After that she was finished with him."

"And he became the Bomb-a-Bar-for-Jesus Guy" Noxia said.

"And he became the Bomb-a-Bar-for-Jesus Guy," Buck concluded.

"I must say, I'm impressed."

"Thank you," Buck replied.

"Buck," Noxia coaxed from her window seat. "You should look out at this sky. It's so blue."

"No thanks," Buck responded without opening his eyes. "I'm good."

"It's a waste," Noxia continued before giving up. "Have you contacted Agent 69 about all this?"

"I already called Muffin. We're keeping William Haggen isolated without any media contact. The longer Raven goes without knowing we know about her son, the longer we keep the upper hand."

"Agreed. Do you think she knows he's the Bomb-a-Bar-for-Jesus Guy?"

"I don't know," Buck said. "But if she does or if she doesn't, it can't help her plans any."

"What are her plans?" Noxia asked.

"I don't know that, either."

"Okay." Noxia lifted her champagne and took a sip. "So what's next? You must have some sort of plan."

"I know that I'm going to go to a meeting of the Rescued Right."

Noxia smiled. Then she began to chuckle. "I get this fiendish delight at the thought of you repenting for your ways, even if it is pretend. Or are you allegedly trying to find the alliterative Heterosexual Highway?"

"Neither," Buck replied. "I'm going to politely ask questions, and that will be that."

"And you think they're going to answer you without any hesitation?"

"I can do it without raising any suspicions."

Noxia laughed. "Please! You're about as inconspicuous as Marilyn Monroe in a monastery."

"Very funny," Buck said. "Why wouldn't they answer a few basic questions? I mean, if they have nothing to hide?"

"And if they do have something to hide," Noxia pointed out. "Aren't you putting yourself into danger?"

"Give me some credit. Besides, it's not their group that I have any interest in whatsoever, it's just one of their members. I don't expect too many problems."

"Famous last words." Noxia smiled. "What am I doing while you're going to your meeting?"

Buck opened his eyes and leaned over. "You're going to get in touch with Muffin and have him set up a meeting of our own. With you, me, and Mr. William Haggen."

"You think you can get him to talk?"

Buck responded with a shrug. "Muffin can't keep him isolated forever. When the media finally gets to tear into him, I get the strangest feeling he's going to shut down altogether. If we're going to get any information out of him, it has to be before that happens."

"Muffin's report says Haggen doesn't say a word except in mixed Bible verses and fortune cookie sayings," Noxia said. "Why do you think he'll respond to you?"

"I have no idea if he will. But we'll have to try. There's something terribly wrong there, and not just homophobic craziness. There's something else. I can feel it, I just can't tell what it is."

"If I had my phone I could make a call and know much more in a matter of minutes," Noxia bemoaned. "But my trip to Quantico shouldn't take that long."

"Let it go," Buck said as he settled back into his seat. He folded his arms and closed his eyes.

Noxia watched him get comfortable before she made her invitation. "Why don't you join me for dinner, my treat. You did a great job, you deserve it."

Buck opened his eyes and smiled at her. "I'd love to," he answered smugly. "I could go for good steak and good wine."

Noxia waited until he once again settled down. "I was thinking of the Gossamer Club." She held her breath and waited for a response.

"Not my first choice," Buck replied, a little hesitant. "I'd rather go someplace else, but hey, if you're paying."

"Oh," Noxia said. "It's supposed to be a crystal-clear night, and I can get us into the exclusive penthouse restaurant." She noticed eye movement behind his closed lids. His left shoulder twitched. "The Sky Room is made of all glass, you know—and from that height there is an amazing view." She watched him chew on his bottom lip and couldn't help but notice his shifting in his seat.

"You know," Buck said, opening his eyes. He turned his head to look directly at her. "I'm really just not in that kind of mood. I think I'll pass. Appreciate the offer, though."

"Really," Noxia said sitting back in her seat. "I thought it would appeal to your inner show queen. With that building's height and view, on a clear day you really could see forever."

"I'm sure it's wonderful," Buck said settling back and closing his eyes. "I'll pass."

"That's okay," Noxia replied, lost in her own thoughts. "We can go someplace else."

CHAPTER SIXTEEN

B uck checked the address scribbled on the side of the folder he carried in his hands. He was in the right place: 501 was painted above the double glass doors. Posters for various nonprofit and political organizations hung in the window. Scanning the display, Buck checked the address once more. He was about to leave, but then he noticed the familiar red flag with the blue cross and lettered insignia of the Sisters of the Southern Cross tucked away in the bottom corner.

He opened the front doors and walked down a long hallway until he came to Suite 9. The Sisters insignia appeared by the upper right hinge. He knocked first before checking the knob, and opened the door, not bothering to wait for a reply.

The room was small, maybe twenty feet long and about ten feet deep. There was a desk with papers strewn about carelessly in the corner. It was the most organized object in the room. Tables overflowing with pamphlets, notes, booklets, and flyers were crammed along the edges, making the small space seem claustrophobic. A pathway had been cleared to allow movement in the tiny room.

A figure sitting at the desk looked up from his work. Seeing Buck, he spun around on his chair. His eyes were wide, and his smile was a bit overly friendly. The bare bulb hanging from the ceiling's center made his face appear washed out.

"May I help you?" the man said in a melodic tone. His blond hair was styled into a faux-hawk. His royal blue button-down shirt was neatly pressed, with just the hint of a bleached white T-shirt underneath. He wore the sleeves carefully rolled up to just below the elbow. The shirt was tightly tucked into snug-fitting, pressed khaki Dockers. His black loafers matched his belt perfectly.

"My name is Buck Miller and I called about finding a friend of mine?"

"Yes, Mr. Miller," the man said. He stood and held out his hand. "I'm Ken, we spoke on the phone." He set up a folding chair next to his desk. It took up most of the remaining free space. With a gesture of his hand, he invited Buck to take a seat. They awkwardly danced around each other until Buck finally was able to sit down.

"Please excuse the clutter," Ken explained. "This is just an office space, and we store a lot of our material here. Obviously, we have our meetings elsewhere." He offered an apologetic smile and sat down, crossing his legs. "Now." He slapped his lap for emphasis. "How may I help you? You're looking for someone?"

"Yes, I'm looking for a friend of mine." Buck put the folder on his lap and untied the binder. "His name is William Haggen, from New Orleans. He's disappeared."

Ken sat rigid, as if carved in stone. His eyes blinked. "Mr. Miller." He cleared his throat. "How well do you know Mr. Haggen?"

"I'd say about four years now," Buck improvised.

"Then you know that William had issues." Ken's voice was smooth and low. "We were trying to help him."

"And how would you do that?" Buck asked.

"I'm sorry." Ken sat forward. "How did you know William again?"

Buck sat against the folding chair's uncomfortable padding. He tapped his thumb against the folder on his lap, biting his bottom lip. "All right," he said. "I'll level with you. Billy was my...*friend*." He paused to let the meaning sink in. "When his mom died, he went through an emotional hell. He was so angry with everyone and seemed to be searching for some sort of answer. That's when he found out he was adopted and set off in search of his birth parents. The last I heard from him was here in Virginia. He wrote a letter mentioning he was getting help at the Rescued Right, so here I am."

Ken listened patiently. He nodded his head when Buck finished, and reached over, patting Buck's knee. His hand remained there for a few moments longer than necessary.

"William did come here, and he was searching for something," Ken stated with a slight smile. "He was looking for a cure to his illness."

Buck didn't try to hide his smile. "Oh." He chuckled. "I knew he was gay, that wasn't the issue."

"Maybe you did know, but that *was* the issue," Ken disagreed. "Billy came to us looking for help. He wanted to find the Lord and travel the path of righteousness. He just couldn't give up his homosexual lifestyle."

"You make it sound like a light switch," Buck said, trying to keep calm. "To be turned on and off at will."

"You may not believe that homosexuality is a choice," Ken explained. "But here we definitely know better. You can't argue, though, that pursuing and acting on those sinful desires definitely *is* a sin." His smile was friendly and obviously pasted on. "As we like to say here, 'You can pray away the gay.' I'm living proof."

"Excuse me?"

"I used to be gay," Ken said. He crossed his legs, in the opposite direction. "But I've seen the path of Jesus. I know his powers and light can heal. I've been with my wife for over two years and have never been happier."

"Congratulations," Buck said, his voice perfectly controlled. "The semantics of it all isn't what I'm here to discuss. What I'd like to know is how well did *you* know Billy Haggen?"

Ken looked at the floor and slowly sat back in his chair. He folded his hands and placed them in his lap. "About six months." His voice was calm and even. "Billy wanted to be cured, and he was close to fully accepting Jesus into his heart." He paused, reflecting a moment, and kissed his knuckle.

"What do you mean by 'close to' accepting?"

Ken sat forward, grinning a crooked smile. He patted Buck's knee again.

"Let me explain the stages we have here at the Rescued Right," he began patiently. Reaching into the desk drawer, he withdrew a pamphlet and handed it to Buck.

On the cover were two doves. The gender implications were obvious—the male dove had a mustache, while the female was wearing lipstick and had long eyelashes. Together they clutched a single olive branch in their beaks. Above the bird heads was a pair of ghostly hands spread palm outward surrounded by a golden halo, and robe-covered wrists that disappeared into a fluffy cloud. The words said in golden, iridescent lettering: *The Rescued Right: Finding the Path to Jesus.*

"Whenever we have new postulants interested in becoming full-fledged members," Ken explained, "there is a series of steps that they must take."

"Become members of what?" Buck asked.

"Full-fledged members of society. Practicing heterosexuality and celebrating God's plan."

Buck sucked in his bottom lip and bit it, carefully trying not to display anything negative in response. "And these steps would be?"

Ken leaned over and opened the pamphlet in Buck's hand. The three-fold brochure spread across his lap, and Ken's finger pointed directly into the printed center. The steps were outlined:

- Must be drug and alcohol free
- Must be wanting to be free of sin
- Must ask Jesus for forgiveness
- Cleanse away all previous connections
- Live free of sin for six months
- Rebirthing Ceremony

"How does someone live free of sin for six months?" Buck asked.

"After they've cleansed themselves from all past sinful connections, they must live in the light for six months before continuing to the next level." Ken smiled and patted Buck's knee. "Living in the light means without any backsliding."

"Why must they cleanse themselves from the past?"

"Mr. Miller," Ken said, "much like any other addiction, it is important to cut oneself off from previous friends who still keep those negative habits and rituals. One of the first steps of any recovery is locating the desired trigger. By removing the past, one can focus on what lies ahead of them."

"I see. And the rebirthing ceremony?"

"Most likely what you think it is." When he crossed his legs again, he readjusted the front of his pants. "We have a community baptism, where the person says his vows in front of our congregation and the Lord. We, in turn, vow to help them along their path and to be there if anyone struggles along the way."

"How many steps had Billy already ascended?" Buck asked.

"William never seemed to have any issues with drugs or alcohol, at least not that I ever noticed." Ken stood up abruptly. "Can I get you something?"

The room was so crowded, and they were seated so close together, that his crotch was almost in Buck's face.

"No, thank you," Buck said, trying to discreetly turn his head and avoid laughing aloud.

"I feel like I'm being rude if I don't offer you something. Would you like something sweet?" Ken paused. "I can get that for you, too."

Buck answered with a smirk. "I always make it a point to eat dessert afterward. It's always better if it's earned." Licking his lips, he took a deep breath and pushed backward with his feet. Buck crossed his legs, ankle over knee, and turned his attention back to the advertisement in his lap.

"So Billy wasn't using drugs. That's good to hear," Buck said. "Did he continue on to the next step?"

Ken slowly took his seat, leaned far back, and kept his legs apart. His elbows rested on the chair's armrest, but his hands lay on his thighs, fingers pointing inward.

"At first, William was very zealous. When I first met him, I thought he was the type to fully embrace the path because he needed to substitute one addiction for another. For him, though, that wasn't the case. Those types usually don't like our rules, and quickly find another substitute. Billy seemed dedicated to the Path of Jesus. Because he wanted to be. He willingly avoided all contact with people of his past. It was never a challenge for him."

"What do you mean?"

"Most people will hesitate turning their back on everything they've known, even when they've hit rock bottom. It's the hardest step for our postulants to make." Ken's voice was calm. His hands remained clenched together. "William never looked back." He studied Buck with a curious expression. "You must have been someone quite special for him to tell you as much as he did."

"I've not had complaints."

Ken smiled briefly. "One day, we had a new person sit in on our group. A big, oafish man, kind of intimidating. Not the sort of man that usually comes into our center, if you understand my meaning? You can see why I was a little leery, but after a few meetings he never caused trouble, and he seemed sincere."

"What do you mean by an oafish guy?" Buck asked.

"To be polite," Ken started, "you have to understand that most of the people that come here, to seek their redemption, are of a certain caliber. Their illness is more…recognizable from the start."

"You're saying the people that come here are flaming queens and diesel dykes."

"To be vulgar," Ken said tenaciously, "yes. But who they are when they come in is hardly the person they are when they finish."

"I have no doubt," Buck agreed. "Do you remember the guy's name?"

"We encourage anonymity here until one is ready to take the first step," Ken explained "They are given a new name once they are rebirthed."

"Did Billy use a different name?"

"He used William." Ken's answer was curt.

"Yeah. That was probably what delayed me tracing him down. This new guy wasn't a sissy?"

"No," Ken answered, flinching at the choice of words. "He was not. William was working in the office here and had just found his birth mother. He never said who she was or mentioned a name. All he said was that she was religious, and that made him more comfortable with his situation. When Lan first came in, as I said earlier, most people were hesitant to get near him. William was not. Not at all, and took him under his wing. But it had the opposite effect."

"Opposite effect?"

"Lan was a devil in sheep's clothing," Ken said. "William continued to embrace his Christian lifestyle, that wasn't the issue. Lan introduced him to the concept of being homosexual *and* Christian. He was taking him to churches that accept the gay lifestyle. There is no convergence; you cannot faithfully practice both."

"And you think this guy, Lan, was responsible for Billy's backslide?" Buck was intrigued as much as he was repulsed.

"I know that a few months after he began to come around, William became more vocal about how the two paths could coincide. He brought books into the meetings that presented ideas that are completely different from what we know to be the Path of Light."

"And you threw him out?" Buck asked.

"Not at all!" Ken was clearly offended. "We'd never do such a thing."

"I didn't mean—"

"We told him that Lucifer can tempt you from the one true path. He was free to follow any road he wanted. We suggested that he didn't present any further temptations to the people willing to walk alongside us. We were never rude about it, but reminded him that our group was governed by our rules, and by God's love."

"People were beginning to question you," Buck said. It was an assessment, not a question.

"Our group was becoming confused from this *outside* information."

"So what happened with Billy?" Curiosity was getting the better of him.

"William and Lan both slid backward," Ken said quickly. He shifted in his chair. "They developed too close a friendship, and despite warnings, they broke the rules."

Buck was incredulous. "They became boyfriends?"

"Yes." Ken's face looked like he'd smelled something detestable. "Then I guess William disappeared. Lan came here looking for him and created a big scene. He was convinced we were holding William against his will and started yelling and tearing up the place. I was here with another member, my friend Janice." Ken pointed to a picture on the desktop. A lumberjack of a woman dressed in denim overalls with a cast on her arm winked out from the frame. She held a thumb up on her good hand. "When I threatened to call the police, he left, and we haven't seen him since, thank Jesus!"

"Any idea where Mr. Haggen could be now?" Buck asked cautiously.

"Anybody's guess," Ken said softly, shaking his head. "I haven't seen him in a while. I only hope that the Lord guides him, wherever he goes."

"Thank you for your time," Buck said. He folded up the brochure from his lap. On the back, in the bottom right hand corner was the address of the Robert E. Lee Hotel. The familiar insignia was next to it.

"You know, Mr. Miller," Ken leaned in and returned his hand to Buck's knee. "We can help you in more ways than you could imagine. It's never too late to find the path to Jesus."

"Thank you for the offer, but I'm good."

"If you open your heart to Jesus, he can fill it with love of the Spirit."

"My heart's reserved for someone else." Buck flashed a smile. He opened the folder, shifting papers, and carefully placed the brochure inside. He stood up to leave. "You wouldn't have a picture of Lan by chance, would you?"

Ken ran his hand through his carefully crafted hair and bit his bottom lip. "Not one of him by himself, no." Ken thought another moment. "Wait, I may have one with him in a group."

Ken stood up and turned his back to Buck. He riffled around the desktop, pushing outward with his butt. He pulled open a drawer and bent over it, searching through until he found what he was looking for. Spinning around, he handed the picture to Buck.

Three people were in the forefront of the picture, while two remained in the background. Two men and a woman were up front with their arms linked over their shoulders, laughing and posing for the picture. Buck recognized the person in the middle was Janice, with Ken and Billy on either side.

Buck searched the photo, trying to find its relevance. The woman in the background on the right side was laughing, half-hidden behind an open sun umbrella planted on the ground. Buck's eyes were drawn to the face of a man on the left side background. Although the body was turned profile, the sheer size made him noticeable. The man's stern face was barely smiling; an awkward grin could be seen if the pixels were examined. The deeply set eyes looked directly to the camera and towered over the three people posing in the center.

"Thanks," Buck replied with a smile, his mind snapping another piece of the puzzle into place. He was looking into a sober and masculine version of the drag queen he'd met in Brussels.

Billy's Lan was Karl Langlier.

CHAPTER SEVENTEEN

L eave it to you," Noxia said with a big smile. "Only you could find a connection between an ex-gay Bomb-a-Bar-for-Jesus Guy in the United States and a murderous Ann-Margret knock-off drag queen in Brussels. I have to admit, that takes talent."

Buck shivered and shook off the visual memory. "Now, that's high praise indeed." He crossed the sterile waiting room to get water from the cooler. Smacking his lips afterward, he crumpled the cup and tossed it over his shoulder into the can.

"Before you get too big for those britches," Noxia said, sitting in one of the offered metallic folding chairs, "let's just figure out where the connection is."

"That would be the million-dollar prize." Buck returned to her side, sitting down in the other uncomfortable chair. "Let's see what we got. On one hand we have Karl Langlier, an established hired hit man with a long history of disturbed behavior."

"Check," Noxia responded. She drew the mark in the air.

Buck gave her a stern look before continuing. "Langlier gets hired by Raven to kill her husband and steal his notes, which he allegedly does. Then he goes to the Rescued Right and meets William."

"Check," Noxia echoed, repeating the gesture.

"Really, stop doing that." His direct glare was emphasized with a firm hand on her knee. "The two get involved with one another, so Karl must have been realizing his own latent tendencies."

"Do you think Raven knew?"

"About him being gay or him going to the meetings? The meetings are in her hotel, but that doesn't mean she knew he was gay." Buck gave up with a shrug. "Maybe she did, maybe she didn't. She knew eventually, she had to." Noxia nodded. "Something happens between them, William becomes the Bomb-a-Bar-for-Jesus Guy, and Karl leaves the country adopting the name Lan Glikërlar. He spies me one night in Brussels and tries to either kill me or detain me for the killer statue to do the job."

"Something's not right there," Noxia said. "Why would Langlier want to kill you or detain you?"

"I got it! What if the statue was really William Haggen?" Buck's eyes were wide with discovery. "Both of them were hired by Raven, at different times, and sent to kill me. They see each other, but after so long it only stirs up feelings for them and ends up in a lover's quarrel, with me in the cross fire—literally!"

Noxia stared at him incredulously. "You really are a drama queen, aren't you? Nice try, but there are a few loopholes with your theory. I could believe that the statue was William, but his physical features differ greatly from the statue's build. And he was here in the States blowing up places. Plus, both of them, and subsequently Raven, would have to have known you were going to be in Brussels. But," she cocked her head pensively, "what if you're right, with all the Langlier stuff, up to the point where he originally meets William? They start whatever together, but William's disappearance isn't due to Karl or Lan or whatever he's calling himself at that time; it's due to Raven? William and Raven have a fight. Didn't Ken say that Lan accused the Rescued Right of hiding William?"

"I see it now." Buck rambled on as if his train of thought hadn't stopped. "Billy comes to find Mommy. Mommy isn't happy Billy is a sissy. He goes to the Rescued Right. It doesn't take. She sends Lan over to keep an eye on Billy, which he does. An eye, an ear, and eventually his lips and tongue. Mommy *really* isn't happy. And then the Raven clips the starling's wings."

"Yeah," Noxia agreed. "But as I said, Haggen couldn't have

been in Brussels to kill you. He was in Virginia blowing up bars and restaurants. A bombing occurred while you were starting your vacation. Then the one after you got back. His pattern has been to plant a bomb the night before the new moon. That's every four weeks or so. He couldn't have been the statue."

"Since we know his patterns," Buck continued, "now all we need is his reasoning. What was it that happened between Raven and William that sent him down the bomber path? And why someone was trying to kill me in Brussels."

"Something tells me you weren't the target there," Noxia said. "The more I think about it, the more I believe you did just happen to be there at the wrong time."

"How do you explain the statue if it wasn't trying to kill me?"

"I can't," Noxia agreed. "Believe me, Buck, while I understand people's desire to kill you, I just don't think that was the case. This time. Langlier must have made several enemies over the years. Maybe it was a hit on him? Or can't your ego handle that?"

Buck stuck out his tongue. There was a rapping at the door. A uniformed man with a funereal face motioned for them to come along.

"You ready to go meet the Bomb-a-Bar-for-Jesus Guy?" Noxia asked.

"You really do like saying that, don't you?"

She grinned hopelessly. "I have to admit it, I really do."

The security guard was waiting. A name badge with a picture boasted the title of Officer R. Martin and hung from over his left chest, pinned to the uniform.

"If you'll follow me, please." His tone was gruff, his shoulders broad and stout, arms moving at his side. He didn't wait for them to answer, continuing to instruct as he walked down the long hallway. "You will be allowed a half hour with the prisoner. He doesn't seem to say much, except in verse and proverbs. You will be seated across a table from him. The bulletproof glass will keep you protected and will allow you to talk to the prisoner. You will be under strict supervision, but the three of you will be the only ones in the room.

Guards will be just outside the door if you need anything. Do not provoke the prisoner. He will be in chains…"

Noxia threw Buck a sideways glance but said nothing.

"You are not allowed to bring anything into the room. You are not allowed to take anything out. You will be searched upon both entry and exit. No recording devices. No cameras. No film. Are there any questions?" The officer stopped abruptly and spun around.

"What is he like?" Noxia asked.

Officer Martin stopped a moment to think. "He's pretty docile. He doesn't struggle much or resist. We keep him shackled because we don't know what he's capable of doing."

"Reassuring," Buck muttered.

Officer Martin put a key in the lock. A loud clanking sound was heard, along with small motors running. He pressed a series of numbers on a keypad and more bolts could be heard separating and opening inside the door. A loud buzzing sound echoed and the red light above the door blinked three times in succession.

Buck and Noxia walked into the plain, sterile environment. A folding table was bolted to the floor in the center of the room and three chairs were around it, two on one side and one opposite. A thick sheet of bulletproof glass separated the room, dividing the table in half. A door with a small window was on the far side, similar to the one they'd entered through. A mirror ran along the wall behind them—most likely a one-way mirror allowing people in the next room to observe. A plastic pitcher of water and a stack of paper cups were left on their side of the table.

No sooner had the door closed and locked behind them in the interrogation room than a red light on the opposite wall began to blink. Two uniformed officers appeared in the door's tiny window. More buzzing sounded. The door opened inward.

A heavily armed officer entered, leading the prisoner, followed by another guard. His legs were shackled at the ankle, as were his hands at the wrist, with a limited range of motion. A longer chain connected his wrist cuffs to the heavy metallic belt he wore around the waist of his electric orange jumper, allowing his arms to hang brutishly in front of him, but only extend six inches outward. Each step was echoed by a loud clanking sound while the light jingling of the links rippled after. He was escorted to the table, where he was chained to the table hook.

"We'll be on the other side of that door," an officer said. "We'll be watching. To make sure everything is all right."

Buck nodded thanks as the two officers took their leave. They rang a buzzer from the inside before another guard came to the door, glanced in, and let them out. When the door shut behind them, it made the room seem infinitely smaller.

William Haggen was in his early twenties but looked twice his age, very different from the picture Buck possessed. The rounded face looked deflated and his cheeks were hollow and hung heavily under his eyes. Dark pupils looked out from the recessed sockets they retreated to, and the eyes were glazed over, allowing him sight into something no one else could see. Originally full of waves and once worn brushed back to reveal a high forehead, what remained of his hair appeared randomly and was shorn prison-short, creating a patchwork of stubbly shadow across his scalp. At his temples were black scabs the size of nickels. He glanced quickly over the two visitors, focusing his eyes on the wall behind and seeing something else far beyond.

"Mr. Haggen," Noxia started. "We'd like to ask you a few questions, if you don't mind."

Slowly, he turned his head. The eyes focused for a brief moment before glazing over once more. He returned his head to the neutral position. After a few moments of silence, Noxia looked at Buck and shrugged.

"Billy," Buck started. "You're originally from New Orleans, aren't you?" There was no answer. "Beautiful city. I was just there for the first time and really enjoyed myself. Ate at some great restaurants. Good times."

A flicker of recognition flashed in his eyes.

"I'd like to talk about why you decided to move from New Orleans to Virginia."

William turned to Buck with the same robotic movement of his neck, keeping his body perfectly still. His eyes scanned over Buck before matching and holding his stare with an unspoken challenge. He shortly went back to staring at the wall. Silence.

"I am but a stranger in a strange land," a voice mumbled. It was low and haunting, with a grating sound.

Buck and Noxia exchanged encouraging glances.

"When did you come to Virginia?" Noxia asked.

William kept his stoic expression. His eyes remained locked between the two of them, fixated on the wall. He said nothing. Under the table Buck tapped Noxia. He gestured with his hand for her to let him try.

"Billy," Buck said. His tone was gentle and paternal. "We know your mother just died, and I'm very sorry."

"And the Fifth Commandment shall be, Honor thy mother and father." He remained perfectly still. His voice added a chill to the room.

"It's never easy to lose a parent," Buck said. "I've been there. I know."

"Honor your father and your mother," he echoed, "so that you may live long in the land of the Lord."

"You found out that you were adopted, didn't you?" Noxia said.

William stared straight ahead, saying nothing.

"Noxia," Buck whispered. "Let me do the talking. He's responding to me, and that's something at least." Sitting up, he focused his attention. "I'd like to ask you about Raven. Raven Evangelista?" There was silence. "Do you know her?"

"Beware of the false prophet that comes in sheep's clothing," he mumbled. "For underneath, they are surely *raven*-ous wolves."

They took notice of the pronunciation.

"Raven was your birth mother, wasn't she?"

"Black of wing and black of heart."

"She wouldn't talk to you, would she?" Buck asked.

A long silence remained. "And among the birds, unclean and detestable to you, every raven of any kind."

"Look, Buck," Noxia whispered. "His quotes are really pretty and all, but this isn't getting us anywhere."

"I disagree." He shook his head and continued. "Billy, do you know a man named Lan?" There was a slight flicker and Billy blinked several times. "He's been looking for you."

Billy's face pulled inward. "And the soul of David was knitted to that of Jonathan, and he loved him as himself."

"Did you love Lan?"

"And Christ said, 'There is nothing from without a man, that entering into him can defile.'"

"Now, that's blunt," Noxia muttered.

Buck motioned for her to follow him. They stood up from the table and retreated to the doorway. William never moved a muscle.

"Look," he said. "He seems to be responding to me a little more, so let me do the talking."

"Go for it," she agreed. "What do you have in mind? He's speaking in badly translated Bible quotes and fortune cookie sayings. What exactly do you think he's going to be able to tell us?"

"I'll fill you in later, but I assure you I have a plan."

She shook her head. "No arguments here." They returned to the table.

"Billy," Buck began. "Did you like Raven?"

"Curse the raven, her ill-betiding croak. It bodes me no good."

"And you felt this way even though she was your birth mother?"

William's head turned, looking directly at him. The eyes glistened in their darkness. His lips curled back into a sneer. Even with his jaw clenched shut, with his lips pulled back, blackened gaps appeared between yellowed teeth. His voice hissed. "A crow may see their chick for its true self. To the raven, her own is always white."

"She wasn't happy with who you are. She wanted you to be something you're not."

William's face calmed down, the tension melting off his concave skin. "And first above all, to thine own self be true. Then thou canst not be false to anyone."

"That's not the Bible," Noxia said. "That's Shakespeare."

"Thank you for stating the obvious," Buck muttered.

William began to softly sing "Jesus Loves Me."

An officer rapped sharply on the tiny window in the door. He glared through the glass and tapped his watch. He held up his hand, palm extended and fingers stretched out to indicate the time remaining. Buck nodded.

"Look," Buck said in a whisper. "I'm going to try a long shot here. I just want you to go with it. Billy," Buck said aloud through the window. He waited a few moments before continuing. "Does the Jesus Injection mean anything to you?"

Noxia shot Buck a curious look. William Haggen slowly turned until he met his eyes. His breathing steadily grew heavier and louder. The blackened eye sockets widened.

"I looked and behold!" His voice was scratchy, slowly raising an octave, taking on an eerie quality. "A whirlwind came out of the blackness. A great cloud, a fire burning, a great brightness about." His face pulled inward and he lowered his head. The shackled hands slowly rose, rattling their chains. "For it is fire that consumes to destruction." His voice grew louder as his hands became fists. He beat them against his legs. "It would wipe out everything I am!"

William Haggen started to rock back and forth in the folding chair. He let out a low, animalistic moan. The cry grew louder until the sound became deafening, ringing off the walls.

Buck and Noxia looked on astounded and stunned. They slid their chairs back, easing away from the table. Officers peered in at the shouting, fumbling with the keys to gain entry. The red light flashed.

"There shall be wailing and gnashing of the teeth. And cast into a furnace of flames!" Billy was shrieking and rocking in the chair, testing the chains that bound him. His fists clutched and unclutched, slapping his legs. Blood spots blossomed through his orange jumper. "Jesus loves me! *Kyrie Eleison!*"

The shrieking became a wailing lament. Three officers ran over to William. Two started unchaining him from the chair.

"Time's up!" Officer Martin snapped at them. They spun around to find him standing behind them. "It's time for you folks to be leaving."

Chapter Eighteen

Noxia made it to the parking lot before she realized Buck wasn't behind her. She turned and searched the building's exit before she saw him approaching, chatting on his phone.

"Sounds good," he said. He chuckled, speaking intimately. "I'll see you tonight at seven thirty. Thanks. Bye."

"What are we doing tonight at seven thirty?"

"We're not," Buck answered. "I am. Just confirming dinner plans."

"In Virginia?" Noxia feigned surprise. "Whoever with?"

"Give the congressman a call," he bantered back. "We can double."

"Something tells me that's not gonna happen." She sighed heavily. "Either way, he's not in town, and I plan on working. Have a good time, just…"

"Don't let it get in the way of the mission," Buck finished. "Yeah, you've been quite succinct with that request. Have you noticed that it *hasn't* gotten in the way? Nor have I given you any grief about Dexter Julian?"

"It's not the same thing," Noxia said. "We're not exactly dating, and I know how to be discreet with my indiscretions. You usually lack in that field. But you're right; it hasn't gotten in the way, so I have no reason to complain."

"Thank you," Buck sternly replied.

"Sorry," Noxia apologized quickly. "And when you're right, you're right. You did a great job in there."

"Yes," he replied with a cocky grin. "Yes, I did." Buck clicked the remote and the car doors chirped open. He slid behind the driver's wheel, and they soon backed out of the parking spot and left through the security gate. Guards opened each of the three gates on their way out.

"What was it that you were saying that got him so upset?" Noxia asked as they drove down the long private driveway of the prison.

"The Jesus Injection? Don't you remember? That was that icon I clicked on that shut down my hard drive. When I downloaded the information from the hotel?"

"Oh yeah," Noxia recalled. "What made you think of that now?"

"It was when he started singing 'Jesus Loves Me,'" Buck answered. "When he started going off again, I thought: 'If he doesn't stop, I'm going to need a shot of morphine to get through this.' Then I remembered the file. It was just such an odd name, the Jesus Injection. I went fishing for information and we caught a big one."

"But what did we catch?" Noxia asked. "We only know that he got extremely upset when you mentioned it. To play devil's advocate, he could have been reacting to anything in that twisted mind of his."

"That's true," Buck conceded. "But I think he was reacting to what I said."

"Hmm," she said pensively. "I think you're right. The medical tests say that he understands what's being said around him. And according to previous records, he has a good IQ." Noxia summarized. "But something scrambled his mind. Brain wave tests were all over the place. One even showed a counter-current."

Buck asked the obvious question. "What's a brain wave counter-current?"

She closed the file on her lap. "It's a particularly strong current that seems to be going against the natural way his brain waves tend to allow him to think. It works almost in reverse, causing so much resistance that eventually, the brain waves conform to the new strand."

"It sounds like a virus."

"Maybe. Sort of a man-made brain-wave virus, if that doesn't sound too science fiction."

"Do you think it's that counter-current that causes him to behave the way he did? All that destruction, somehow trying to destroy something within himself?"

"Could be," she said as they drove on. "I don't know. There are still too many tests that need to be done. His mind works, but not the way it's supposed to work."

"Like when there's a virus in the computer hardware?"

"Yeah, actually," Noxia said, nodding. "It's mixing his mental files up to where they're coming out in gibberish. There was a lot he said in there, it just needs sorting through."

"It's easier for some to sort through than others," Buck teased. "I don't mean that cruelly, it's just that you're not gay."

"What the hell does that have to do with anything?" Noxia shifted in her buckled car seat as best she could.

"It's just that being a heterosexual, your brain works in a different way than someone who is gay."

"Oh my God," Noxia said with a laugh. "You're heterophobic!"

"Hardly," Buck argued. "Remember when I said that membership has its advantages? Well, this kind of insight to another gay mind is one of them."

"Buck," she replied. "I'm as gay-friendly as they come. Although I've had a relationship with a woman I wouldn't call myself bisexual, but you can't tell me that gay people have some privileged insight because of the gender of who they sleep with."

"Noxia," he explained. "When you hear Cole Porter's song 'You're the Top,' you hear a witty and clever patter song."

"Yeah. So?"

"I hear a complete listing of gay innuendo and *double* double entendres."

"I think you're begging on that one," Noxia said with a laugh.

"I've told you before, membership has its advantages."

"Advantages maybe," she agreed. "But special insights? I don't *think* so!" Noxia wagged her finger dramatically between them. She sat back in the car seat, giggling at the conversation. "What's wrong? You're sitting there like someone walked on your grave."

"Nothing," he said too quickly. He shook it off and got back to the subject at hand. "Be that as it may, Billy still responded to me."

"Did you notice the markings at his temples?" Noxia asked, eager to avoid another discussion. "Those are burn marks. He came into the prison with them."

"Which I think ties into what he was saying."

"He was saying Bible quotes."

"What Bible quotes were they?" Buck waited for the answer and got silence. "All of the references to Jonathan and David in the Bible? He was telling us his own love story."

"Buck," Noxia said. "People have argued that interpretation for centuries. How can you be so sure?" He shot her a look. "Okay. Let's assume you're right. What have you gained from this, mighty Joseph with your amazing Technicolor insight?"

"Whatever the reasons that brought Lan to the Rescued Right, it all changed when he met Billy," Buck explained. "They got involved. Just like we thought. And I agree with your theory. I'm positive that Raven was somehow the cause for Billy to go off the deep end."

"What was the damning evidence?"

"Billy's reaction to the mention of the Jesus Injection."

"But what is it?"

"I don't know," Buck replied. "But you can't help but notice the strong reaction we just got."

"The howling was quite disturbing."

"He barely said a word before any of that," Buck pointed out. "But once I mentioned the Jesus Injection, his response was textbook—literally. It was right out of the Book of Ezekiel. Ezekiel is all about a great happening in the sky, a vehicle of fire and windstorm, with lightning flashing. Some have interpreted it as biblical proof of UFOs. Remember that book *Chariot of the Gods?*"

"I know of the title," Noxia replied. "But I do believe it was before my time. Besides, I know you're not saying William was abducted and brainwashed by an UFO. So what are you talking about?"

"I don't know, Noxia," Buck confessed. "There's something there. Something that Raven did that caused fires in the sky and lightning to flash. Something that took a normal gay man, scrambled his brains and transformed him into another completely different and confused individual."

"The Bomb-a-Bar-for—"

"Enough already!" They drove a few moments without either one of them speaking.

"How do you know so much about the Bible anyway?" she finally asked. "All that can't be from *Jesus Christ Superstar* or *Godspell*, and you don't exactly strike me as being overtly zealous."

"I'm very spiritual, Noxia," Buck defended. "I just prefer to keep my path private. Besides, when people use the Bible as a weapon against you, there's little choice but to learn it well enough to fight back."

"Amen to that," Noxia agreed. She exhaled heavily and stretched her arms out with a yawn. She held out her hand, wiggling her fingers. "Let me have your phone."

"Why?"

"Because my original one was stolen," she said with a patronizing tone. "Because I haven't gotten another one issued to me yet. Because I'm going to have to make a few calls tonight and the hotel line isn't secure. And most importantly," she shifted so her entire body was facing him, "do you really want to be disturbed tonight? I mean, any more than you already are?"

"Good point." He reached over and grabbed the phone from the car's cup holder. He handed it over.

"I'm just looking out for your happiness." She immediately started going through the phone book. With a chuckle, she pressed the Call key and held the phone to her ear. "You actually have him under Muffin?"

"That's his name."

She shook her head. "Oh my God." She tried to stifle her laugh. She reached out, lightly clutching Buck's arm. "I actually got his voice mail."

"What can it say?" Buck asked with gleeful curiosity. "He's always yelling at me to be secretive."

"Oh. It's just the automated confirmation of the phone number. And of course," she hung up the phone, "no voice-mailbox has been set up."

"What did you expect?" Buck asked. "I could have told you he wasn't in the office. Muffin's latest experiment went wrong, and now some repairs are being done."

"When?" Noxia asked. Doubt wrinkled the tops of her brow.

"You mean I actually know something that Noxia von Tüssël doesn't?" He feigned great shock. "Didn't you get the call?"

"With what phone?" she snarled.

"Point made."

After several moments of silence, she reached over and turned on the radio. With little adjustment, the music of the eighties poured forth from the speakers.

"I have my iPod, if you'd rather?" Buck offered.

"No, thanks," Noxia said. She settled into the corner against the car door. "I've had my fill of Broadway show tunes for the moment, thank you." Neither one spoke over the music of Duran Duran and Tina Turner as they drove back to the hotel.

❖

Noxia took over the main room of the hotel suite as Buck showered. Her laptop was open and had just finished booting up when she heard the shower's water turn off. She sat comfortably, in a pair of jeans and a sweatshirt, viewing her notes. Sipping on a glass of rich burgundy, she slipped into her work, becoming lost within the flow charts.

Buck puttered behind her back. His soft singing kept him as occupied as her computer notes.

"Muffin called," Noxia said without looking up. "Office is repaired, but it's going to stay closed until next week sometime. He was unspecific."

Buck coughed to get her attention. "Well, how do I look?" He stood before her, arms raised and outstretched. It took an effort to pull her focus away from the computer screen.

Black Prada loafers, black Armani slacks, dark socks. A forest green D&G T-shirt brought out his hazel eyes. The subtlety of the V-neck cut directed attention to his chest. His brown hair was carefully brushed up, from either side of his head, and smoothly met in the middle.

Noxia made the sign of the cross at him and turned back to her notes. "Go forth into sin, my son. Go with my blessings." Her brow became heavily lined as she studied the screen. She was missing something right in front of her. She began again, starting at the top and reading all her jottings about Dr. Raven Evangelista. Noxia's mind refused to focus and kept returning to the burn marks on either side of William's head. All those comments of fire and lightning—the answers were there, if she only looked carefully.

"A shame you're not going out with the congressman," Buck said.

Noxia didn't bother to look up. She raised her arm and waved good-bye. Then she turned her hand over and flashed her middle finger at him.

"Very nice. And a good night to you, too."

Noxia heard the door open and close. She picked up the phone and ordered the almond chicken salad off the room service menu. After a few moments, she sighed heavily, enjoying finally being alone. At least Buck was out of her hair and she could concentrate on some factors that continued to bother her. *If only he invested as much time on work as he invested in his—*

Investments. Noxia bolted to the edge of the sofa. A few strokes and all her notes were hidden, clearing the computer screen. She pulled up a new browser and typed in the web address for Riding the Wave.

"Investments." She whispered the sacred mantra. She read over the pages, picking at every written word. "Brain waves. That's it." She looked up at the wall, staring at a framed scenic photo, not seeing a bit of it. "She's harvesting the technology from Riding the Wave for something else. That's why she's so heavily invested in the company."

With a few deft strokes of the keyboard, the notes on Dr. Raven Evangelista appeared in full. She devoured the pages with fresh ferocity for finding what was hidden there. Noxia pulled up her notes on Dr. Shoulwater and placed the facts side by side with those of his former wife.

"She's using his notes to create something new," Noxia thought aloud. "Some cure, but not for AIDS." Images of the burn marks filtered through her mind. They floated like darkened circular wraiths.

Noxia opened a fresh page in her browser. She searched an unending list for photos of medical burn marks at the temples. The number of pages seemed infinite. Her fingers danced over the keys, becoming more specific with her search engines. A new display of photos opened. As she glanced over them, her eyes fell onto one particular photograph toward the bottom right of the screen. She clicked on it and the picture tripled in size.

The burn marks looked the same as the ones on the sides of William Haggen's head. Tiny circular marks just about the temples. Feeling her heart picking up speed, Noxia scrolled down to see if the medical procedure was listed. Centered under the photo in clear black print, it said: "The scorching left can be a factor in ECT treatments. Usually temporary…"

"ECT." Noxia rolled it through her mind. "Electroconvulsive therapy? Why would Raven want to use that?"

She scanned over several articles until she found a potential answer. It was listed in a paragraph on the possible side effects about ECT.

> …*with effects including memory loss, both retrograde and anterograde. Some of it may be recovered, as this is usually short-lived, but prolonged usage can further damage the memory until huge sections are erased. Patients may be susceptible to suggestions and…*

She sat back on the sofa, her thoughts racing. In her mind she tried to piece the possibilities together. They floated before her, meshing and changing their order like a giant jigsaw puzzle with no flat edges to form a frame. The hardest part was finding the first two pieces to fit—once they did, the others began to snap into place.

"She's trying to find a cure for"—Noxia forced her mind to think through the absurdity—"for being *gay*?" The thought made her laugh out loud, but it soon quickly died. "Brain waves. Lightning flashing," she muttered. "ECT burns. She can't be that insane?"

The more Noxia thought about it, the more sense it made. Raven's status as her political agenda grew. Her interest in Riding the Wave and hosting the Rescued Right; more connections thundered into place. The picture was growing more horrific, and as absurdly science fiction as it sounded, one thing rang clear.

It is plausible.

"That's where she gets her guinea pigs from, the Rescued Right," Noxia deduced. She felt a chill running up her arm. "Those poor, desperate people trying to change who they are. They didn't know how much they had to lose. I'm betting there have been other disappearances from different chapters."

A sharp knocking from the door interrupted her.

"That's one crazy woman." Noxia said, shaking her head. She stood up, closing the computer, feeling distracted, exhilarated, and frightened by the theories racing through her mind. She crossed to the doorway, her new discoveries creating a greater hunger.

"Just in time. I am one hungry lady!" She threw open the door. "Shit!" was all she managed before the figure dressed in a skeleton's costume pushed her back into the room and clamped the chloroform-soaked cloth against her mouth.

Noxia went limp instantly.

CHAPTER NINETEEN

B uck rang the doorbell to the brick town house and waited. He held the flowers behind his back, rocking in place and humming "Everything's Coming Up Roses." Glancing at his watch, he noted he was precisely on time. He studied the door, waiting for it to open. After a few more moments, he pressed the bell again, cocking his head and listening. The chimes echoed, muted through the heavy wood, and he withdrew the paper from his pocket to confirm the address.

Pressing the doorbell a third time, the wheels in his mind started turning. True to his nature his thoughts jumped to the furthest extreme, and visions of Richard being held as Evangelista's captive flashed through Buck's mind. Hesitantly, he reached into his leather jacket and was curling his fingers around the gun when another thought occurred.

"Maybe I am a drama queen like Noxia says." Buck smiled at the thought and withdrew his hand to ring the bell.

The door suddenly opened and Richard jumped, letting out a startled yelp. His hand clutched his chest through the button-down lavender shirt. "You scared me," he said, laughing off the awkward moment. A look of shock crossed his face and his eyes grew wide, as if he'd seen a ghost. Pulling on a welcoming smile, Richard stepped aside with a hand sweep, welcoming Buck into his home.

"You?" Buck answered as the door shut behind him. The sound

echoed off the small foyer. "I was beginning to think I had the wrong address, or the wrong night." He followed Richard up the stairs to the main landing, admiring the view as they went.

"Yeah," Richard muttered. "I mean no, you have the right address and night. Evidently."

"These are for you," Buck said, handing him the spring bouquet. "Are you all right?"

Richard glanced away before answering. "Yeah," he answered, shaking off whatever rode his shoulders. "I'm just having an Alzheimer's day and am totally running behind schedule." He gestured to his own appearance. "I just got out of the shower and barely had time to get dressed."

"My bad luck that you had the extra time, then," Buck said. Stepping closer, he casually wrapped an arm about Richard's waist, pulling him in. They kissed. Their lips touched softly and then pressed together before slightly opening, their shallow breathing growing deeper. Richard pulled away.

"Let me give you the grand tour," he said quickly. "Dining room and kitchen," he said, gesturing to the formally dressed table next to them, and the room beyond. Taking Buck's hand, Richard brought them into the main area. "This is the living room, bathroom, and the stairs go up to the master bedroom."

"Don't I get to see that?" Buck asked with a salacious raise of his eyebrow.

"Maybe if you're a good boy," Richard replied.

"I'm always a good boy."

"You can be pretty bad," Richard said slapping the seat of Buck's pants. "If memory serves correctly."

"It does," Buck automatically responded, and shook his head. "Sorry, it's something Noxia and I do, it's a bad habit."

"No, no," Richard said. They sat down on a blue overstuffed sofa, their backs to the kitchen. "I'd like to know more about your bad habits."

"That could be arranged." He leaned in for another kiss.

Richard pulled away. "I forgot I have champagne. I'll be right back." He bolted up, going to the kitchen.

"Do you need help?" Buck called out as Richard disappeared around the corner.

"Nope. I got it." The sound of a champagne cork popping emphasized his point.

Buck looked around at the fireplace across the room from him. Pictures lined the mantel in assorted frames, presumably family and friends. He stood up to look them over, noting how much warmth pictures could add to a room's atmosphere.

"Would you like a glass of champagne?" Richard offered. He came back carrying an ice bucket with an open bottle nestled within. Between the fingers on his other hand, he carried two flutes by the stems. He placed them on the table. "I'll be right back." Richard returned to the kitchen.

Buck filled the two glasses and waited for Richard to return. Gazing around, he noticed a small photo album among several assorted books and magazines lying on the shelf below the glass tabletop. He retrieved the book and started thumbing through the pages.

Photographs of dinner parties and events filled the first part of the book. Close-up pictures of food platters were beautifully captured. Cakes and pies had been cut to display the inner layers, and steam rose off bowls of soups.

"Hey," Buck called out over his shoulder. "These pictures are fantastic! Are they of jobs you've done?"

"You don't need to go through that," Richard said. He carried a glass platter covered with raspberries and strawberry slices. Putting them on the table, he sat down next to Buck. Their knees touched. "Fruit with chocolate-infused balsamic vinegar drizzled over."

"That sounds delicious," Buck said, glancing up. "There are some great photos in here. Are you blushing?" He closed the album, putting it aside and playfully knocking knees with Richard.

"No, I'm not blushing."

"You are just too cute," Buck said. His hand crept out, lazily tracing the side of Richard's leg. As his fingers drew higher, Richard's thigh flinched. "Are you ticklish?"

"Stop it," Richard protested. "You'll make me spill the champagne." He reached out and quickly grabbed the glasses. He leaned forward and handed one to Buck, who quickly put it down and crawled on top of him.

"So you *are* ticklish," Buck said. His fingers threatened to attack, stopping short before actually making contact. Richard squirmed with every movement.

"Come on," he pouted. "That's not fair, I have a glass in my hand."

Buck took it from Richard's fingers and put it on the tabletop. Richard waited until Buck put the glass down before throwing him against the sofa. Using his hands, he pinned Buck down by the inner elbows.

"Now, that wasn't fair," Buck said. Richard leaned down and kissed him. "Okay, maybe it is." Buck's hand slid down Richard's back.

"Do you think I'm that easy?" Richard asked. He sat up and moved Buck's hand from behind. Richard raised his index finger and waved it like a metronome in Buck's face. Playfully he chided, "I don't *think* so!"

Buck's body went rigid.

"Are you all right?" Richard slid off Buck's chest and moved to the opposite end of the sofa.

"Yeah," Buck said, nodding and trying to make light of the situation. "Something just walked over my grave."

"Are you sure you're all right?" Richard asked as Buck drank half of his champagne in one gulp.

"Yeah," Buck replied. "It's just a stupid thing of mine."

"What is it?" Richard asked playfully. He moved closer and reached out, resting his hand on Buck's ankle.

"Just a stupid phobia of mine. It's nothing, really." He pointed to the photo album. "Which job was your favorite?"

Richard stared at him for several minutes before reaching

across and picking up the discarded album. He let the moment slide away as he became more focused on the pictures he was hunting for.

"Well," Richard confessed sheepishly. "I love old movies, so there are actually two that were my favorites. One was a benefit I did for Debbie Reynolds. She was a hoot. The other was for Ann-Margret. Now she…Okay!" Richard shut the book. "You did it again! You completely froze up for a minute. What's up with that?"

Buck's face was flushed. His eyes roamed the room trying to find something to focus on. On three occasions he opened his mouth to speak, but closed it instantly without a word. Acquiescing to the look Richard was giving him, Buck took a deep breath and coyly smiled.

"If I tell you, I'll have to kill you."

"I'll take my chances," Richard said with an impish grin.

"It's a stupid phobia that makes no sense to anyone else but me," Buck started. "It's completely irrational, and I'm fully aware of it."

Richard sat snuggled into the corner of the couch. His legs were folded in front of him, adding to his boyish looks. He wore a small smile as he waited.

Buck couldn't help but be charmed. He finished off his glass of champagne. "Okay. Again, this makes no sense."

"You've said that," Richard winked.

"I had this dream many years ago," Buck began. He squirmed in his corner of the couch, opposite from Richard. "You know that I'm a big theater fan?"

"Ah yes," Richard replied. "You've made that very clear."

"Okay then. I dreamt that I was dating Andy Margret, the brother of Ann-Margret."

"Does she really have a brother with that name?" Richard asked.

Buck leaned forward and patted Richard's knee. "Really not the point here. In the dream she had a brother, and his name was Andy."

"Okay," Richard said. He winked again. "You were dating Andy Margret."

Buck smiled and nodded. "Anyway, I broke it off and Andy was very upset."

"His loss is my gain," Richard said, refilling the flutes and raising his glass in a toast.

"Thank you," Buck responded. "But again, not the point."

"Well," Richard teased, "what is the point?"

"The point is," said Buck, enjoying the playfulness between them, "that Andy was so hurt and ticked off that he used his sister's clout. And *she* had me banned from every live theatrical performance in the world from elementary school up to Broadway, and including London's West End."

Richard clasped a hand to his mouth, swallowed, and coughed. "I almost had champagne coming out my nose."

"Look," Buck said playfully pouting, "I told you that it makes no sense to anyone else."

"And you think that Ann-Margret has that kind of power?"

"In the dream she did," Buck answered defensively. He crossed his arms. "Shut up. It was scary. Every time I went to get a ticket, she'd pop out of the box office like a redheaded jack-in-the-box. She would wag her finger in my face, like you did, and say in the same exact tone: 'I don't *think* so!'"

Richard did his best not to laugh. He held up his finger and examined it before looking at Buck. "And this is what triggered you?"

"Hey," Buck protested. "To this day she scares the hell outta me. You try being a show-tune queen and *never* have seen the movie of *Bye, Bye Birdie*."

"She's really the nicest person you'll ever know," Richard said, baiting him. "I can get you in touch with her if you want to work through some of that."

"Sounds wonderful," Buck said with a sneering smile. "And afterward, we can find a *Titanic* survivor and hold their head underwater to help them through that."

Richard chuckled and leaned forward to kiss Buck on the lips. "That is the stupidest thing I've ever heard." He kissed Buck softly. "And you are the silliest man I've ever met." They kissed again. "And I think you are absolutely adorable."

"If you like that," Buck whispered and reached out to take Richard's face in his hands, "you're gonna love the story of how I blame Rip Taylor for my fear of confetti." This time, Buck kissed Richard.

A timer from the kitchen rang softly.

"I'm hearing bells," Buck said. "How about you?"

"Now, that's perfect timing," Richard responded. "I'll be right back."

Richard stood up as Buck stretched out on the sofa. Reaching over, he retrieved the photo album and flipped to view the second half. Pictures of banquet tables and trays of food gave way to photographs of people posed like famous statues. Richard appeared in several.

"When did you do the modeling?" he called out as Richard gathered things in the kitchen.

"Oh, that," came the reply, modesty clearly in his tone. "I did some posing for some art classes in college. One thing led to another and for a time, to pay for cooking school, I was a male model."

"Handsome," Buck said aloud. "Very handsome indeed." Picture after picture slowly flipped by. He stopped on photo of a Roman discus thrower. The body was arched, bent almost in half, muscles flexed. The sinewy arm pulled behind, holding the disk and ready to lurch into action. Each detail of the muscular back led Buck's eye downward, and without hesitation, he studied the curve of Richard's buttocks.

With great admiration, Buck muttered, "You could chip a tooth on that."

The words echoed in his brain. The context was familiar. Something else went through his mind, something beyond the photo before him. There was a memory flashing of another statue: the statue in Brussels, the one that killed the drag queen. Buck had said those exact same words about the statue of the Barber's Guild: the statue that tried to assassinate him, the one that got away.

Buck reexamined the photograph, hoping to find some flaw that would separate the two in his mind. Considering himself a connoisseur, Buck looked over the curvature of painted flesh. There could be little mistaking something so beautifully shaped as the curve of his ass in that photo, or the ass of the Barber's Guild statue.

Why would Richard want to kill him in Brussels?

Suddenly the pieces fell into place and the full picture began to take shape. Noxia was correct, and his ego wouldn't allow him to believe it. He wasn't the target in Brussels. That was just coincidental timing, like Noxia and Muffin had tried to tell him over and over again. The statue was there to kill the drag queen, Karl Langlier, all along. Raven wanted to silence the man who killed her husband and get revenge on the man who led her son astray. The scene replayed in his mind. Langlier's last words echoed loudly.

"Three. One. Four." Buck mumbled the words aloud. It wasn't a date. It was an agent's name. "Three one four," Buck said again. It was right in front of him, and he'd been blinded all along. He heard imaginary glass shattering as realization settled in, and a chill raced up his body. He looked down at the photograph of the discus thrower, shaking his head. Not wanting to believe it was true, he felt the disappointment ripping him apart from inside out. There was no denying it.

"Agent 314," he bemoaned.

"Very good, Buck," Richard interrupted. "Or should I congratulate Agent 98 for figuring it out."

Buck looked up to see Richard holding a gun pointed directly at him. "Three point one four, the number for pi, Richard Pye. Surely you could have thought of something more original than that?"

"Why?" Richard asked taking a step closer. "It managed to keep you off the track for this long." He tossed a pair of handcuffs over to him. "Why don't you put these on? Arms around the table leg, if you don't mind."

"Handcuffs on our second date," Buck said. "Usually I wait

until date three." He slid his arm between the glass tabletop and the metal shelf holding the books underneath.

"Show me your arms, to make sure they're secured!" Richard ordered. Buck yanked on the chain to prove he was bound. Richard walked around the sofa to make certain. Once assured, he lowered the gun.

"It's a shame," Richard said, his white teeth shining like pearls from their golden nest. "I was looking forward to having sex with you at least one more time."

"If you'd rather do that, I'm game."

Richard moved around behind him. "What's to stop me from doing both?" His lips brushed Buck's neck. The flesh prickled beneath the softness of his lips.

"Because then," Buck said with sharp breath, and through clenched teeth, "you'd be a murderer and a rapist."

"True," Richard said. "But you know what they say, 'In for a penny...'" He stopped the kissing; his lips paused just above the skin of Buck's neck. "Don't worry, you aren't worth it."

The butt of the gun crashed down behind Buck's ear, knocking him unconscious.

CHAPTER TWENTY

B uck's head throbbed in pain. It felt like a bowling ball had been attached to his neck. Lifting his head took great effort, the pain thundering through his skull. His eyes struggled open, causing new, shattering waves of agony to wash over him. Buck was sitting in a straight-backed chair, arms tied behind his back, with another rope tied around his waist. As his blurred vision fought to focus, his body fought queasiness. He let his head fall back and it collided with someone else's skull. Another round of hammering took place inside his head.

"Ow! I'm glad you're awake, but could you watch it?" the voice said from behind him.

It took Buck a moment to recognize it, recovering from his daze. He tried to look around but the bindings gave him a limited viewpoint. To his left, there was a door. To his right stood a wooden bureau stretching from the floor to the ceiling.

"Buck?" the voice asked after a moment's silence, seeking confirmation. "I assume that's you. Are you okay?"

"No," he responded sharply, regretting it immediately as another wave of pain shot through him. "It's Julie Andrews and I'm feeling just supercalifriggin' great. Noxia, what are you doing here?"

"There was a knock at the door," she explained, "and I thought it was room service. When I opened it, our friendly skeleton guys reappeared and jumped me."

Buck was astonished. "You? You made a careless mistake?"

"Really, Buck. You don't need to give me shit about this now."

"No?" he answered. "Chances are neither one of us is going to live long enough to get out of this room. So tell me, if now isn't the right time, when is?"

"There are times I really hate you."

"You can hate on me later," he said. "Right now you can tell me where the hell we are and what you know."

She sighed. "I only woke up minutes before you. And have no idea."

He looked around to see what he could. "No windows, so I'm guessing we're in a storage unit, possibly a basement or garage. Have you seen anyone else?"

"I've only seen Raven and two other guys. They just left. There could be more."

"Great," Buck moaned. "Not exactly what I had planned for this evening."

"Hey," Noxia asked. "What happened to you? Did they grab you on the way to Richard's house?"

"Nope," Buck said, trying to be elusive.

"On the way back?" She sounded surprised. "Is Richard all right?"

"Oh," Buck answered with a sarcastic snort, "I think he's doing better than all right."

"You have such an ego."

"Thank you, Noxia," he responded. "I like the way you think. Unfortunately, our date officially ended when he pulled a gun on me and knocked me out."

"Before or after he saw you naked?"

"You're really not funny, you know." Buck knocked his head backward, colliding with hers. He winced as the pain shot through him. "It was a set-up, all along. The statue in Brussels wasn't there to kill me. He was there to kill Langlier, to ensure his silence. You were right. Richard was the statue. And I was starting to really like him, too."

It all became clear to her in an instant. "Of course! The number connection, three-one-four! *Pye!* It seems so easy now."

"A little credit here," Buck protested. "It's easy once I explained it to you."

"Buck," Noxia replied calmly. "We're tied up, back to back. Most likely we're going to die. Do you think credit and who is one up on the other is really the bigger issue here and now?"

"Maybe not," he replied. "But I figured it out, just for the record."

"You really want to play this childish game now?" Noxia said. "Here's one for you. While you were out trying to get a piece of Pye, I was at the hotel figuring out some major things myself. Any idea what the Jesus Injection is?"

"As a matter of fact, I do." The voice took them both by surprise. "I'm so sorry to hear that you do, too."

Raven entered the room with two men in tow. One walked with a limp, and Buck recognized one of the skeletons from New Orleans. The other was Terje, his broken nose almost healed. Raven held a gun pointed at the two agents.

"What's the matter, Raven?" Buck taunted. "Your two friends there gluttons for punishment? Didn't get enough in New Orleans, so they're back for more?"

"Just let me at him," Terje said. The other pounded his fist into his palm.

"Fair match," Buck said. "You there, with two friends to help. I'm strapped down in a chair with my hands tied. I only have *her* at my back."

"Thanks, Buck," Noxia said. "Thanks a lot."

"I could go on watching you two snipe at each other all day," Raven said. "It's really quite amusing. But, alas, I have things to do. First, I need to know: Which of you is going to get me into your agency's building? I know my files have been downloaded somewhere in your office, and I need to get in to retrieve them."

Silence.

"Which agency's building?" Buck asked. "My antique dealership in California or her brokerage firm?"

Raven smiled back. She looked over to Terje and signaled with a jerk of her head.

Terje joined his fingers, cracking his knuckles over his head, and walked over to them. The back of his hand flew out and smashed into the side of Buck's face. The force knocked his head back, causing it to collide with Noxia's skull.

Buck pulled himself together and sat up as best he could. His tongue darted out and wiped away the blood trickling out the corner of his lip.

"You know," he said. His breath was heavy and he closed his mouth to swallow hard. "You are so going to regret that."

"Yeah?" Terje drew his hand back and repeated the action from the other side. "Say it again."

"Buck," Noxia said. "Antagonize him all you want, but could you at least do it when I'm not tied to you?"

"I'd listen to your bitch," Terje said.

"Oh no, you did not!" Buck said with a hesitant warning. "You don't want to call her that. She hates being called the B-word. In fact, she gave me a warning not long ago. Remember, Noxia, on the plane?"

Buck moved his finger as best as he could. It nudged up against Noxia's and he scratched her with his fingernail.

"Buck, dear," Noxia said picking up the clue. "Do us all a favor, and shut up!" She tried to reposition her fingernail to get the razor's edge pointed against the ropes. The finger made contact with his binding, but quickly lost it. She tried again, making little progress, but at least it was something.

"I'd listen to the bitch, Buck," Terje taunted.

"Now you're pushing it," Noxia warned. "Buck, since you've done it twice already, can I kick his ass now?"

"Sorry, Noxia." Buck played along. "This one is all mine."

Terje smiled, laughing at them both. Raven's smile was more studious. She kept the gun pointed and watched them with a hawk's sharpness.

"You do have all the fun," Noxia said. Her fingernail scratched away at the thick rope, but the effort was failing.

"You never forget the first time do you, Terje?" Buck cooed. "It was in the bathroom in Virginia that I first kicked your ass. You know, the night Raven's son here blew up that gay bar?"

"Oh," Noxia said. "You mean the Bomb-a-Bar-for-Jesus Guy."

"Really?" Buck asked her in a sarcastic tone. "When he said he was looking for that faggot, it was Billy they were looking for, not me."

"I told you so," Noxia replied. "You're not the only faggot that causes trouble."

Buck ignored her and continued. "The second time Terje got his ass kicked was in New Orleans. You probably didn't recognize him, Noxia, because he had the skeleton costume on at the time."

"Oh yeah," Noxia said. She continued to try to cut through, but the angle was too bad and the ropes too thick. "I see that bony resemblance now."

"Enough of your games!" Raven cried. "I don't have time for this. I want to know. How do I get into your office? The elevator doesn't go all the way up, and I know there are several floors more. Now tell me, or I shoot her in the head." Raven stepped forward, placing the gun's barrel against Noxia's temple. "I won't ask you again." She cocked the gun.

"Okay," Buck said. "You need a key to get onto the penthouse floor."

Raven kept the gun pressed against Noxia's head. "Paul, go through our lovely lady's purse. See if you find any keys."

Paul limped out of the room.

"How could you, Raven?" Noxia asked. "How could you destroy the mind of your own son?"

"He may have been a son to me," Raven snapped. She pressed the gun's barrel tightly against her head, scraping the skin. "But he was also an abomination unto God."

"To turn your back on him like that?"

"God told Abraham to send the handmaid Hagar and their son Ishmael out into the wilderness. I would not defy God."

"God gave Ishmael an entire nation," Buck pointed out. "What did you give your son?"

"Abraham's son was innocent," Raven said. Her eyes were narrowed, and her blinking increased. "Mine was a sinner."

"And what does God have to say about people who use electroshock and brainwashing as a way to control others?"

"Are you serious?" Buck asked. "That's what the Jesus Injection is? Good God, woman! You're more twisted than I thought."

"Well," Raven smiled, "isn't that the crow calling the Raven black." She laughed.

"How do you plan on using this injection, Raven?" Buck asked. "Do you think they're just going to line up and present themselves?"

"They have so far," she answered with a malicious smirk. "Why do you think I started the Rescued Right? There will always be those who hate themselves enough to try just about anything to be someone else."

"How many others?" Noxia demanded.

"A few here, a few there," Raven said. "Every experiment has trial and error."

"And you have no conscience about destroying their minds like you did with your own son?" Buck said.

"I wouldn't say destroyed," Raven said. "I prefer to think of those few as being the pioneers in a scientific experiment that will change and save the world!"

"I doubt this is what your husband would have designed his cure for," Noxia reprimanded.

Raven pushed the gun's barrel, nudging Noxia's head. She smiled down at her captive.

"My former husband designed a cure for the wrong illness," Raven said. "HIV is God's scourge. It's not a virus, it's a detergent, designed to cleanse away the sins of those who go against God's laws."

"And you think you can fix where he went wrong?" Noxia asked.

"Exactly," Raven said perfectly calm. "Riding the Wave showed me the way. They are on the verge of creating something incredible if they only have enough nerve to take it to the next level. That's the problem with public companies; you have to pander to the public. It'll be years before they get to the point of discovery—when it took me only six months to figure it out."

"And you really think that you're going to have success with this? Didn't your son show you enough reasons why this won't work?"

"Mr. Miller." Raven smiled. "He was a fledgling experiment. I've gotten much better, and with greater success. You will soon find out what the true power of Christ can do."

"If it's making me a brainwashed zombie, no thank you."

"You know, Mr. Miller, I've had about as much from you as I'm going to take."

Paul came back into the room, immediately going to Raven's side. He held up a small metal ring containing eight different keys. "This was the only keychain in her purse."

"What do you need all those keys for, Noxia?" Buck asked.

"Not important right now," she replied.

"We'll never tell you which one it is, Raven," Buck said. "So you're just shit out of luck!"

The confident grin that spread across Raven's lips was not what he was expecting.

"Am I, Mr. Miller?" Raven answered calmly. "Am I really? I'm standing here with a gun pointed to your friend's head, and I'm the one out of luck? You misunderstand my intent, Mr. Miller. Let me help you understand."

Raven pulled the trigger on the gun.

The pistol's hammer snapped down loudly, echoing through the room.

"Next time," she said, sounding quite pleased, "there will be more than just an echo on these walls."

Raven kept her eyes locked on Buck and Noxia, making sure they saw her every move. With a quick flick of her wrist, the handgun's chamber fell open. Holding up one at a time, she presented each of the six bullets before placing them into the chamber.

"Now, Terje," Raven said. She cocked the gun and pointed it at Noxia's head. "Untie her, carefully. We wouldn't want Mr. Miller to get loose. Not yet."

Terje reached to his belt and withdrew a knife from its sheath. Slowly, he turned the blade over to let the light glisten off the sharpened, jagged edges. He looked into Buck's eyes and pulled the knife up to his own throat, the point under his left ear. Using the smooth edge, he drew it across his trachea, eventually letting the edge pierce a tiny prick under his other ear. The droplet of blood dribbled down the silver blade.

"Could you be any more melodramatic?" Buck said snidely.

"Do you mind not being snarky to the man with the sharp knife?" Noxia snapped.

Terje grabbed Noxia by the neck and roughly pulled her forward. His hand slid down between the two of them. After a few coarse cuts, Noxia pulled her arms forward, rubbing her wrists.

"Where are you taking her?" Buck called out. "You already have her keys."

"Do you think I'm that stupid, Mr. Miller?" Raven said. "We have them, but I don't know which one to use, and there's no telling what waits for us. Besides, I'm sure the lovely Miss von Tüssëll's company will be perfectly enjoyable. Especially if there are any further problems—there or here." She looked directly at Noxia. "That really is a ridiculous name."

"It's not ridiculous," Noxia said.

Buck responded. "It's German!"

"Either way," Raven continued. "Any problems and we can assure you, it will be the end of her. Tie her hands and give her to Paul."

Terje tied Noxia's hands behind her back. He pushed her over to the other assistant. Paul caught her and held her still, her throat locked in his elbow and his gun pressed into her ribs.

"What about me?" Buck asked.

The smirk that crept across Raven's thin lips was pure malice.

"You?" Raven said, like a child with a bag of candy asked to share one piece. Her eyes slowed their blinking as they narrowed on him. "You will find out what the Jesus Injection really is, firsthand. When you wake, you will be ready for your rebirth."

Raven nodded to Paul to usher Noxia from the room. She handed the gun to Terje, whispering into his ear. He smiled at Buck, making the break in his nose more noticeable. Raven left the room, leaving only the two of them.

"Alone again," Buck said. "Naturally."

Terje said nothing. He turned the gun slowly in his hand until he held it by the barrel. He bounced the handle against his palm before raising it above his head and coming toward Buck.

"Not again!" Buck complained as the gun butt made contact, knocking him unconscious.

CHAPTER TWENTY-ONE

B uck awoke with a sense of déjá vu. He was still in the same chair, his body restricted and bound, sitting in the same secluded room. The difference was this time he was alone, and his head hurt even worse. He could feel his wrists' bindings around the chair back, and he tugged on them to no avail. A low humming rumbled from somewhere, sounding like the purr of an electronic cat. The sound vibrated in his ears. He drew his legs up to a sitting position.

There was no telling how long he'd been unconscious. Or how long it had been since Raven took Noxia. He started thinking out his next move.

Get out of here at once. His mind dictated the easiest first. *What then? Catch up to Raven and Noxia, but how? Raven wouldn't risk taking Noxia through public transportation.* A brief glimmer of hope filtered through Buck's mind, especially after the last time he'd been with Noxia in an airport. He delighted himself with the fantasy of Raven being strip-searched, and shuddered at the visual. *That would serve her right, Noxia knows a lot of people and could possibly get away.* He eventually rationalized with the truth. *They can't fly, Noxia's being coerced.*

His mind tried to function, but it was still clouded from the two forceful attacks to his head. The humming sound was starting to irritate him.

They have to drive in a private car, Buck concluded. That was almost as good. If they were anywhere in the vicinity of the Robert E. Lee Hotel, driving back to the Agency's office would take at least five to ten hours, depending on traffic and driving speed. That would give him time.

"Christ is the redeemer..." came a singing voice blasting out of hidden speakers. The sound thundered all around for a moment, and then the volume lowered. The song continued singing about the glory of Jesus in a country drawl, and Buck felt as if he were sitting in on a Southern tent revival.

The door opened and Terje came back in. He glanced at Buck, giving him little other acknowledgment. The tall blond went to the dresser and fumbled with the locked latch, pulled the doors open, and slid them back into the sides of the dresser.

There was the source of the humming sounds. A machine was vibrating loudly as power surged through it. Four triangular lights formed a large red circle at the center. Two of them were completely lit, with light flickering in the belly of the third. Colored bars lit up, and lined gauges were scattered over the surface, registering the charges and pulses.

"You woke up earlier than expected," Terje said. He picked up a plastic squeeze bottle and a large stick with a cotton swab attached at the end. "The worse for you. The better for me."

He squeezed a yellowish orange liquid out of the bottle and onto the cotton swabs. He rubbed them in tiny circles on the sides of Buck's head and around his temples. The liquid felt cold as it dribbled down his face.

"Could you be a little careful with that stuff," Buck said, "I have oily skin and don't want to break out."

"And Christ will bring his love..." finished out the song. There was a momentary pause before another gospel began twanging through the speakers. "Honor and power to the Lord..."

Terje continued to apply the conductor. "Have you made peace with Jesus, you sorry-ass faggot?"

"No," Buck said, "Not with him. I did make peace with Jesus

you sorry-ass hick, though. Or was it Jesus you sorry-ass redneck? I get them mixed up."

"That's funny," Terje said without so much as a smile. He finished applying the conductor. "As it is written in Job," he quoted, "'He will fill your mouth with laughter, and your lips with shouting.'"

Terje put the plastic bottle down and turned back to the machine. The third red triangle was fully lit. The fourth started to flicker.

"So what's going to happen here, Nurse Ratched?" Buck asked. Nervousness crept into his voice. "Do I sing songs from *Next to Normal* as I fly over the cuckoo's nest, or send *Postcards from the Edge*?"

"We wait." Terje's calm was unsettling. His fingers tapped the unlit triangle, sparks of red igniting deep within. His joy in what he was planning to do was evident in the smooth way he glided about, preparing his task.

"Aren't those machines a little barbaric?" Buck asked with an uneasy laugh. "Aren't there more efficient ways in modern medicine?"

"Yes," Terje answered. "And yes." His fingers took control of a machine knob and clicked it hard.

The humming sound sped up, raising an octave. The fourth light flickered at a faster frequency. It finally stayed on.

Terje's smile broadened. He reached into the cabinet and withdrew what looked like a set of headphones with rounded ends instead of ear cushions.

"What a friend we have in Jesus..." an unseen singer assured.

"Any final words before rebirth?" Terje said, the headphones in his hands. His eyes were wide, the gray-blue colors dully reflective.

"How about *Hell No!*"

Buck stood up, the chair coming with him. With a quick twist of his body, he slammed the legs of the chair into Terje's hip. The surprise impact caused him to drop the electronic headphone piece, stumbling back a few steps.

That was all the time Buck needed. He took a step closer, spinning around with greater force and slamming the chair into the side of the bureau. The hindquarter of the wooden chair smashed apart, splintering across the room. The rope around his waist fell slack as the remaining chair parts slid away. His hands remained tied behind his back.

Terje staggered back a few steps from the initial blow, but recovered quickly. Buck charged forward. Terje tried to jump out of the way, but Buck's head connected with his hip, and both were sent spinning in opposite directions. Terje was thrown into the corner between the walls and the cabinet.

"Glory! Shout Hallelujah! Glory!" commented the speakers.

Buck tumbled to the ground. Using his shoulder to break his fall, he rolled on his side and got to his feet. Terje was momentarily trapped in the corner. Buck charged forward, crashing full-on torso to torso. Terje was flung back into the siding, restricted by his position. Buck used the force of his own weight to pin Terje against the wall. He pulled his head back and slammed it into Terje's forehead.

Terje's head flew back, bouncing off the wall behind him. As his skull rebounded, Buck reared his head back and pounded into Terje again. A third round caused Terje to collapse against the wall, sliding down to the floor. A quick shot from Buck's knee connected with the side of Terje's head, assuring his surrender to unconsciousness.

"I am saved! I am saved!" the speakers shouted.

"Amen," Buck commented, panting heavily. "Amen to that!"

Buck stood completely still, trying to assess his situation. His heart raced. His breathing came fast and heavy. A smith's hammer crashed heavily in his head, banging out a painful tune. He closed his eyes, trying to focus and gather his plan of action. Slowly it all subsided—the throbbing in his head, the pounding heartbeat, and the racing breath—until he regained control.

His eyes opened. Terje was not moving, and was not about to. Buck stepped over the body and approached the machine. He scanned for a power source, finding a red switch in the bottom left corner. He turned around and his fingers lightly danced over the knobs until he found the one he wanted. He snapped it off. The machine's humming died down to silence.

Buck let out a heavy sigh. A wave of relief washed over him, bringing a chill to his body and causing perspiration to break out down his spine.

There was nothing in the room except for the broken chair, the machine, and two people, one of whom was thankfully unconscious. With a concentrated effort, Buck backed himself against the cabinet corner. He rubbed his bound hands up and down the sides, hoping that friction would either wear down the ropes or heat them up enough to cause them to fray.

After relentless efforts, the ropes began to pull apart. Buck increased the speed and finally broke free of the binding. He shook his arms as they hung at his side, letting the blood flow fully return to his wrists and hands.

Buck approached the door with caution. Doubtful there was anyone there, but not pressing his luck, he leaned in, cupping his ear to the door, listening for anything on the other side. Hearing nothing, he was quite assured that if anyone were there, they'd have come to Terje's aid before this. He hesitantly reached out, turning the knob.

The door opened into another empty room. Padding lined the walls to ensure sound wouldn't travel beyond them. A refrigerator hummed softly in the corner, and miscellaneous chairs littered the carpeted floor. A sofa was kept spotless; a bed pillow lay on top of a blanket on one end. In the center, three chairs sat around an abandoned table. Noxia's purse lay on its side, the contents scattered out across the tabletop. In the corner stood a small table with nothing on it but an MP3 player, set in a loading dock. Speaker wires ran out the back and up the wall and disappeared into the ceiling.

Buck went immediately to the small table and picked up the music player. He turned it off and the gospel singing ceased.

"Thank God!" he muttered and turned his attention to the table in the center.

Buck scanned over the contents poured out from the purse.

What was there was minimal: a few makeup essentials, a credit card, some loose change, and about twenty dollars in small bills. He picked up the discarded bag and inspected the inside. Along the back lining, hidden under a small flap, was the zipper he had hoped for. He reached in and felt the rectangular object through the material, then opened the zipper and pulled out the cell phone.

It was his cell phone. The one'd he loaned to Noxia before his date with Richard. He turned it on and cursed the phone's slow processor, along with his own impatience. The screen came to life; the mask from *Phantom of the Opera*, offering a row of options at the bottom. Unfortunately, there were no connection bars. Buck looked around and found the exit nestled in the far corner, camouflaged within the soundproof padding. Quickly, he took the cash that was scattered on the table, gathering each dollar and coin, and picked up the credit card with a wicked grin.

"Thanks, Noxia. This one's on you."

Buck cracked the door open, squinting in the bright light from outside. Shielding his eyes, he found his guess was correct. They had been in a storage unit, one among many. Peering through the opening, he saw no one moving among the buildings. He stepped out into the light, closed the door behind him, and moved quickly away, trying to look as casual as possible. He couldn't be sure when anyone would be coming back, or how many there would be.

Crossing down several alleyways, Buck felt confident he could finally relax. He held up the cell phone and, to his absolute delight, found two of the six bars lit up in the corner. There were only two, but they were enough. He found the GPS icon. It took a few moments to pull up, but after a couple of refining choices from the menu, Buck was able to find his location on the map, the Hoarder's 4 U Storage Facility, in the far west limits of Fairfax, Virginia. He made a note of the address.

Switching the phone's applications, Buck flipped through the contact list and made his selection. He remained still, afraid of losing the connection, and scanned either side of the alley for any signs of life. The phone only rang once before an agent picked up the line.

"This is Agent 98, Buck Miller," he said into the phone. He thought about his fastest connection options. "I will need flight arrangements out of a DC airport to Home Base immediately. Any airport, whichever can get me there the fastest!" That was all he was allowed to say on a cell phone. Once he heard the confirmation, Buck disconnected the call. The next call was to information.

"What city, please?" the nasal voice inquired.

"Fairfax, Virginia," Buck said. "Any cab company, I'm not particular, just connect me direct. Thank you." He waited a few moments, listening to the phone being connected and ringing on the other end. "Yes," he said once it was picked up. "I'll need a cab to take me to Dulles Airport. Yes, right now please, I'll be standing outside Hoarder's 4 U Storage Facility. Yes, that's the address. No bags, I'll be waiting out front."

Buck hung up the call and locked the keypad. He shoved it into his pocket. Giving a final glance down the alley, Buck took off toward the other end. He broke into a quick-paced jog, weaving his way down the paths and following the signs to the main entrance.

CHAPTER TWENTY-TWO

Noxia stood in front of the elevator waiting for the car to come down to the lobby. The building was empty due to the weekend, and not even lobby security was around during the day. Paul stood directly behind her, his gun pressing into her back. Raven waited impatiently behind them, tapping her foot. Her mud-colored hair, disheveled from the long drive and frizzy from the humidity, made her appear like a mad scientist.

"Will you cut my hands loose now?" Noxia asked. "After that eternal car ride from hell, it's the least you can do." She felt battered from being kept in the car with her hands tied behind her for so long. The muscles in her arms and hands ached from cramping, and her body felt run-down.

Paul looked at Raven for a signal and got none. The elevator doors opened and he nudged Noxia in with the barrel of the gun.

"Don't you think you may need me to have my hands free?" Noxia pointed out as the elevator doors closed. "Where am I going to run to?"

"Push the top button, Paul," Raven said. They were the only words spoken during the ride up.

The doors opened on the fiftieth floor to the wall painting of the setting sun. Fresh flowers stood in a vase on the table directly in front. Blocking the car doors with her body to keep them from closing, Raven turned to Noxia with a self-righteous smile.

"Now," Raven said, her voice low and calm, "how do I get to the top floor?"

"This is the top floor," Noxia answered. Her voice and composure were equally calm.

"No," Raven said. Her expression didn't change. "It's not."

"Hey, Paul pressed the button, not me," Noxia argued. "There's nothing higher."

Raven looked at Paul and held her hand out. He dug his hand deep into a pocket and took out a small black object. Raven held it up in her hand. It was a black rectangular device, like a remote control. She turned it over in her hand, pressing a button on its side. It chirped several times in succession and let out a last, solid sound. She held it out to Noxia to see the large red number 2 floating in the center of the screen.

"See that?" Raven asked condescendingly. "That is a simple device that was installed on my computer system a long time ago. It's something that my late husband developed before he died."

"Before you had him killed, you mean."

"Before he died," Raven insisted. "It's a program called 'Snitch' because it reports when anyone has entered my personal computer files without my personal passwords. It also attaches itself through the download and sets a tracking device to my own private monitor." She held up the black box in her hand.

"Now, this says that two unauthorized downloads exist of my personal files. You see, there were three, but we retrieved the one from the laptop in your hotel room."

"And that's why you broke in and stole the computer?"

"Not me!" Raven said with a fiendish implication. "But I'm pretty sure the computer is now keeping your cell phone company in a recycled electronic center somewhere." Her face grew clouded. "Your phone was better locked than the computer."

"Leave it to Buck to not guard his property."

"Yes," Raven hissed. She turned the tracer around, admiring the function of the device itself. She tapped a code number from the side panel, and the screen changed format. She stepped away from the car doors, allowing them to close. The elevator remained stationary.

"Now, this tells me where the two remaining downloads are," Raven explained. "The tiny green dot means that one is out there, but currently can't be traced." She smiled wickedly at Noxia. "We know where that one is, and it will be obtained shortly. This red dot shows that we are within a hundred yards of the other download."

Without warning, Paul grabbed Noxia and threw her into the elevator car. She stumbled back, hitting the handrail. He pinned her head against the back of the car, choking her by pressing his arm into her throat.

"Look, bitch," he seethed. The stench from his breath was foul. "How do we get to the top floor?"

Noxia brought her knee up sharply between his legs, making direct contact with his genitals. Paul bent over, releasing his grip on her throat. "How many times do I have to tell you," Noxia said. "I hate being called a bitch!" Noxia took one look over at Raven's pointed pistol and knew there was no escaping the elevator car.

The smile on Raven's face was a curious one, her mouth slightly ajar. She turned her head from the disturbance in front of her, to the button panel by the car doors. When she looked back to face them, her grin grew much wider. The speed of her blinking eyes increased.

"Paul!" she snapped at him. "You're a bloody fool. Come here." He pulled himself upright and moved to her side. "Take out the key chain, and see if one fits right here." Raven tapped the small cylinder lock above the dormant numbers.

Paul did as he was told. He found the small bike lock key and studied its teeth and two prongs. Moving closer to the wall, he inspected the lock and decided they matched. As he was about to put the key into the lock, Raven reached out to touch his arm, stopping him right before the key made contact.

"Wait," she said with a scrutinizing look. Her upper lip peeled back, revealing uneven, coffee-stained teeth in the form of a sharpened smile. "Give her the key. Make her use it. If there are any tricks, then we all suffer together."

Noxia took a step forward, taking the keys from Paul's hand. She selected the cylinder key, inserting it into the lock, and momentarily paused. With a deep breath, Noxia gave the key a firm twist to the left. The elevator motors hummed into action and the car leapt upward.

Paul's face remained filled with pain and rage from Noxia's kick. His eyes stared heated daggers, doing his best to pierce her breast—in more ways than one. Raven's lips wore a satisfied, smug smile. The elevator glided to a halt and the doors slid open.

The reflection off the stark white walls of the fifty-second floor lit up the entire elevator car. Paul stepped out first and moved immediately to the side, keeping an eye on Noxia as she exited, followed by Raven. There was no way to go but toward the end of the hallway, the back wall beckoning to them, reflecting the brightness.

"Move," Raven ordered in a harsh voice. She pushed the gun against Noxia's back, forcing her down the hall. "Pull the handle, Paul," Raven commanded as they came to the dead-end. He did as he was told, but the drawer remained hidden and shut. "Now what?" Raven snapped. Noxia didn't say a word. "Paul," Raven commanded. "Search the wall."

Paul immediately went to the corner, pressing himself against the wall. His hands slowly glided over each reachable square inch, his fingers moving as if caressing a lover. It didn't take him long before he stumbled onto something embedded. He traced the outline and he leaned in, finally seeing the hidden button as if it were an optical illusion.

"Here," Paul said. His fingertips drew an outline around the button so Raven could see.

"Very good," she said, sneering. "Noxia, would you be so kind." Raven moved to the side so Noxia was completely in front of the handle and the wall button. She kept the gun positioned at Noxia's head. Paul stood behind her to make sure she couldn't back away.

Noxia found the button with little effort. Her fingertip circled it with an uneasy motion, hesitating before pressing it. The drawer's outline manifested from its seclusion, the handle ready to be pulled.

Raven gave the gun a stunted jerk, motioning for Noxia to continue. Noxia leaned over, resting her head against the wall, and pulled open the drawer. Raven's eyes widened as the retina scans' light reflected upward. Once Noxia allowed the red beam to record her eye patterns, the door appeared. Raven's delight was written in the astonishment of her muddied brown eyes. She took a step back and motioned for Noxia to open the door.

As the heavy door opened, the lights instantly flashed on, flooding the room with bright fluorescents. Raven nudged Noxia into the room and was followed by Paul. The outside door closed, leaving the three of them in the computer room.

The five-by-five rows remained empty, all the chairs pushed up to their respective desks. All the stations were bare except the one computer in the far corner of the back row.

Raven took out her tracking device. She pressed the side buttons and the black rectangle chirped loudly, several times in quick succession.

"And we have a winner," Raven said. She looked past Noxia toward the one computer, success written on her face. Motioning forward with the gun's barrel, Raven nudged Noxia down the center aisle, two rows stretching out on either side. Every movement Noxia took was reluctant, stalling after each reluctant step, and they barely got past the first row before Noxia halted altogether.

"Why would I go any farther?" Noxia said. "You see the computer. You can get it yourself."

"Noxia," Raven said. "I'm not a stupid woman, so please stop insulting my intelligence. I'm going to keep you until I get what I want. Then I'll shoot you. Not before then, so just continue along."

Noxia took one step and then stopped again. "You'll need the password to get into the files, no matter what. Otherwise you're just staring at a screen saver."

"You'll tell me the password," Raven said. A chill reached out and touched the nape of Noxia's neck.

"Why would I tell you that, when you just said that you're going to kill me as soon as you get what you want?"

"Because I'm growing very weary of you," Raven said with a heavy sigh. She continued her explanation, her voice full of confidence. "And you are absolutely right, I can get into the computer at this point myself. Smash it, if I choose to. But I'm thinking that if I touch anything major or pick something up, there may be an alarm. If I use the code and erase the computer's files, there's less chance of being exposed. Don't look so amazed, I thought this one out. Now I'll ask you again to proceed."

Raven pulled the gun's hammer back, cocking the handgun. She held it up against the back of Noxia's head. The cold barrel made Noxia's skin prickle and break out in a cold sweat.

"So the deal's this," Raven continued. "If you don't tell me the password, I'll blow your head off right here. They'll scrape your brains off all these desks when the team arrives in the morning. If you tell me the password now, I'll let you live. It's that simple."

Noxia stood perfectly still. She closed her eyes and took a deep breath. Slowly, she turned around, standing in place until she came face-to-face with Raven. The gun's barrel remained pointing directly at her, now aimed at the center of her forehead.

"And why would I believe you now?"

"Because, Miss von Tüssëll, you have no other choice."

"And what's to stop you from killing me the minute I give in?"

"Life has no guarantees, Ms. von Tüssëll," Raven said with a cocky shake of her head. Her eyes blinked every other second. "But a thief trapped against the wall has no other way to run. Believe me when I say this will be the last time I ask. What is the password?"

Noxia stared back at her. The coldness of the gun's steel

matched that of the insipid brown eyes she stared into. Noxia bit her bottom lip and knew there was no other choice.

"It's Buck's full name," Noxia confessed, conquered. She lowered her head and looked at the floor.

"That's it?" Raven asked. A touch of doubt remained in her tone.

Noxia picked up her head and looked directly at Raven with an innocuous expression. "This is Buck we're talking about."

Raven nodded, understanding with a smirk. "So simple that no one would ever think of it. Thank you. Kill her." Raven turned to Paul and handed over the gun.

"What?" Noxia exploded. "You just said if I told you…"

"Do you really think I got this far by playing by the rules?" Raven started down the side aisle, heading toward the computer station against the wall. "Kill her!"

Noxia looked at Paul. His crooked smile spread maliciously across his face.

"Not today!" Noxia leapt forward and knocked into Paul's gun hand. The pistol flew out across the room, leaving him without a weapon. Turning around before he even knew what happened, she took off toward the back of the room and the conference door she knew was hidden there.

"After her!" she heard Raven yell.

Paul's slight limp allowed Noxia the lead and advantage she needed.

"Row two, row three," she counted as she ran toward the back. "Row four, and jump." Noxia hopped over the floor space between rows four and five. She landed and fell against the back wall, bracing her landing. Her fingers nimbly punched in the code word.

"Fuck!" Paul yelled as his foot hit the electronic trip wire set up across row four. The invisible beam cut deeply into his ankle, sending him rolling into the side desks.

Raven looked back, distracted for the moment. Her line of vision traced from Paul's fall, to Noxia disappearing into the back conference room, and then to where the computer sat unattended.

Once the heavy door closed between her and her assailants, Noxia knew she was safe, at least for the moment. She darted across the room and slid between the pulled shade and the one-way viewing glass.

Raven reached the computer station and stood up tall, triumphantly. Her hand reached down behind the monitor. After a moment, the screen burst into light and Raven looked up, a smug smile smeared across her face. Her eyes were wide, and they blinked as if she were about to have a seizure. Raven glanced around, looking for any signs of where Noxia disappeared. She was gone. Time was running out. No one was there except Paul, rolling on the ground and clutching his bleeding ankle, moaning.

Raven pulled out the station's chair and sat down. The monitor's screen bathed her face in blue-white light, giving it even more of an eerie appearance. She positioned her hands over the keyboard, and prepared to type in the correct code word: B-u-c-k-M-i-l-l-e-r.

Noxia watched from behind the thick Plexiglas of the one-way mirror. Her nose and the palms of her hands were pressed flat against the viewing surface. She held her breath with anticipation. Noxia watched. She waited. And above all, she prayed.

Chapter Twenty-three

B uck arrived at the agency's office in record time. The flight was
ahead of schedule and, if his good luck stayed with him, he
might be able to arrive before Raven and Noxia. If they drove here,
it was possible that he would be ahead of them. Most likely, Raven
had already been and gone, but he felt like he must at least make an
effort. He shuddered at some of the things Raven might do to Noxia
once she had what she wanted.

He entered the building and made his way over to the elevator,
trying to appear as calm as possible for any security cameras. The
lobby was empty, which made things easier, no interference with
the general public. Pressing the button, he pushed his hands into
his pockets to keep control over the nervous energy that caused his
fingers to flutter. His right hand closed around the elevator key and
his finger pad touched the prongs inside. The feeling of the small,
cold metal made him feel more confident.

The elevator numbers counted in reverse, halting on the lit "L"
for the lobby. The car doors noiselessly slid open, and Buck stepped
in. He leaned on the handrail, trying to catch his breath as the doors
slid closed. After a moment, he heard the doors slide open again.
Before he could turn around, Buck felt the rounded steel of a gun
barrel pressed against the nape of his neck. He immediately stood up
straight and put his hands in his pockets.

"Now, I'd recognize the back of your head anywhere," Richard said smoothly. "Step forward to the back of the elevator," he dictated. "And take hold of the handrail where I can see your hands."

"Richard," Buck said calmly, controlling the surprise in his voice. His hands remained in his pant pockets. "Isn't that short for Dick?"

"As you well know," Richard shoved Buck forward with one hand and stepped into the elevator, "with me, it's never short for anything."

The elevator doors closed. Richard pressed the button for the top floor.

"How did you find me here?" Buck asked. He turned around to face Richard, leaning back on the handrail. "You weren't with Raven when I was about to be brainwashed."

"No," he answered. "I was waiting to see if you would live or not. I'm so sorry to see that you did. Now, take your hands out of your pockets. Place them on either side and grab metal."

Buck glanced up as the numbers ascended. An impish expression crossed his face. "Don't you want to reach into my pockets and take my hands out yourself?"

"Uh-uh," Richard said, pulling out his index finger and wagging it in front of Buck's face. "I don't *think* so." His impersonation was perfect.

"That was a low blow," Buck muttered with a heavy shudder. "I told you that in confidence." Richard's smile only broadened.

Without taking either his eyes or the pointed gun away from Buck, Richard reached into his back pocket and withdrew a set of metal handcuffs. He held them up and spun them around the fingers on his free hand.

"I'm sure you know what to do with these," Richard said. He tossed them over, purposely aiming for Buck's head.

Buck freed his hands to catch the cuffs in midair and avoid being hit. Something small glimmered in the light and fell to the floor, lost among the dark hues of the fake tile elevator floor.

Buck caught them, feeling their heavy weight in his hands. "Usually, I'm not the one in the handcuffs," he said nonchalantly.

He held them out as an offer, a drop of blood beading on the edge of his fingertip. "Are you sure you wouldn't want to give them a try? I could make it worth your while."

"If what I sampled in New Orleans is the best you have to offer," Richard said, his grin as malicious as his words, "then I'll pass. Just put on the cuffs."

Buck opened one end and put it around his wrist, but didn't snap them shut. "How did you even find me here, anyway?"

"You're really not that clever," Richard answered. "When you downloaded Raven's files onto the flash drive and then your phone, you also downloaded a virus that sent a tracer back. We knew your every move."

Buck's mouth opened into an oval as comprehension settled on him. "Which is how you found me on the streets of New Orleans?"

"Exactly," Richard said.

"And knew where my computer was…" Buck put it all together.

"Very good."

The last piece thundered into place. "And why Noxia was kidnapped. She had my phone. That's why you seemed so surprised when I showed up for our date—you weren't expecting me for dinner!" Buck studied Richard with both admiration and sheer repulsion. "You are a first-class bastard."

"Sticks and stones," Richard muttered. "Now close the cuff on your wrist. Be a good little boy and do what Daddy says."

"Under different circumstances," Buck said after a moment's hesitation, "these cuffs, those words—it could have been a much more pleasant scenario."

"Been there. Done that." Richard's smirk matched his sarcasm. The elevator doors opened onto the fiftieth floor, the sunset painting casting orange hues over the elevator's opening.

"Top floor," Buck said. "Men's department. Suits, shirts, slacks, and other sundry items."

Richard stared at him point blank, with no expression at all. His reflective black eyes looked at the handcuffs, still not clicked shut, and then back to Buck's eyes. Richard raised the gun and cocked the pistol.

Buck snapped the handcuff around his left wrist.

"Your finger is bleeding," Richard said.

"Yeah? You threw the cuffs a little hard."

"Wimp," Richard answered, shaking his head.

"It's a shame," Buck said with a click of his tongue. "You were fun, too."

"Too bad I can't return the compliment."

"Richard," he replied, exasperation in his voice. "There's no need to be hateful. You know I was better than that."

"Mmm, not really."

"Harsh," Buck said. "For that lie alone, you will have to die."

Richard laughed and stepped into the elevator car to let the doors close behind him. "That's really good. I'm holding the gun on you and you're plotting *my* death."

"You are kind of asking for it, you know," Buck said with a grin. "You were asking for it the other night, too, weren't you?"

Richard replied calmly, "Consider it the gay man's way of faking orgasm."

Buck's eyes grew narrow as they searched Richard over. "You bastard."

"You say the sweetest things." He motioned to the cuffs with the barrel of the gun. "Put your arm through the handrail and cuff your other wrist. I really don't want to have to worry about you. Through the rail, Buck. Now."

Buck threaded his arm between the metal railing and the elevator wall. With a final look at the pointed gun, he surrendered and snapped the cuff onto his other wrist.

"Yank on it," Richard commanded.

"Not without dinner," Buck responded. He pulled up his arms, demonstrating his captivity.

"Where is the key to get to the top floor?" Richard asked.

"I don't know what you mean," came the coy answer.

Richard pointed to the elevator's wall panel, his finger tapping the cylinder lock. "I have been up and down this elevator for over forty-five minutes. This lock is the only thing I can think of, so I can only assume that this is it."

"I don't have to tell you what happens when you assume, do I?" Buck chided.

"If you are what you eat," Richard quipped, "then that makes us even. Where is your key?"

"Okay, Richard," Buck answered, giving way to defeat. "The truth is I don't have it with me."

"Come on," Richard said incredulously. "Do you expect me to believe that? Why else would you be here if you didn't have the key to get to the top floor?"

"I was expecting to meet up with Noxia," Buck responded. "She has her key."

"Not anymore," Richard said. "Raven and Noxia went upstairs about an hour before you even got here."

Buck's eyes grew wide. "Then why are you still here?"

"Obvious, isn't it? I'm waiting to take care of you. They haven't come down yet, so I'll just bring you up to them. Raven will be delighted."

"I don't get it, Richard." Buck said. "Why? Why in the world would you follow a crazy woman like that? Don't you know she has an insane idea that she can cure homosexuality? She's using shock therapy to destroy people's minds, and her own twisted zealous version of the Bible to build it back up. She's not going to settle with you being the exception. Why would you want to help a woman like that?"

"It's not that crazy an idea," Richard said calmly. "There happens to be merit in it. People can be cured."

"For a real, medical necessity I can understand the use of ECT," Buck said. "Being gay isn't reason enough to have your brain fried by electricity."

Richard lowered the gun, secure that Buck's arms were locked. He studied Buck as if he were a foreign organism, newly discovered under a microscope.

"It must be nice to be you," Richard said.

"Actually, it is," Buck readily agreed.

"You can be that self-confident and happy with who you are."

"That's kind of what gay means, isn't it?"

"You probably were never told no as a child, were you?" Richard's eyes narrowed as they probed deeper. "You were one of those kids that had family support. Never got teased by the other kids for your skin color, your heritage, or effeminate nature. You probably never questioned your sexuality? Never had a problem accepting who you are?"

"Don't cry for me, little Tina!" Buck argued. "You're not going to make me feel bad for being self-confident. You don't know a thing about my childhood. We've all had shitty times growing up! Bullies dump on the weaker kids, I don't make the rules and it hasn't changed. There's always going to be someone to beat down on you. Get over it! It doesn't mean you have to be a self-loathing hypocrite."

"I'm not a hypocrite," Richard said, offended.

"No?" Buck argued. "Than what do you call seeking a cure for being gay and yet still sucking my cock?"

"A *small*," he let the word linger, "backslide on the road to recovery. God forgives all. He's cured me once. He can do it again."

"I feel sorry for you, Richard," Buck said sincerely. "I honestly do. You are so self-loathing, you've denied yourself any kind of happiness. Do you think that's what God had intended for you, a life of denial? A life of depriving yourself of love?"

Richard's lip twitched into a grimace. "You can ask him when you see him. It shouldn't be too long before he sends you directly to hell."

Richard planted the gun flat against Buck's temple. He leaned in and kissed him hard. His tongue forced Buck's mouth to open, and after a moment's invasion, Buck surrendered to the conqueror.

Richard pressed his body tight against Buck's, one hand caressing his body while the other held the pistol to his head. Richard hungered for more as his hand crawled down Buck's stomach and farther below the belt. He traced the hardening form within Buck's jeans and gave it a firm squeeze. His fingers traveled over, across Buck's hips, and down his legs.

"What's this?" Richard asked. His eyes grew wide with excitement.

"My ass!" Buck replied, nipping at Richard's bottom lip.

"The keys," Richard said. "And your cell phone."

Wearing a winning grin, Richard placed his knee directly below Buck's crotch, bracing himself against the wall. Keeping the gun pointed, Richard used his free hand to dig into Buck's pocket to fish out first the keys and then the phone.

"Aha!" Richard exclaimed.

"My sentiment exactly," Buck commented. "There is no way after that kiss, and after the way you felt me up, that you can say I'm bad in bed!"

Richard gripped the key carefully. "Buck," he said calmly. "If your dick was half as big as your ego, you'd be a much better lover."

"Richard," Buck said in the same mocking tone, "you are the original dick joke."

Richard leapt forward until they were nose to nose with each other. Buck never blinked, and Richard's breathing was hard and angry.

"Buck you!" Richard's fist flew out and collided forcefully with Buck's head, knocking him to the floor.

Richard opened his hand and let the phone fall. It bounced twice on the ugly tile before settling with a spin. Richard lifted his leg and brought his heel down hard, smashing the phone's casing into several pieces. He continued to stomp the bigger pieces until there was nothing worth salvaging.

"Raven will be happy to know that the last copy of her stolen files has been destroyed." Richard stepped backward until he was at the front of the elevator. He watched Buck, doubled over, listening to him trying to catch his breath. The sight made Richard's sneer grow. With an easy motion, he put the key to the cylinder lock and pushed it in.

Buck knelt on the floor, coughing and trying to get his breath. His hands were wrapped tightly around the handrail, clutching it to keep from sprawling on the floor.

Richard laughed at the sight. His teeth shone like pearls in the dim elevator's light. The key's handle stuck out of the lock, waiting to be turned. Richard's golden fingers took hold and with a firm grip, he twisted the key to the left.

The elevator hummed and moved into action. The passengers felt the jolt as the car ascended the two remaining floors. The light panel blinked with no numbers illuminating, chiming the first floor as it passed by without stopping. The car rocked to a stop. Another chime sounded, acknowledging the arrival at the next floor. The doors remained closed.

Richard put one hand under his gun arm to brace it, keeping it steady. "Good-bye, Mr. Miller." He pulled back the gun's hammer. "I think we're done."

"I think you're right," Buck said. "We're done." He smirked and gave Richard a quick wink.

The entire elevator car began to shake, as if from an earthquake. Richard stumbled across the floor, crashing into the wall. As his shoulder collided, another jolt struck the elevator, shaking it again. Richard was thrown in the opposite direction, tripping as he went. His arm hit the railing and the gun flew from his hand.

Richard fell down on his hands and knees. His wide, black eyes registered fear and shock as he braced himself. He gave Buck a quick look of surprise and scanned the floor for the gun. It lay in the middle of the car.

They both saw it at the same time. Buck reached out with his foot, trying to get a hold of the gun with his shoe heel. Richard dove forward, landing on his stomach.

The elevator stopped moving. The sounds of metal gears grinding scraped away, echoing loudly all around. The floor shook. A large crack started at one end and tore down the center. It made its way straight toward Richard's head, disappearing briefly underneath and continuing until it connected with the far side.

Another set of gears turned. For a brief eternal moment, silence filled the car. The two men looked at each other. Richard waited, letting out a short gasp before a much slower and longer breath. An awkward smile appeared, more from nerves than anything else, as Richard realized the worst was over. When he looked into Buck's eyes, he realized he was wrong.

The lights blacked out.

Buck felt the floor fall out from under his feet. For a split second his body was airborne, free falling. The cuffs about his wrists yanked him to a halt, digging into his flesh as his body weight pulled him downward.

Richard's screams echoed in the darkness. They grew dimmer as he fell farther into the darkness below, his cries reaching upward. They stopped suddenly with a muted, dull thud from many floors below.

Buck hung in the darkness. A cold chill blew all around him as he remained swinging by the metal cuffs on his wrists. He reached upward, grasping at the metal railing. which was still connected to the elevator wall. He tried using it to pull himself up, but his feet could find nothing to get traction on in the blackened shaft. A dim light came through the bottom of the closed elevator doors, signaling they were on the next floor. From where he was hanging, there was no way he could attempt to get the doors open.

A loud rumbling crashed down from above his head. Billows of rolling smoke poured out from the floor above, cascading down the elevator shaft.

Buck closed his eyes and held his breath, trying not to breathe in toxic fumes. His fingers gripped the metal bar frantically, but his sweating palms made his hands slick, and it was difficult to keep his grip.

His hands slipped. For a quick moment Buck thought he was going to fall down into the darkness. The chain of the handcuffs caught him, cutting into his wrists. His legs dangled in the darkness, causing the metal links to scrape along the handrail. The force from his legs swinging pulled him a few inches down the handrail.

Slowly and carefully, he moved his legs back and forth, letting the force of the swinging pull him another inch farther. When he eventually shimmied down to the corner, Buck used his strength and pulled his legs up. On the second try, his heel caught the side handrail, and he was able to pull himself up. The position wasn't much, but it gave his wrists a short break from the metallic assault.

The elevator doors above him grumbled as metal struck against metal. They squealed their displeasure as they were forced open. Thick black and gray smoke poured into the shaft, causing Buck to cough and lose his grip. He fell, swinging in the smoke and darkness.

"Damn it!" Buck yelled as the metal cuffs bit into his wrists.

"Buck!" a voice bellowed down through the thickness. "Is that you?"

"Get me the hell out of here!" he yelled up.

Somewhere through the haze, a white light flickered. A form appeared, silhouetted by the light behind. The figure leaned out into the smoke, reaching down.

Buck saw a hand coming toward him through the darkness. He tried to swing his legs to make contact, but couldn't reach it. The force sent him scuttling away, farther down the handrail. A blinding light shone down the shaft. It slowly scanned the wall until it found him, dangling connected to the rail. The light came down, into his eyes, temporarily blinding him.

"Buck," the voice boomed down toward him. "Are you all right?"

"Just hanging out, Noxia," he hollered up to the familiar voice. "Are you okay?"

"I'll survive."

There was a long pause.

"Ah, Noxia?" Buck hesitantly inquired.

"Yeah?" came the voice, assuring him she was still there.

"Can you do something to get me out of here?"

"Sure," came Noxia's lighthearted tone. "It should only be a few moments longer."

Something told him it was going to be longer than he expected. Something told him this was petty revenge.

Chapter Twenty-four

B uck watched the two of them sitting at a cozy banquette in the far back of a hole-in-the-wall restaurant. Both the food and the service had a reputation for being good, and the waitstaff for being discreet. The table's location practically guaranteed them privacy not only from the guests, but from server interruptions as well. Noxia and Muffin kept their heads down, talking intimately, and didn't notice him until he was almost at the table.

"And what are you two conspiring about?" Buck said.

"It's about time you showed up," Noxia said, looking up from the table. "Agent 69 and I were taking bets on if you got lucky on the way over and were going to blow us off."

"Never twice in the same mission, my dear. It's gauche," Buck quipped back. He slid into the booth next to her, putting her in the middle. "And I think we can agree that's one thing I am not."

"God forbid," Muffin added from the other side of Noxia.

"God forbid," Buck concluded.

A waiter dressed completely in black appeared at the table with an ice bucket and a bottle of champagne, the bottle gaily painted. Three glasses, carried upside down by their stems, were held in his other hand.

"As you requested, sir," the waiter said to Muffin. "A bottle of Perrier-Jouët when the gentleman arrived."

The server set up the stand next to Muffin and opened the bottle with a sharp pop. He poured out the first glass, offering it to the stout man, and then poured out two more for the others. Once finished, he offered a slight bow and left them alone.

Muffin held the glass in the air over the table. Noxia and Buck followed suit with their own champagne flutes.

"To a job well done," Muffin said.

"To a job well done," the other two echoed. All three of them sipped their champagne.

"What's that?" Noxia asked, pointing to a thick leather bracelet around Buck's wrists. "On both wrists? You going for the biker look?"

"Not quite," Buck answered. "The ligaments in my wrists were a little torn. You know, from hanging in handcuffs for so long? My doctor recommended that I wear these braces to keep the muscles steady so they can heal."

"You mean to tell me," Noxia said, trying to suppress a giggle and the impish sparkle in her eyes, "that all joking aside, you really are a limp-wristed gay man?"

"Nice," Muffin said with a wink.

Buck protested. "Don't they make me look butch?"

"If you have to ask," Agent 69 said over his champagne glass, "the answer is no."

"And Muffin gets the point," Noxia said.

"Okay," Agent 69 said, with a change of subject. "Enquiring minds want to know. What happened in the elevator?"

"Go ahead," Noxia encouraged with a sip of champagne. "You've shown us your leather Wonder Woman wristbands, now tell us what happened."

"Well," Buck started, "Richard had me at gunpoint. I knew that sooner or later, I was going to be coerced into giving him the key. So I put my hands in my pockets to stall for time."

"How was that stalling for time?" Noxia asked.

Buck looked at her incredulously. "I'm extremely cute and boyish when I stand with my hands in my pockets."

"No, really." Muffin chuckled. "You mean that actually worked?"

"Thanks for your support," Buck commented before giving in with a heavy sigh. "Fine. My hand was in my pocket because I was trying to call for help on my cell phone with one hand."

"That sounds more like it," Noxia said.

"There's no reception that high up in an elevator," Muffin interrupted.

"Now you tell me!" Buck said defensively. "Anyway, my other hand was fingering the prong in the key. I broke it off. It cut deep under my fingernail, too. It hurt."

"The broken key activated the trap door," Muffin finished. He turned to Noxia next to him and stage-whispered, "I figured I'd get the story rolling a little faster or we'd be here all night."

"Thanks for taking my thunder, Muffin," Buck complained. "But yes. That's what happened. Richard fell fifty-two floors down the elevator shaft. I was cuffed to the rail, praying that it would support my boyish frame."

"I'm amazed," Noxia said, "that you could find the key in your pocket and break off the prong without being noticed."

"Hey," Buck said. "By the time I was fifteen years old, I was a master at keeping my hand in my pocket without letting anyone know what I was up to."

"I'm sure," Muffin said.

Buck motioned toward the champagne bottle, a request to refill the glasses. "I want to hear what happened with Noxia and Raven."

"She was just about to tell me when you walked up," Muffin said.

"There isn't that much to say," Noxia said modestly. She leaned back against the banquette's cushion, champagne flute in hand. "I knew that Raven would kill me as soon as I gave her the passcode to get her files back. I knew she'd kill me if I didn't. Then she'd just destroy the computer, and it all would have been for nothing."

"What did you do with Paul?" Buck asked.

"I'm getting to that," Noxia said, the parental tone creeping back into her voice. "Paul wasn't going to be much trouble unless he had a gun. When Raven gave him hers, I didn't have a choice. I had to take my chances. I have learned to count on Muffin's protections." She gave Agent 69 a brief kiss on his cheek. The Hitchcock doppelganger blushed. "All I needed was to get Paul disarmed. Once that was achieved, I took off.

"I ran right for the conference door," Noxia continued, after a little sip. "Paul followed me. He ran right into the one trip wire Muffin always sets. Between the damage already done to his ankle and the power of the trip wire, it almost severed his foot from his leg. How high did you have that thing set anyway?"

"Rhino, I think." The pear-shaped agent shrugged. "Maybe Grizzly."

"Whatever it was," Noxia slid up to the table, leaning on her elbows, "I'm just glad it works."

"Then what happened?" Buck insisted.

"You are just an impatient child, aren't you?" Noxia smiled at him before shaking her head and taking a deep breath. "I made it to the back wall. Paul was crippled and wasn't getting up. Raven was unarmed and wasn't about to take me on in single combat."

"I heard that!" Buck said with a nudge of his glass. "You're practically a one-woman army."

"Make that a two-woman army," Noxia said. "I'd definitely work with you again." She blew him a kiss.

"Can we please save the banter for later?" Muffin asked.

"Anyway," Noxia said. "I knew I was safe once I was in the conference room." She shook her head. "I knew what was going to happen, and yet, I couldn't look away. I had to see it. It's true what they say about train wrecks—we all have to watch it play out before our eyes. I watched her every step, and you know what? I almost felt sorry for her."

"What happened?" Buck pounded his fist on the table, making the glasses shuffle. Muffin reached out and grabbed his glass just in time to keep it from spilling. "Sorry," he said, quieter. "What happened?"

"Raven went to the keyboard," Noxia reported. "She sat down. Typed in the code word and," Noxia raised her fist and extended her fingers in a sweeping motion, "boom! The code activated the defensive mechanism. It exploded right in her face. She never knew what hit her."

"That's why all that smoke came billowing out when you opened the elevator doors!" Buck exclaimed.

"That's it all right," Noxia reported. "Muffin, that is one powerful explosive computer. It shook the viewing glass in the conference room!"

"I do need to turn down the voltage on that," Muffin muttered to himself, making a mental note. "Don't go above two on that meter."

"There's practically nothing left to that room," Noxia said. "I waited about twenty minutes for the smoke to clear and the shrapnel to settle. I picked my way through the debris, trying to make my way to the stairs. Then I heard a scream, like someone falling."

"That would have been Richard."

"When I opened the elevator doors and looked down," Noxia continued, "I saw you hanging by your wrists."

"How did you get Raven to use the one computer that was still booby-trapped?" Buck asked.

"It was the only computer in the room."

Buck was about to ask a question, but hesitated. His mind churned through a few theories before he shifted his train of thought. Noxia offered only a smile, while Muffin sat back, leaning against the cushions, enjoying the scene.

"Out of curiosity," Buck asked, hesitation in his voice. "And I know I'm going to regret this. How did you know the password? Muffin wouldn't tell me."

"I was wondering when you'd get around to that," Noxia said with a smile.

Buck leaned forward to see Muffin. "Why did she get to know it and not me?"

"When did you need to know it?" Noxia asked.

"Not the point." Buck focused on her, scrutinizing. "What was the password?"

"Muffin was really clever here," Noxia said, "giving credit where credit is due."

"Yeah, Muffin's a real peach," Buck said, getting irritated. He asked again with more insistence, "What was the password?"

"Muffin programmed the computer to blow up if anyone entered a code with a double letter. Words such as 'Mississippi,' or 'bookkeeper,' or…"

"Or," Buck's mind began mentally churning, "or my full name? Did you use my name as a booby trap?" Muffin and Noxia both immediately looked away from him, avoiding eye contact. "Oh, I can't believe you."

"Thank goodness you never do office work. I guess we were just lucky, eh?"

"You know, Noxia," Buck said, "you are a royal bi—" He stopped himself as she spun around challenging him with a staredown. "Big pain in the ass! What if I decided to use that computer?" he complained. His indignation was abundantly clear. Noxia and Agent 69 gave each other sideways glances and laughed.

"Buck," Noxia said in between giggles. "When have you *ever* done any kind of keyboarding office work, never mind touched a computer in that office since the day you started? And you certainly wouldn't have started at *that* computer station, either way."

He folded his arms across his chest with a petulant huff. "That's because you all use PCs and I'm a Mac guy."

"You would think it would mellow him out," Noxia said, turning to Muffin as if Buck wasn't there. "Hanging by his handcuffed wrists, fifty-two stories up over an elevator shaft. You'd think he'd have a better appreciation of life."

"Go figure," Muffin added.

"You took your own sweet time getting me the hell out of there, too, I might add," Buck sullenly said. He held up his arm, showing the leather cuff. "I have to wear these for a month. Any idea what goes with leather wristbands?"

"A tambourine?" Muffin shot out.

"A handlebar mustache and a soufflé recipe," Noxia guessed.

"And the point goes to the lady! That's a tie at one apiece," Muffin yielded. They smacked their palms together over the table.

"I lose what could have been the love of my life," Buck mumbled to no one in particular, "I almost have my wrists ripped off, and they make leather daddy jokes at my expense. I can't believe this."

"Buck." Muffin reached over Noxia and patted him on the arm. "You're too easy."

"That's what Richard thought," Noxia replied.

"And there's the win! Game. Set. Match." Muffin held his palm out for a replay.

"If you two are done making jokes."

"You'll take your marbles and go home? Get over it," Noxia said. She threw her arm about Buck's shoulders and gave him a sincere hug. "Richard was a double agent and played you like a free spin on a slot machine. It wasn't your fault."

"It's happened to us all," Agent 69 reported.

"Think of it as," Noxia thought a moment, "a rite of passage. Happy bar mitzvah!"

"But Richard was hot!" Buck said with a childish pout. "He was sexy! He was a chef!" Buck pounded on the table. "He was a gymnast! He could move his body like Gumby, damn it! Why did he have to be a bad guy?"

"Okay, your Royal Whineness," Noxia said. "It was fun while it lasted, but hello!" She wrapped her knuckles on Buck's head. "He tried to kill you. Not once, but twice! Not such a nice boy."

"But I liked him," Buck mumbled.

Noxia withdrew her arm and patted Buck's hand with a maternal gesture. "Don't worry," she assured him. "There will be other gays and other days."

"Many others, no doubt." Muffin chimed in.

"Many, many others," Noxia continued. "Let's face it, Buck, you're a man slut. But somewhere out there, in all that whoredom, the odds are good that there will be at least one guy that won't try to kill you."

Buck looked up at her with eyes dramatically wide. He clasped his hands together, pressing them against his cheek. "Do you really think so? Really?"

Muffin looked from one to the other, shaking his head at the both of them. "You are a pair of sick enablers. You know that, right?"

"Maybe," Buck said. "But we enable each other, so it works out."

"How will the explosion be explained?" Noxia asked. "I know the Agency has several different offices and will just move. But the damage couldn't have been limited or restricted to just the top floors. The elevator is destroyed."

"It's a lot easier to explain than you would imagine." Muffin puffed up with self-appointed pride. "We fed it to our news station, the one that's never correct, and it's explained easy enough." He paused for dramatic flair. "It was a delayed and desperate, final bombing of the…" Muffin cued Noxia with a gesture.

"The Bomb-a-Bar-for-Jesus Guy," she finished.

"Exactly," Muffin said. Buck rolled his eyes. "We release William Haggen from our custody to the FBI. No one knows the truth about our office, and no one needs to. Any damages to the building will be paid for by insurance, and overly compensated by us."

"That seems far-fetched," Buck said.

"The whole thing seems far-fetched," Muffin said. "That's why we leak what we want through the media."

"It's odd to think," Buck said, "that this whole thing started with a cure for HIV." The thought sparked another one, and then another. "Out of curiosity, were you able to find any records of Dr. Shoulwater's notes on the HIV cure? I mean in Raven's files, maybe?"

"Unfortunately not," Muffin replied. "Whatever files were transferred still remain in four places: Raven's personal files, and there's no way we're going to get into them at this point." He held up a finger for each location he rattled off. "Then there's your laptop, which was stolen and presumed erased or destroyed. And the downloaded files on the computer in the office. Noxia's already told us about that one."

"Richard smashed my cell phone, so that took care of the last download," Buck said. "There was a tracer on those files when I downloaded them. Then it got transferred to my phone, and Raven and her thugs were able to follow it. That's how they found Noxia in the hotel, thinking it was me."

"Did I thank you for that?" Noxia asked.

"What about the other computer?" Buck asked Muffin, ignoring Noxia altogether. "The one we viewed Raven's files on in the conference room? Wouldn't that have a copy of what we saw on it?"

"That never downloaded," Muffin said. "We just viewed it through the network from the other computer."

"And it's a good thing you didn't download it," Noxia said. "Otherwise, Raven would have known there was a room back there and might have been more anxious to get to it and me."

"Was Langlier involved in Dr. Shoulwater's murder? Or was it really an accident?"

"Good question," Muffin answered. "I don't know. I don't think any of us will ever know. We still have only our theories that they were somehow connected, but at this point, no evidence. It's highly probable. Until actual proof comes along, that's all we'll have to go on."

"That sucks," Buck said.

"It does," Muffin agreed.

"And Raven?" Noxia asked. "Raven's a major player. How does someone like her just simply disappear from public view?"

"People disappear every day," Muffin said. "That's not nearly as difficult as you think, Agent 49."

"Noxia, please," she said politely. "You know, I think I'm going to keep this name for a while. It's kind of grown on me."

"I still think it's ridiculous," Muffin mumbled.

"It's German!" Buck and Noxia answered simultaneously. They laughed together, enjoying the good friendships and the warm feelings shared at the table.

"How will the Sisters of the Southern Cross ever get along without Raven?" Buck asked.

"You know," Noxia said, nodding with thought, "I bet they get along better without her. I wouldn't be too surprised if they pulled back on their overly zealous politics and concentrated more on civic duties, like they originally intended. It's a better feather in your hat if you can build a community back up rather than separate and pull it down."

"Very well said," Muffin cheered.

"I wonder what will happen with the Rescued Right?" Buck asked.

"Groups like that are like mosquitos," Noxia said. "For every one that goes away, you know there will be more coming soon. All with the same annoying intent."

"And I'll swat 'em down, every time." Buck flashed his full smile.

"And that's all?" Noxia asked. She sounded disappointed.

"All involving me, maybe," Muffin said. "But there's still a matter involving the two of you. I believe the two of you had a bet? The mission is officially over. Time to lay your final card on the table."

"That's right!" Noxia said. "And I can't tell you how much I'm looking forward to a first-class trip to Belize. I need it!" She rubbed her hands together in anticipation. "You're awfully mellow about this, Buck."

"No reason not to be," he answered calmly. He wore his self-assured, full smirking smile.

"All right, then," Noxia said. She spoke slowly with controlled and eager anticipation. "The first day, on the plane to Virginia. You were really on edge and uncomfortable."

"I had just been cavity-searched thanks to you and your friend Timmy," Buck said. His interruption only served to give Noxia fuel.

"More than that," she said. "I asked if you wanted the window, you said no. You did the same thing on every flight." She paused. "You've done that on every flight we've ever taken together. That's point one." She waited for some sort of acknowledgment.

"That's true," Buck said. Neither his expression nor his tone revealed anything. "I prefer aisle seats. It's easier when you have to get up and go to the bathroom." His face was completely non-emotional, except for an indiscernible, impish grin.

"When we've gotten into an elevator," Noxia continued, "you hold on to the back rail, even if it's only a few stories."

"It's called a handrail," he answered. "That's what it's there for, for holding on."

"Maybe, but you grasp it. Tightly." Her face lit up as her excitement grew. The glimmer in her eyes burned bright. "Most people in a glass elevator enjoy the view. You turned your back immediately upon entering. I don't think you looked out even once. That's point two."

"I was talking to Randy Hardin," Buck said. "His was a much better view to look over."

Noxia's eyes narrowed and she craned her long neck forward, like a cat ready to pounce.

"When I invited you to go to the Sky Room, at the Gossamer Club? It's one of the best restaurants in the United States, yet you declined."

"I told you then it wasn't my first choice," he pointed out. "But I also said I'd go there if you insisted."

"So the fact that it's on the thirty-fifth floor, and completely surrounded in viewing glass, had absolutely nothing to do with your not wanting to go?"

Buck sat back in the banquette cushion with a heavy sigh, folding his arms across his chest.

"Did you have an accusation to make?" he asked with a smug smile and a cocky shake of his head. "Or are you just fishing?"

"Okay," Noxia said. She sucked her bottom lip in, softly biting. "I'm guessing you have acrophobia, the fear of heights."

"Okay." He accepted her guess with a nod of his head and an arched eyebrow.

"I'm right, aren't I?" Her stunted smirk grew into a smile. "Yeah, I'm right. You know it, too!" She shifted to face him directly, leaning her arm on the table's edge.

Buck looked into Noxia's face. He saw in her eyes the fierce determination and resourcefulness that he admired so much about her.

"You got me," Buck quietly said. "You got me."

Noxia slapped the table with both palms. She sat back, a superior smile spreading across her lips. Muffin watched the two of them, saying nothing.

"I knew it!" Noxia's smile was triumphant. "You may be a tough nut to crack, Mr. Miller, but never underestimate Miss Noxia von Tüssëll."

"Oh well," Buck said. "I guess I underestimated you one too many times. But must you be such the sore winner?"

"Are you kidding me?" Noxia answered. She refilled the glasses with the remainder of the champagne. "If the situation was reversed you'd be on the table doing a little dance, and you know it!"

"Were we talking about me?" Buck asked.

"Right there! That's exactly what I'm talking about," Noxia said. "You think you're so sly. So cocky and can never lose. Guess what? Pucker up, buttercup, you lost. Maybe next time you won't be so bloody arrogant. Just remember, Buck. I do know what scares you. And gloating privileges were included in the prize package."

"Okay. That's fair," he said lethargically. "I may not like it, but a deal's a deal. I'll buy your two first-class tickets and my two in coach. I'll make the resort reservations this week as soon as you get the name of the resort to me. I assume the congressman's name is as easy to spell as it sounds?"

"Oh," Noxia said, sounding like a pixie. "I'm not taking the congressman."

"Why not?" Muffin asked.

"Too many hassles." Noxia dismissed it with a wave of her hand. "This would be way too much of a private event for a man who needs to keep a public image."

"I'm sorry it didn't work out," Buck said sincerely. He reached over and took hold of her hand.

"Thank you," Noxia said. "Who are you bringing on the trip? Way back there in…coach." She choked on the word and poorly stifled a giggle.

Buck smiled salaciously. "Yet to be determined. Auditions will be held soon."

"Incorrigible," Noxia said, dismissing him with a headshake.

"And you?" Buck asked. "If the congressman is not in the picture, who are you bringing?"

Noxia's lips played with a coy smile. "I've decided to take a girlfriend of mine."

"Oh?" Buck raised a surprised eyebrow.

"Just a good friend of the family, more like an old auntie," Noxia said. "She's an actress friend and just finished a long project, and I know she could use the vacation." The sounds of Beethoven's Fifth rang out. Noxia dug deeply in her purse for the phone. She glanced at the caller screen. "Excuse me." She motioned for Buck to slide out. "I need to take this call."

Buck sat back at the table and slid next to Muffin. "Why are you looking at me like that?"

"You know, Agent 98," Muffin said softly, "you're not nearly the bastard you like others to think you are."

"I don't know what you mean." Buck drained the last of his champagne.

"You may have known Agent 49 for many years so far," Agent 69 said. "And you may know each other for many years to come. And you may think you know each other very well. But I still know you better."

"What are you talking about, Muffin?" Buck played with the glass flute in his hand.

"You and I both know you are *not* afraid of heights."

"That's not..." Buck started, but saw Muffin's stern expression and knew he was caught. He took a deep breath and succumbed. "You can't ever tell her. I've put her through the wringer, not only on this mission, but on a few others, too. I guess you could say I owe her one. As long as she doesn't get too crazy on the day I have to be her servant."

"Still," Muffin said, a hint of warning in his voice, "I would be careful. She has a way of having the final say."

"Eh," Buck said with a wave of his hand. "It's only for twenty-four hours. I'll survive. Aside from that, it's still Belize."

"You're a good man, Agent 98," Muffin said.

"Yeah? Well don't tell anyone."

"Tell anyone what?" Noxia said. She stood by the table's edge. "What aren't we telling someone?"

"Nothing," Buck said, waving the subject off with a sweep of his hand. Muffin smiled at Buck and gave him an understanding nod, assuring his personal silence.

"I have to get going," Noxia said. "I have vacation plans to make and a new wardrobe to buy."

"Yeah, yeah," Buck said, pulling on his sullen face.

"You know, Buck," Noxia put a hand lightly on his shoulder, "I appreciate it enough that you acknowledged my win. If you don't want to do this, you don't have to."

"Really?" Buck asked incredulously. "That's very nice of you."

"And also a crock of shit!" Noxia said. She bent down and kissed his cheek. "Get out your credit card, Bucky, Mama's going to Belize."

Noxia turned to exit, fluttering her fingers over her head as she walked away.

"The two of you really should be committed," Muffin said. "There's no explanation for the relationship you share with one another."

Buck laughed. "Does there really have to be?"

EPILOGUE

Buck exited the shower with a trail of steam following behind. The mist filled the bathroom with its warm breath, fogging the mirror. He toweled off and wrapped himself in the plush cotton bathrobe that hung on the back of the door. Running a hand through his damp mop of hair, he brushed it aside, for once not caring about his appearance.

Leaving the bathroom, he glided through the master bedroom, its earth-tone colors beckoning him to sit and relax. The window was open. The Indian summer hadn't ended, and the early evening breeze carried a hint of the autumnal weather to come. Buck was in his own apartment and felt safe and secure. For the first time in a long while, he relaxed.

The main room housed an overstuffed pewter-colored couch against the back wall and a reclining easy chair facing the bay windows and the mountain range view beyond. Settled on the table, between the couch and chair, were several small remote controls, neatly lined up according to frequency of use. Buck picked up the second one and pressed three separate buttons.

Audra McDonald's singing filled the room. Buck smiled at the angelic soprano's choice of songs from the Depression Era and let another layer of tension melt away from his body. Picking up the smallest of the remotes, Buck made another selection and the gas fireplace roared to life, adding to the ambience of the room.

The last of the tasks were almost finished. His routines after finishing a mission were precise and ritualistically followed. From the fine crystal cabinet, Buck selected one of the Baccarat glasses and filled it halfway with a rich Bordeaux left open to breathe twenty minutes earlier. The Château Lafite Rothschild was from the year of his birth. Buck believed that all major accomplishments were in need of celebration, and this was his way to reward himself for a mission well done: privately and with complete hedonism.

Extinguishing all other lights, Buck sank deep into the sofa cushions, letting the firelight's glow cast its spell over the room. Carefully, he flicked the edge of the crystal, letting the perfect-pitched ringing echo off the walls. The scent of the rich tannins teased his nostrils and excited his taste buds with anticipation.

The first sip of wine, under these circumstances, always tasted like pure, sinful pleasure. He closed his eyes to feel each sensation as the wine rushed into his senses.

If a man's home was indeed his castle, Buck felt that his was impregnable.

Buck opened his eyes, replenished, recharged, and refreshed. A buzzing sound vibrated, and his personal cell phone danced on the table. He reached for the phone and saw the call was from an unlisted number. Very few people, and then only those within his close inner circle, had this phone number, and all of them would have shown up on caller ID. Curiosity winning over hesitation, he answered the phone.

"Hello." Buck listened carefully.

"Hello," a sultry voice answered. "May I speak to Mr. Buck Miller?" There was a certain familiarity to the sound, but he couldn't identify it yet. She was definitely an older woman who still had sex appeal in her voice.

"Speaking," he answered with curiosity.

"We've never met, but we have a mutual friend. You know her as Miss Noxia von Tüssëll."

A chill swept over Buck's skin, causing the flesh to crawl. The hairs on his neck stood at rapt attention.

"Noxia and I have been friends for years," the woman continued. "She's been an absolute dear and has invited me to go with her, and evidently you, to Belize for a week's vacation. She says that it's all-inclusive and first class. I can't say thank you enough. Especially since we haven't met."

The room felt uneasy to Buck. He heard a proverbial rumbling as he felt an earthquake shake his private world.

"Listen to me rambling on when I haven't even told you my name," the woman said softly. "My name is Ann-Margret. I'm an actress. Wait, what's that, dear?"

Buck could hear shuffling on the other end of the phone. Two voices were quietly discussing something, but he couldn't make out what it was.

"Okay, I'll tell him," Ann-Margret finished to her friend. "I'm supposed to raise my finger in the air and shake it. What? No, wag it at you. And give you this advice: 'If you think you could underestimate my friend Noxia, I don't *think* so!'"

Buck remained perfectly still with the phone pressed to his ear. He stared ahead blankly, seeing nothing. He disconnected the call and the sounds of laughter that were coming from the other end. His arm fell to his side and the phone slowly slid from his hand.

Buck bit his bottom lip, shaking his head slowly from side to side. He closed his eyes and chuckled, finally understanding the adeptness of her abilities and the vastness of her connections. His chuckle changed into a giggle. Then it developed into laughter.

Buck reached for his glass. "To Miss Noxia von Tüssëll," he said, raising it in salute. "You bitch." And drank in her honor.

About the Author

Eric Andrews-Katz was born in New York. When he was twelve years of age, his family moved to Florida without asking his opinion. Eventually, he studied creative writing at USF before attending the Florida School of Massage. Since moving to Seattle in 1994, Eric has built a successful Licensed Massage business (The Massage Guy™), and lives with his partner, Alan. Eric is a contributing writer for the *Seattle Gay News*, where his theater interviews and reviews frequently appear. Other works can be found in these anthologies: *So Fey: Queer Fairy Fiction, The Best Date Ever, Charmed Lives: Gay Spirit in Storytelling, Gay City Anthologies* Vols: 2, 3, & 4. Eric is also the co-editor for *Gay City vol 4: At Second Glance.*

Eric can be found at: www.EricAndrewsKatz.com or reached at WriteOn530@gmail.com.

Books Available From Bold Strokes Books

Timothy by Greg Herren. Timothy is a romantic suspense thriller from award-winning mystery writer Greg Herren set in the fabulous Hamptons. (978-1-60282-760-8)

In Stone by Jeremy Jordan King. A young New Yorker is rescued from a hate crime by a mysterious someone who turns out to be more of a something. (978-1-60282-761-5)

The Jesus Injection by Eric Andrews-Katz. Murderous statues, demented drag queens, political bombings, ex-gay ministries, espionage, and romance are all in a day's work for a top secret agent. But the gloves are off when Agent Buck 98 comes up against the Jesus Injection. (978-1-60282-762-2)

Combustion by Daniel W. Kelly. Bearish detective Deck Waxer comes to the city of Kremfort Cove to investigate why the hottest men in town are bursting into flames in broad daylight. (978-1-60282-763-9)

Night Shadows: Queer Horror edited by Greg Herren and J.M. Redmann. *Night Shadows* features delightfully wicked stories by some of the biggest names in queer publishing. (978-1-60282-751-6)

Secret Societies by William Holden. An outcast hustler, his unlikely "mother," his faithless lovers, and his religious persecutors—all in 1726. (978-1-60282-752-3)

Wyatt: Doc Holliday's Account of an Intimate Friendship by Dale Chase. Erotica writer Dale Chase takes the remarkable friendship between Wyatt Earp, upright lawman, and Doc Holliday, Southern gentlemen turned gambler and killer, to an entirely new level: hot! (978-1-60282-755-4)

The Jetsetters by David-Matthew Barnes. As rock band the Jetsetters skyrocket from obscurity to superstardom, Justin Holt, a lonely barista, and Diego Delgado, the band's guitarist, fight with everything they have to stay together, despite the chaos and fame. (978-1-60282-745-5)

Strange Bedfellows by Rob Byrnes. Partners in life and crime, Grant Lambert and Chase LaMarca are hired to make a politician's compromising photo disappear, but what should be an easy job quickly spins out of control. (978-1-60282-746-2)

Into the Flames by Mel Bossa. In order to save one of his patients, psychiatrist Jamie Scarborough will have to confront his own monsters—including those he unknowingly helped create. (978-1-60282-681-6)

Fontana by Joshua Martino. Fame, obsession, and vengeance collide in a novel that asks: What if America's greatest hero was gay? (978-1-60282-675-5)

The Dirty Diner: Gay Erotica on the Menu, edited by Jerry L. Wheeler. Gay erotica set in restaurants, featuring food, sex, and men—could you really ask for anything more? (978-1-60282-677-9)

Sweat: Gay Jock Erotica by Todd Gregory. Sizzling tales of smoking-hot sex with the athletic studs everyone fantasizes about. (978-1-60282-669-4)

The Marrying Kind by Ken O'Neill. Just when successful wedding planner Adam More decides to protest inequality by quitting the business and boycotting marriage entirely, his only sibling announces her engagement. (978-1-60282-670-0)

Calendar Boys by Logan Zachary. A man a month will keep you excited year-round. (978-1-60282-665-6)

Buccaneer Island by J.P. Beausejour. In the rough world of Caribbean piracy, a man is what he makes of himself—or what a stronger man makes of him. (978-1-60282-658-8)

Twelve O'Clock Tales by Felice Picano. The fourth collection of short fiction by legendary novelist and memoirist Felice Picano. Thirteen dark tales that will thrill and disturb, discomfort and titillate, enthrall and leave you wondering. (978-1-60282-659-5)

Words to Die By by William Holden. Sixteen answers to the question: What causes a mind to curdle? (978-1-60282-653-3)